THE DANCER

A FORBIDDEN BILLIONAIRE ROMANCE

VIVIAN WOOD

AUTHOR'S COPYRIGHT

This book would not have been as special or nearly as well-loved without my beta team — Patricia and Amanda particularly! I would also like to thank Antje, Jeanette, and all my other eagle eyed early readers... you all are the bee's knees!

Want to hear a playlist of songs that inspired The Dancer? Click here to see it on Spotify.

1. Supercut (El-P Remix) — Lorde, Run The Jewels
2. Hallucinate — Dua Lipa
3. Bad At Love — Halsey
4. Mykonos — Fleet Foxes
5. Naked Eye — Luscious Jackson
6. The Scientist — Coldplay
7. Slide — Goo Goo Dolls
8. PILLOWTALK — ZAYN
9. Where Have All The Cowboys Gone? — Paula Cole
10. Dance Yrself Clean — LCD Soundsystem
11. break up with your girlfriend — Ariana Grande
12. Summertime — The Sundays

Enjoy the book!

1

KAIA

*T*hirty one days.

Today marks precisely one month since Calum broke things off with me. I can still hear him, even now.

We are letting you go, Kaia. I won't need your services anymore.

My services.

Which meant my body. My excitement. Even my virginity.

He was so cold and callous when he said it, so detached. It was as if I didn't matter in the least.

Like I hadn't laid against his chest, both of us fully naked, and listened to his heartbeat galloping frenetically.

Like we didn't spend countless hours teasing, torturing, and tormenting each other with pleasure.

Like I never surrendered my virginity to him in the first place.

I swallow, tears pricking my eyes as I move through the afternoon heat. If I don't hurry, I will be late. Even

1

though I know that, I don't move any faster. My hesitance about meeting up echoes around in my head as I stride onward.

I blow out a breath, turning my head to check my reflection in the mirror-like surface of the sleek downtown Manhattan skyscraper as I walk past. A stranger looks back at me.

Thin, blonde, wearing one of the little black dresses that Calum bought for me and oversized black sunglasses. She walks with grace, I would say.

But even as I toss my hair and look away, I know that I'm lacking. In what exactly, I can't put my finger on.

Something that made Calum crumple me up and throw me away. I spent a week sobbing inconsolably, trying to parse out what exactly it was that made him end not only our agreement, but to terminate my employment with the New York Ballet. And after all that, all I know are the facts.

I'm not a ballerina anymore.

Not warming anyone's bed.

Not a virgin, either.

I'm like a ship that has been cut free from its anchor, exploring the sea listlessly, unmanned and unmoored. In the mass of turmoil and uncertainty that have followed my firing, I only have one place to turn.

Acid sloshes around in the pit of my stomach at the thought.

The building that I am hurrying toward looms just ahead. I pull my sunglasses off as I open the doors. A sleek granite wall greets me, with a young woman standing

2

behind an ultra-modern white hostess stand. She glances up, smiling pleasantly.

"Welcome to Feast. Do you have a reservation?"

I tuck my sunglasses in my handbag, nodding. "Walker."

She bows. "Of course. If you will follow me…"

She leads me through a towering doorway into a very upscale restaurant. White linen tablecloths, luxurious black booths, a fancy bar that runs along the back wall. At this hour, the place is almost empty. But though I can't yet see him, I can hear my father telling a story at full volume. His booming voice and bombastic style of speech are still very much intact.

I wince, steeling myself. The last time I saw my dad, he was fleeing out the back door of the theater. Running away from Calum, who I thought was actually going to kill him for laying a hand on me.

How long ago that seems now.

Following the hostess around a corner, I'm surprised to see my entire family sitting in a large circular booth. My mother sees me first, making a soft noise of pleasure. She gets up from her seat and opens her arms.

I gladly step into her embrace, hugging her hard. "Hey mom."

She kisses me on the cheek. "Hello, Chickadee." She pulls back, looking me up and down. "You look very grown up. And very thin."

Her lips flatten a bit on the last word. She's worried about me, as I suppose a mother should be.

I smile shyly, tucking a strand of my hair back. "You look good."

Actually, there are shadows under her eyes that say she hasn't slept well recently. But she's still my beautiful mother. She gives me another hug and my heart squeezes against my chest.

"Serena!" my father bellows. "Christ, sit down, will you?"

She instantly moves away from me, obeying as she has for twenty years.

My sister Hazel and my dad are seated next to my mother. Hazel smirks at me, giving me a once over. She's wearing a bright pink dress and looking like the cat that ate the canary.

My dad is dressed in his usual khakis and white polo, sprawled out in the booth with no regard for anyone else's comfort.

"Dad. Hazel," I greet them.

My dad looks at me, smiling coldly. "Kaia. Have a seat."

He flicks his fingers toward the empty seat in the booth. I duck my head, swallowing as I do as he says. My mom sits down across from me, reaching across the table to take my hand.

"It's so good to see you."

Hazel rolls her eyes. "God, mom. You act like she's your perfect little angel. You have blinders on where Kaia is concerned."

Mom looks at her, her smile strained. "I think we've heard enough of your opinion, Hazel. Why don't you go back to scrolling through your phone?"

Hazel shoots her a glare. Only a second later though, she does exactly that.

Dad adjusts himself against the black leather booth. "Did you bring me a check, Kaia?"

I flush. Of course that's the first thing he's interested in. Digging in my handbag, I pull out an envelope and slide it across the table to him.

He squints at me as he rips the envelope open. His eyes travel down to the dollar amount. Two hundred and fifty thousand dollars. A jaw dropping amount of money, every penny that he asked for. He arches his brow and folds the check in half, putting it in his wallet.

I keep waiting for some kind of acknowledgement. Maybe even a thank you? After all, most daughters couldn't come up with that kind of money.

Honestly, I wouldn't have been able to either. But then Calum dumped me. And suddenly, I had nothing else to do with the money sitting in my bank account.

Dad looks at me skeptically for a half a minute. I squirm under his gaze.

"We should talk about you working out a payment plan," he says at last.

My eyebrows fly up. "Excuse me?"

Hazel looks up from her phone, grinning at me. Dad ignores the sudden tension crackling from me, looking around the restaurant.

"Yeah, I've recalculated the costs of just what you owe me recently. You know, what with interest and balances accruing. I don't want to fall into a trap where you disappear for a while and only come around when you can scrape together a little cash. I think it would be better to do something more frequent. Sunday dinners, you come over with ten thousand dollars every week. I mean, it's only fair."

My jaw drops. "Dad, you said that you owed three hundred thousand to the mob. I managed to get most of that money together at very great personal cost..." I pause, gulping. "I can't believe you have the nerve to demand more!"

My sister raises her phone, snapping a picture of me. She giggles. "My friends are going to think it's funny, watching you lose your shit."

"Hazel, the adults are talking," my mother sternly corrects her. "Another word and I'll make you go wait in the car."

Hazel sticks her tongue out at my mom. I'm too floored to pay attention to their bickering. All my focus is on my dad, who seems uninterested in the conversation. He's busy trying to get some service.

He cups his hands to his face. "Waiter!"

"Dad!" I say, my voice rising in pitch. "I just handed you a check for a quarter of a million dollars. And your only response is to tell me it's not enough?"

My dad completely ignores me. A waitress comes rushing around to our table, flushed. "What can I get you?"

Dad narrows his eyes at her. "Top shelf bourbon, two fingers worth. And food menus."

"Of course."

He slides his gaze to me, a sneer appearing on his lips. "Only three menus. One of us is not staying to eat. She probably has some preparations before she goes out, walking the streets, hanging out on the corners like a fucking whore."

6

My face immediately goes red. The waitress licks her lips, her eyebrows jumping up. She backs away slowly.

"Uh, yes sir," she says, looking to me. As if I have answers. As if I can help control the situation.

I press my lips into a thin line and drop my gaze. Inside, I'm practically screaming at myself.

Why did I come here? Why did I just give my dad basically all of my money? What did I hope to accomplish?

Acid rises in my stomach.

"It really is wonderful to see you," my mom says softly. She's trying to make things better by pretending like everything is normal.

I raise my eyes to meet hers, my eyes tightening. "Mom, I just paid dad two hundred and fifty thousand dollars because he owes it to the mob. I was afraid that the mob would hurt you and Hazel if I didn't find the funds. Kill you, even. Things aren't normal, no matter how much you pretend they are."

My mom's cheeks color slightly. She runs her hands down her beige dress, clucking her tongue. "I'm sure that your father is only asking for what's fair. Isn't that right, Robert?"

Of course. My mom is supportive of me, but only so far. When forced to choose between me or my dad, my mom will always choose his side. No matter how outlandish my father's demands get, it seems.

My lips twist. I feel sick.

"I notice that no one seems to want to investigate where I got the money from."

My dad pins me with a look, arching his brows. "You

only have one thing worth selling. I assume that you sold your body. Am I wrong?"

My face burns. "You are a piece of work."

Hazel snickers, looking up at me and dad. "You were right about Kaia selling herself like a prostitute."

The waitress appears with a stack of menus, handing them out. She slides one in front of me, smiling nervously. "Just in case you decide to stay for lunch."

I bob my head. "Thanks."

She vanishes. My dad reaches over and grabs the menu from in front of me, his expression petulant.

"I'll expect to see you this Sunday afternoon. Maybe you can take the weekend to reflect on how you should be more thankful and show gratitude to me." He smirks. "And try to bring cash next time. Checks are so cumbersome."

I grit my teeth. "So that's it? No pat on the back. No good job. No words of thanks for saving your ass. No mention of the fact that you showed up at my school and lost your damn mind. Just the expectation of me paying you again and again?"

My dad gives me a look, opening his menu. "You're being irrational. When you break down the numbers, really consider what you owe me—"

I stand up, shaking my head. "I can't believe that I came here. If I were smart, I would go straight to the bank and tell them to issue a stop payment on that check."

My dad's expression goes black. "I wouldn't even say that out loud if I were you. Wouldn't even think about it. Because you are worthless to me unless you can pay me back. You might as well be dead."

I blanch, though I know that he'll say pretty much

8

anything to rattle me at this point. He's still my father, still the person that I used to depend on for everything. Hearing him call me worthless is a knife to the gut.

"Coming here was a mistake." I grab my handbag, pulling it onto my shoulder. I step out of the booth, looking at my mom.

She's crying, but she's also looking pointedly away from me. A lost cause, not a port in the storm that is my family dynamic.

"Bye, Mom," I say.

Her lip quivers and she darts a glance at me but doesn't say a word. My father leans close to the table, spreading his fingers out on it.

"I didn't say you were dismissed."

My breath leaves me in an audible huff. "You won't see me again."

His face reddens. "I'd better. I have several men to introduce you to. It's time that you settled down—"

I turn, unable to listen to any more. He is legitimately crazy. I knew that before I even stepped foot inside this restaurant...

But forgiving and forgetting has always been a huge part of my life.

As I start to walk away, I hear my father's shout.

"Don't make me come find you, Kaia! Kaia! Come back—"

I start to run, tears blurring my vision.

CALUM

I stride through my high end Manhattan apartment, wearing a scowl that has become a permanent fixture on my face lately. I'm dressed in light gray sweatpants and a loose, dark tank top. Ready for the gym.

Ready to sweat out all my anger and angst and disgust with myself.

I push open the swinging door that leads into a vast echoing space that is my home gym. Lucas is already inside. He's dressed in black shorts and a white t-shirt, his dark hair long enough that he wears a headband to keep it out of his face during our workout.

He's chatting with a tall, incredibly built black man in tiny gray shorts and a gray tank top. His name is Otto, he's Austrian, and he happens to be the best Crossfit trainer in New York City.

Lucas says something that makes Otto grin. I walk up to them, casually stretching my arm behind my head.

"There you are," Otto says, his voice booming. He

consults his watch. "Are you two ready to have your asses kicked?"

Lucas groans a little. "This is Calum's thing. Go easy on me. I am still sore from seeing you two days ago."

Otto grins, walking toward the middle of the gym's floor. "We will all work hard enough to get punished. Then I will whip up protein smoothies as a reward."

Lucas gives him a disgruntled face. I jog in place, ready to start.

"Let's go!" I insist. "What do we start with today? Jump rope? Jumping jacks?"

"That's the attitude that warms my heart. Today we start with one hundred lunges!"

Lucas shakes his head, putting his hands on his hips. "You don't have to sound so fucking gleeful about the fact that you're about to murder us, Otto."

I'm impatient. "Let's go."

Blowing out a breath, my brother moves about five feet away from me and then faces me. We start doing deep lunges, which are absolute killers on my hamstrings. No pain no gain though, I suppose.

"So did you end up doing anything last night?" Lucas asks, wincing as he lunges. "You know. Talk to anyone, go anywhere. Do anything but work or work out?"

I shake my head. "Nah. I was on the phone with Taseki until ten p.m. last night. I actually drifted off in my office again. Blame it on the high intensity interval training."

Lucas wipes away a sheen of sweat from his brow. "You know, for a billionaire, you live a surprisingly ascetic life. You're surrounded by every luxury and yet all you do is work out and work. You might as well be a hermit."

I pull a face, starting to breathe hard. "You don't need me hanging around you while you meet women left and right."

He snorts. "No, I don't. But I'm tired of you brooding all the damn time. It's been a month since you broke things off with Kaia. Don't you think it's long past time that you fucking got back out there?"

At the mere mention of Kaia, I bristle. "You talk a big game for somebody that never sees the same woman twice, Lucas."

A grin bursts over his face. "Don't be so jealous, brother. You too can live a blessed life. You only need to say my name at the door of every sex club in New York."

I shake my head, chuckling. "No thanks, man. I have nothing against kink, but I'm no exhibitionist. The idea of acting out every sick fantasy in front of other people? No thanks."

My brother laughs. "Your loss."

Otto has been quiet, presumably counting the number of lunges. My hamstrings and my ass burn through the last few reps. Sweat starts to drip off of me.

"Okay," Otto says. "That should be a hundred."

I push myself just a little further, doing one extra set of lunges. When I'm done, I head over to pick up a hand towel to mop my face and grab a bottle of water.

"Fuck," Lucas says, wiping himself off with another towel. "I need you to get laid so that I don't have to do these high intensity training sessions anymore. I like being shredded but damn, it sucks when I'm in the moment."

"Come on. We don't want our heart rates to drop too much," Otto says. "Let's do ninety sit ups."

Taking another long pull from my water bottle, I carry another hand towel over to the center of the room. Then I get on the floor, assuming the position.

Lucas drops beside me, muttering. Otto starts counting and we begin.

"I heard that Jack was fired," Lucas says after a minute.

That's news to me. I slide a look of surprise at him. "Yeah?"

He chuckles. "Apparently someone with a massive amount of buying power shorted his company's stock. You wouldn't know anything about that, would you?"

I don't go for the bait, even though we both know it was me. "He was a fucking bastard. He hid behind a religious mask but he was a fucking creep. I'm not sad to see him go."

Lucas grins. "The company is basically worthless now. I had my broker sweep up everything that's left this morning. We now own all of the remaining company."

"Hmm," is my only comment.

"That's ninety! Take five minutes and then we hit the pull up bars," Otto says.

I do a final sit up, dragging breath into my lungs. Jumping up, I wipe my face with my towel and then offer Lucas a hand up. He takes it, shaking his head at me.

"Hey, how has that private investigator that I recommended been working out so far?"

Grabbing my water bottle, I nod slowly. "Good. O'Neil has already dug up a shit ton of stuff on Honor. Believe it or not, she has made a ton of fucking enemies in her life." I grin, pouring water into my mouth. "I can't wait to rub her nose in it and see how fast she runs away."

Lucas nods, wiping away sweat. "Good. You have to fight fire with fire."

I sneak him a look. "I might have had O'Neil do some checking up on Kaia, too."

He is mid-swallow when I say it. He looks at me, his eyes narrowing into a glare. "What? Why?"

I shrug. "My lawyer has been calling her, trying to get her to accept a final payment. But she hasn't picked up. I got curious."

"Don't take this the wrong way, but it kind of sounds like you want to be in control of the situation."

I scowl. "Who doesn't like control? Especially when you have more money than god and spending a little gets you exactly what you want."

"It doesn't sound like it's working out the way you had planned. I guess sweet little Kaia isn't going to play by the rules you've set out."

I scrunch my face up. "You might be right about that. Even O'Neil has had some trouble following her trail."

Lucas looks at me, tossing his sweaty hair back. "You should just leave her be, Calum. I know that you felt you had to break off your little arrangement—"

"It would have gone sour eventually," I cut him off. "Trust me, when there are women and a lot of money involved, it always does."

"Well, regardless. You broke things off. And yet you are still fucking moping around your apartment and checking up on her."

I shoot him a glare. Taking a final pull from my water

bottle, I stretch my hamstring. "O'Neil said that she just applied to dance with Emerson."

He blinks. "Yeah? I mean, if I had left New York Ballet and was looking for a new home, that would be where I went first. They are the next biggest dance company. Really the only competition for NYB."

I suck in a deep breath. "You think I should make a call to them?"

He looks at me like I've grown a third head. "To Emerson? What are you going to say? I really like fucking this ballerina? You should hire her?"

Otto jogs over, ignoring the dirty look I'm shooting at my brother. "Time for pull ups."

I'm glad for a break from being interrogated. Stalking over to the bar, I start to execute pull ups, my arms burning with the effort. When I'm done, my arms feel like jelly. I can't draw in a full breath to save my life.

Lucas finishes half a minute later, gasping and shaking his head. "Enough! Please, five minutes…" he begs Otto.

Otto smiles. "Only five."

Lucas turns to me, breathing hard.

"We have to get you out of this very nice black hole you've created for yourself. Seriously. Why don't we go out tonight? We can even go to the bar downstairs if that's what you want."

I steel my expression, showing him nothing. But inside, I remember all too well the first girl I tried to pick up after Kaia. I worked my charms effortlessly. Got her back to the bathroom, practically panting with desire. But when the time came to actually fuck her?

I caught sight of myself in the mirror. Looked at myself for a long time.

And then I turned and left that girl in the bathroom without saying a word.

I don't tell my brother a word of this. That's not how conversations usually go between us. But I do clap him on the shoulder.

"Another time," I promise.

He rolls his eyes. "When is this going to be over?"

Otto cuts in. "The sooner we start doing burpees, the sooner they are over."

Lucas groans, grabbing a fresh towel. "Kill me."

"I'll do everything but that," Otto fires back. "Are you ready?"

I grab a fresh towel and get ready to really sweat. "Lay it on me. Make it hurt, Otto."

Otto grins and rubs his hands together. "Let's go!"

After that, I'm wrapped up in my own world of not being able to breathe and every muscle screaming with pain. But inside me, a longing for Kaia is still lodged in my chest.

3

KAIA

I stand just to the left of the stage, my heart in my throat. My pointe shoes are laced up, I'm in pale pink tights and a stark white leotard. I'm sweating so profusely that I can almost feel the dampness at my lower back. I'm not even under stage lights.

I just never thought I would get this chance again. When I applied to be a dancer at Emerson, it was a hail mary, an outside shot. And yet here I am, stretching my hamstrings, ready to dance for their hiring panel.

"Kaia?" the stage manager asks. When I nod she waves me onto the stage. "Break a leg."

She says it with a wink, hurrying off the stage. She's encouraging and warm to me even though she doesn't know me from Adam.

What a difference that is from New York Ballet and Calum's stage managerial style.

I stiffen my posture and walk out onto the stage, beaming. Inside I am a mess of nerves and doubts. But ballet has prepared me for the pageantry of this moment.

I smile easily under the bright lights. Walking to the little X marked with black tape, I look out at the audience. It's all women from what I can see. Another huge difference from NYB.

One of the women calls out to me. "What's your name, please?"

"Kaia Walker," I say, projecting my voice into the theater.

The woman glances down at her clipboard, scribbling something. Then she clears her throat.

"Kaia, you were most recently at New York Academy of Ballet?"

My smile falters for a spilt second. Should I reveal my brief tenure at their competitor?

No. Let them judge me based on my dancing alone. I nod my head. "Yes."

Another of the three women chimes in. "What will you be dancing for us tonight?"

My heart beat starts to race. "Aurora from Sleeping Beauty. Act Two, Scene Two."

Eyebrows rise. The judges look at each other for a moment. I've chosen a very difficult part with a particularly hard solo as my audition piece. Hoping to wow them, I guess. The first woman speaks up again. "Go ahead whenever you are ready."

I raise my arms in a delicate arch as the music begins to play. A wide smile teases my lips. My heart in thundering against my ribcage.

I start dancing, quickly and flawlessly executing the pirouettes and jetés. Under the bright stage lights, time

18

stops altogether or maybe speeds up to hyper speed. It's really difficult to tell.

I try not to dwell on it. Kaia fades away for a few moments. In her place, I'm Aurora, seeking her true love.

I finish with the biggest grand jet possible, flying and floating across the stage. I have that same thought, that I'm actually a good dancer.

Not the best, maybe. But I should be able to get a part as a member of their *corps de ballet* with this performance. Right?

I strike a pose, lifting my eyes toward the three women that stand in the rows. One is whispering to another. The third frowns as she makes furious notes.

The first woman straightens and applauds very briefly. "Very nice, Kaia. Thank you. I think we all would like to see you back for another audition…"

Another audition. That's the process when you aren't fucking one of the stage managers, I guess. I curtsy deeply and mumble my thanks, turning and rushing off the stage. Already, the stage manager is calling the next girl.

I hear her voice call faintly. "Brigid?"

Slowing my exuberant footsteps to a walk, I turn the corner. I'm expecting maybe a stagehand or a costumer to look up and distractedly point me in the direction of the changing rooms.

But no. Instead there is a lone man dressed in head to toe black. His dark hair is ruffled. His blue eyes pierce right through me. His shoulders are ruggedly large, his hips slim, his expression unreadable.

I halt suddenly, my hand flying up to cover my heart.

My heart hammers in my chest. My lips part, a question forming.

"Calum?"

It comes out gentle and soft. But my fists ball up, my fingernails biting the delicate skin of my palms.

He stands there, his blue eyes pinning me in place. For the longest time he doesn't say a single word.

Anger starts building deep inside me. My smile slips away, only to be replaced with a scowl. In the static silence between us, I hear a quiet echo of his last words.

I no longer need your services.

The sour taste of bile rises in the back of my throat. I turn and try to rush past him. To be as done with him as he is with me.

He reaches out, grabbing my elbow hard so that I can't get past him. I look up into his handsome face, my expression twisting with the physical pain his touch brings me. His fingers burn into my skin like red hot brands.

I give my arm a yank. But of course, I'm much less strong than he is. He looks down at me, his five o'clock shadow grown into scruff, his ice blue eyes chilling me with one hard glance.

"Don't," he rumbles, giving me a shake. "I just came to check up on you."

I screw up my face, this close to spitting at him. "Let me go, Calum. You gave up the right to check on me when you walked away a month ago."

A muscle ticks in his jaw. His lips thin. His eyes are electric and alive with the raw energy that seems to course between us. For a second, he pulls me closer. Like he's hovering on the brink of violence.

His eyes dip down to my mouth, setting me ablaze. Just that one little thing is enough to remind me of how those gorgeous lips once nibbled at my neck, how those big hands made me burn with need.

I lick my lips, jerking my arm again. "Go to hell."

He releases me suddenly. I almost tumble backward because I am leaning away from him as hard as I can. Catching myself, I smooth out my expression.

Make it as cold and unfeeling as him.

I turn away, moving down the darkened passage.

"Kaia!" he calls after me. He sounds aggravated.

He has no right to be, though. He has no rights where I am concerned at all.

Calum's hand lands on my shoulder, spinning me around.

I hiss at him, bristling. "What are you doing? Can't you see that I don't want to talk to you?"

His eyes narrow. I could be crazy, but I swear that for a second, he looks guilty. "I want to know why you won't take the money I am offering you."

I fold my arms over my chest, protecting myself. "Maybe I don't like being told what my affections were worth. Maybe I don't like the feeling of being paid to keep quiet. Either way, what does it matter to you?"

His brow furrows. "Kaia… you don't understand. I didn't mean to hurt your feelings."

A cold little laugh bursts from my lips. "You have the strangest way of showing it."

His lips twitch. "It's not about you at all. You're…"

Calum's eyes travel down my body. I can sense his hunger as he takes in my tits, my hips, the vee between my

21

legs. And god help me, when his gaze stops and stays right there where my pussy is, I subconsciously clench.

Damn if I don't experience a little thrill of being wanted again, even if it's by someone as cold and cruel as Calum. I know what he can do. What he can make me feel. How he can make me come and come and come.

Apparently my body hasn't gotten the message that Calum and I are through because though I press my thighs together, I feel my pussy growing wet for him.

His gaze travels back up to my mouth. His fingertips dig into my shoulder as he starts pulling me closer. My breathing grows more rapid; my heartbeat roars in my ears.

I want to feel his kiss more than anything. But I haven't forgotten how it felt to have Calum look at me and say that he doesn't want me anymore.

My hand comes up, slapping him on the cheek hard and fast. His eyes widen. He raises his hand, touching his cheek.

I shudder, wrenching my shoulder out from his grasp. "I'm not some toy that you can take down from the shelf whenever you feel like playing, Calum. I know you are richer than Croesus, but I'm not a street walker. I have some dignity, if you'll let me."

He scowls. "I'm telling you, beauty. I broke things off with you because I was being blackmailed…"

Holding up a hand, I shake my head. "I don't care. I don't want to see you again." I pause, dragging in a shaking breath. "And don't you dare call me beauty. Not after tossing me aside."

With that, I turn away, moving swiftly down the

passage. I hear Calum calling my name. But there are tears gathering in my eyes and I'm too fucking proud to let him know how deeply he's hurt me.

4

CALUM

*E*veryone lives with regrets. Every single person has a few moments that they replay when they should be sleeping. Wondering if they had just said or done something differently, the outcome would have been much better.

The early morning light breaks through the gaps between the towering buildings of downtown Manhattan. As they slide by my chauffeured car window, I find myself ruminating on mistakes and regrets. I have always been a leader, always felt certain about making multimillion dollar deals that would affect literally hundreds or thousands of my employees.

But just now, as I stare out the window, I must admit to having made a mistake in dealing with Kaia. I've done so many gutsy boardroom deals in my lifetime, with little or no eye toward the feelings of anyone else involved. I always felt like anyone who whined about a merger or a new direction was ungrateful and unreliable.

But looking into Kaia's face after she slapped me? The

hurt and fury that I saw dancing in her eyes was itself a blow. It was only at that moment that I really started to feel like I might have fucked up.

More than that. I was tantalizingly close to pulling her into my arms and kissing her anyway. I missed the shape of her small body pressed against mine.

But what am I supposed to do about it? How can I make Kaia come back to me?

I don't have an answer for that yet.

The limousine pulls up outside the New York Ballet. I get out, stretching. The building itself is no work of fine art; in fact, from here, it looks like an oversized cement brick. It's funny that it hides such a gem inside; the ballet has really been my touchstone, my grounding influence in a materialistic world.

Slowly making my way up the broad gray steps, I check my phone. I stop when I see a message from Devereaux, the private investigator I sometimes use. I asked him to check up on Honor, to find any kind of dirt that I could use against her in my blackmail battle.

My lips curl up as I scan through the documents he's sent me. It's the first time I have felt like smiling in ages. Gripping my phone, I look up and push open the huge glass door of the NYB.

I trot up the stairs, nearly running smack into a distressed-looking Emma. She smoothes a hand down her charcoal pants suit and gives me a wide-eyed look.

"Honor is derailing a dress rehearsal by throwing a fit about her costume," she grits out. "I have no idea what you two have worked out between yourselves. But she's even harder to work with than before! She's really giving prima donnas a bad name."

I flash her a grin. "I'm going to take care of her right now. And by take care of her, I mean fire her. You'd better have a good dancer in place as her understudy."

Emma's brows rise. "I think so. We... lost... Kaia. So I put Ella in as Honor's understudy."

I give her a hard look. "Do you want Honor fired or not?"

She nods quickly. "Yes."

I straighten my tie, smiling grimly. "Okay then." I brush past her.

From the click of her heels on the granite floor, it becomes clear that Emma follows me toward the auditorium. But I'm focused on the task at hand. When I throw open the double doors to the high-ceilinged space, I'm immediately confronted by a red-faced Honor.

She's standing in the middle of the stage, hands on her hips. All the other dancers are sitting down on the stage, riveted by the drama that is unfolding. One of the male dancers casually films the fight on his phone. Gathering evidence for a future lawsuit, maybe.

Honor yells at Sam, the diminutive silver haired man who hand sews all the costumes. He's as pale as a ghost and trembling like a leaf.

"If you can't make the costume in exactly the way I'm telling you to make it, I think you should quit your job right now!"

Sam tries to speak up. "But Honor, it's hardly my fault that your measurements keep changing—"

She stomps her foot petulantly. "Is it too much to ask

that you use corseting to make the size of my top fit better? Jesus!"

"But corsets aren't recommended for women who are... in your condition," he argues.

I stride down the aisle, clapping my hands. "That's enough," I boom. I feel all eyes turn toward me. "Rehearsal is dismissed for the next hour. Sam, you can return to your work backstage."

Sam sends me a wide-eyed look but doesn't argue. He just looks relieved as he scurries off. In the wings, all the dancers begin getting up and walking backstage.

Honor levels a black glare at me. "And just what do you think you're doing?"

My lips twist. "My job. The New York Ballet asked me to stage manage. And for the last month, I've been allowing you to run things as you saw fit."

Honor rolls her eyes and crosses her arms. "You haven't been much of a stage manager. And even Bas hasn't been at the last couple of rehearsals—"

"Shut up," I say loudly, cutting her off. "You're fired."

I feel Emma at my right elbow. She clutches my arm excitedly when I announce it, but I keep my eyes on Honor.

Honor's lips curl upward into a sarcastic smile. "Are you insane? Surely you have lost your senses. You can't fire me."

I straighten on of my starches cuffs. "Yes, I can. If anyone wants to know why, I'll just ask around for video of you berating and belittling a staff member in front of everyone. Something tells me that people will rush to provide evidence."

She makes a sour expression. "I think you have forgotten that I know things about you. Things that would see you not just fired from your position here, but probably tarred and feathered too."

A thin smile spreads across my lips. Out of the corner of my eye, I look at Emma. "Give us a minute alone."

Emma is looking at me a little suspiciously. But she nods nonetheless. "I'll go check on the rest of the dancers."

She turns and vanishes out the doors, leaving Honor and I the only two in the cavernous theater. I stalk toward the stage, already pulling my phone out of my jacket.

"I had my private investigator do a little digging on you," I say. "Call it due diligence on my part, before I signed a single check over to you."

Honor comes over to the edge of the stage, looking down at me haughtily. "And your investigator found nothing, because there is nothing to find."

I give her a tiny smirk. "You're right. Honor Laurent is a dedicated ballerina and has nothing besmirching her record of excellence."

She narrows her gaze on my face. "And still, you interrupt my rehearsal with this foolishness."

I look down at my phone screen. "I had my investigator dig a little deeper. And he found a name you might recognize." I spear her with my gaze, relishing the moment. "Jessica Pavlova. Does that ring any bells?"

Her breath leaves her in an audible gush. It's like I knocked the helium from her balloon; she loses the smile and her entire posture seems to shrink. She grimaces and bares her teeth.

28

In her beautiful face, her expression looks incredibly sharklike. I'm taken aback by the very fact that only two months ago, I would've done anything for attention from this woman.

It's funny how such a small amount of time changed my view. Meeting Kaia didn't hurt, either.

"I don't know who you've been talking to, but they are wrong," she says. "I've never even heard that name."

A cold laugh bursts from my lips. "No? It's funny, Devereaux seemed to think that Jessica Pavlova was mixed up with the Russian mafia."

Honor looks at me, every nerve standing at attention. "You're wrong."

But her voice cracks. Her whole being seems to reverberate finely. She's obviously scared shitless.

I make a show of composing a text. "I have a phone number for a Stanislav. Does that sound familiar? Hmm, what should I tell him?"

Honor clambers down off the stage, suddenly dead serious. "Calum... you wouldn't. There are things you don't know..."

I frown down at my phone. "Let's see. How about something simple? 'Jessica Pavlova is dancing under the name Honor Laurent'. What do you think?"

I turn the phone to face her. She reaches out and slaps it out of my hand. It flies into the blue velvet covered seats and I glare at her.

"That's not very good behavior."

She grabs my arm, her nails biting into my skin. "What do you want?"

My lips curve upward. "I want you gone. I never want

to hear your name again. No one that I know should ever see your face. Get out of New York. And most importantly, I am not signing the birth certificate for your unborn kid."

Honor looks angry. But she also keeps checking behind herself, as though I've told the Russians where to find her already. She grips my arm.

"If I go, you won't say anything to the Russians? Not even a hint?"

I shake her off, brushing my sleeve. "I'm glad you've just completely abandoned any pretense. And no, what would be the use of having this juicy little morsel if I just pulled the trigger right now? I thought you understood how blackmail works."

She wraps her arms around herself, her face puckering. "Fine."

I cock my head. "Fine what?"

"I agree, okay?! I'll leave New York City."

I chuckle. "It's your funeral if you don't. If I even think you're still around, I'm calling in my chit. The Russians don't give a fuck if you're pregnant. They'll kill you anyway. So if you want to live to see that baby grow up—"

"All right!" Honor says.

I just stare at her for several seconds. She stares back, ebullient. I check my watch.

"Did I mention that you have exactly one minute to vanish and never been seen again? I guess not. That minute starts…"

Before I can even say now, she pushes past me and starts running toward the double doors at the back of the auditorium. I grin and saunter after her, making it to the doors before I spot Emma.

I arch a brow at her. "That's what you wanted, isn't it?"

Two bright spots of red appear in her cheeks. "Yes. But…" She turns, looking at where Honor just hurried by. "What did you say to her?"

The corners of my mouth lift. "Don't worry about that. Go tell the understudy that she's now the solo."

Eyes wide, Emma nods, rushing off toward backstage. And I just stand here for a second, my heart beat picking up.

Now I just need to figure out how I'm going to make Kaia come back into my bed…

5

KAIA

*T*he buzz of my cell phone ringing brings me swimming up from the depths of murky sleep. It's early, too early for anyone to be calling. I reach out of my bed and feel around on clumsily made milk crate turned bedside table. Finding the phone, I yank it to my ear, keeping my eyes closed.

"Hello?" I mumble.

"I'm calling for Kaia Walker," a woman says lightly. She pauses. "It's Emma Rosenberg. I'm the director at the New York Ballet."

My eyelids open. In the same electrified movement, I sit straight up, breathing a little hard.

"Yes?" I squeak. My cheeks heat and I push the hair back from my face. "I mean... I know who you are. What can I do for you?"

She clears her throat faintly, amping up the tension I feel. "Well, I was calling to offer you your place back at NYB. It seems that there was some sort of administrative error on our part?"

It's as much a question as an answer.

My eyes go wide. My mouth opens. I shove back my hair again. "An administrative error?"

Empty-headed? Yes. But it's all I can think of to reply.

There is a distinct pause. I get the feeling that she's not doing this on her own. At length, she sighs.

"Yes. Well, the NYB would very much like to correct the administrative error... would you be willing to join us at rehearsals this week?"

My mouth screws to the side. "Did C— I mean, did Mr. Fordham put you up to this?"

I've accidentally struck a nerve, it seems. "And if he did? What does it matter how you got here or who asked for you to return? The question is whether or not you want to dance with us."

My cheeks fill with heat. "Of course, Miss Rosenberg. It would be an honor to return."

I can almost her thin lipped smile through the phone. "Good. We'll see you early on Wednesday."

Before I can say anything else, she disconnects the phone call. I stare at my phone blankly for a moment. My alarm clock begins blaring suddenly, making me panic for a moment.

It's seven in the morning. The time I normally get up for my morning run.

I turn my alarm off and toss my phone on the bed. Exhaling quietly, I press my face into the bed.

Sucking a breath in, I allow myself one single scream of excitement. After all, I worked my ass off to dance at the NYB. Getting it back is unexpected and nearly sweeter than the first time I heard that I was accepted.

But then I sit up, giving myself a shake. It's not final until I actually walk into dance class on Wednesday. I can't go getting my hopes up.

Not over an opportunity with Calum as a backer.

Not quite knowing what to do with myself, I make myself a cup of coffee and start getting dressed. I throw on my favorite pair of pink nylon shorts, a black sports bra, and an oversized blue tank top.

I down my coffee, my mind still swirling. Administrative issues?

It sounds like Calum was right there, directing her as she made the call to me. It does sound just like him to be so controlling.

In my mind, he stands over her, looking so domineering and stubborn, his icy eyes glinting. A chill slides down my spine.

A month ago, I would have called the sensation anticipation.

Grabbing my ancient iPod, I put in headphones and then tuck a key to my apartment in my shoe. I thunder down the stairs, swinging the front door wide.

I see dark-suited Calum stretched out in the doorway a little too late. I'm already in running mode, halfway out the door.

I smack into him hard enough to knock the air from my lungs. He saves me from going sprawling down the stairs by pure muscle strength; grabbing me by the arms, he braces both of us against the hard concrete of my stairs.

I look up at him, shocked. "What are you doing here?"

Calum licks his lips for a moment, the tiniest smirk on

his face. He rubs his hands together, his gaze dropping to my body. He cocks his head.

I fold my arms across my body. There's some possibility that I've got enough adrenaline pumping through my veins just now to make my nipples hard.

I don't want him to think that I am so stupid as to still want him... no matter how good he might seem in that suit right now, looking at me with such a devilish glint in his eyes.

"Fuck off," I say at last, wrenching myself from his grasp. I step back into my apartment, trying to keep my face neutral.

I definitely don't want Calum to know that the second I saw him, butterflies burst to life low inside my stomach.

He moves closer, his lips twitching. "I couldn't stay away. I missed you, beauty."

I school my expression just to keep my jaw from dropping. My heart skips two beats, stuttering in my chest.

"What?" I say, trying to come off as indignant.

He leans in the doorway, jerking his thumb over his shoulder. "My limousine is waiting to take us wherever you want to go."

He tries to take my hand. I smack his arm. "Quit that," I order. "If you think that you're just going to waltz back in and I will just fall back in bed with you, I think you have another thing coming."

He bites his lip, reaching out to skate his fingertips up my arm. My whole body visibly shudders. I grow warm all over.

Calum pins me in place with his arctic gaze, smirking.

"You have missed me too. I can tell. You're so tense that you're about to combust."

I glare at him. "I am not."

Clenching my jaw, I try to take another step back. My body is practically begging me to stay, to welcome him to come inside. To fuck his brains out.

But my brain is too smart for that. I haven't forgotten those words. "*We are letting you go, Kaia. I won't need your services anymore.*".

"You just thought that you would show up here and what... I would be happy to see you?" I ask, shaking my head.

His smirk slides away, replaced by a little frown. "I assumed we would resume as before. I mean, if it's the contract you want, if it's money—"

"It's obviously not money!" I say, my voice rising. "Otherwise I would've answered your lawyer's phone calls."

He tilts his head, not quite understanding. "Then what? I went to a lot of trouble to fix things so that we could resume our..." He pauses. "Our understanding."

"Our understanding?" I echo. For a moment, I have the urge to shove him out of the doorway and shut the door in his face. "I'm not one of your bimbos, Calum. I'm not a Barbie doll. I'm a human. Cut me and I'll bleed. Say that you don't want me, and I'll believe it."

He squints. "Wait, this is about your feelings still?"

Making a frustrated sound, I turn and reach for the door. Calum is too quick for me though. He uses his sheer size to keep the door open.

"I'm sorry. I'm not a machine. You can't just turn the

36

dials and turn on a sexy, happy song. What you did, what you said… it hurt me." I thump my fist against my heart. "When I'm trying to fall asleep, I still hear the words you said to me, over and over again."

His eyebrows lift. "That's what you have a problem with?"

"Yes!" I cry, feeling emotional.

He screws his face up for a minute. "Jesus, Kaia. I mean… what do you want me to say? I already came here, hat in hand. I told you that I missed you. I asked for you to come back to me…"

I shake my head slowly. My eyes start to mist over. "No. You told me that we could resume our understanding, whatever the fuck that means." I hug my torso, scowling at him. "I don't have a lot of self esteem, Calum. But even I want you to call the thing between us a relationship. Even I know that missing me isn't really enough. What about the next time you decide that you're done with me?"

That seems to shut him up. He narrows his gaze on my face, considering me.

"This?" He motions between our bodies. "You don't find this just anywhere, Kaia. We have the right kind of hunger, the right kind of passion, the drive. I've been looking for this chemistry for a long fucking time. And I'm not giving it up just because you said no this time."

I tilt my head and frown at him. "What does that mean?"

He smirks and leans in close, until his lips are nearly touching my ear. "It means that I don't forget, beauty. I can't forget how good I can make you feel. You have come for me over and over before; you'll do it again soon. I'll be back."

He kisses my ear ever so lightly, so quickly that I barely have time to register and recoil. He's already drawing back, that slick smirk on his lips. I see his eyes sparkle once more.

And then he turns and trots down the stairs, leaving me agog.

6

CALUM

I cast my gaze around the luxurious apartment, squinting. Every detail must be perfect, every last extravagance seen to. The sleek black furnishings that were here have been replaced by softer-looking crushed pink velvet and teak wood. The bed, once nakedly on display, is now sheltered by screens, peeking coyly out of a white lace canopy. Gone are the stage and pole; in its place is a small dance studio, complete with mirrored walls and a hardwood floor.

This space, once given over to my particular tastes, has now been completely redone to suit Kaia's needs. A kitchen has been built out in one corner of the vast space. The walls have been repainted in soft pastel colors, reminiscent of those that I noticed in her apartment.

With the late afternoon sun coming in the huge wall of windows, the place is completely transformed. Well, except the wall of sex toys. After the wall was repainted and the shelves swapped out for antique teak ones, a few toys were carefully placed on the wall for display.

Handcuffs, a huge dildo, a jeweled butt plug, and sleek black clitoral vibrator. Just to remind Kaia of what I promise to do to her while she's here.

There is a distant chiming sound. My head jerks around to where I've had a new security system installed. I stride over and touch a couple of buttons, pulling up a screen.

There is Kaia, entering the apartment's elevator with a frown. She's right on time.

Stepping outside the apartment's door, I wait for her.

Thirty seconds later, I watch her walk in. My entire body tightens as I look at her. She's wearing a short pink babydoll dress and tall white stockings and owning every inch of the look. With her long blonde hair split into two pigtails, she has me hard before she even turns those green eyes on me.

Her mouth twists. "What am I doing here, Calum?"

I smirk a little. "I thought about what you said yesterday. You said you wanted to feel like I saw you." Walking toward her, I look her up and down.

A blush rises in Kaia's cheeks. "That was a fraction of what I said," she says softly.

I take her by the hand, gently pulling her toward the doorway. "Come see."

She swallows and frowns, her brows drawing down suspiciously. "Calum…"

Reaching in my pocket, I pull out a tiny black box with a white satin bow wrapped around it. When I hand it to her, she takes it haltingly.

"What is it?"

I give her a bemused look. "Open it."

She drops my hand and unties the ribbon, then removes the lid. Inside, nestled in black velvet, is a shiny silver skeleton key.

Kaia glances up at me. "What does it lead to?"

I jerk my head toward the apartment's door. "This apartment."

She bites her lip, shaking her head. "This is generous, Calum. But it doesn't solve anything between us."

My lips twitch. "You don't even know what you're turning down, beauty. Come and see."

She gives me an exasperated look. Yet still, she lets me tug her toward the door. I catch a whiff of her perfume as I lead her into the apartment. Kaia always smells so damn enticing, fresh and clean and feminine. That scent goes to my head and reminds me of just what is at stake as I hurry her onward.

As soon as we step through the door, I hear the sound of her inhaling sharply. Seeing the changes I've made, she pulls her hand from my grip. I turn and look at her, raising a brow.

Her pouty little mouth is open ever so slightly. Her green eyes are wide, scanning the scene in front of her. A note of puzzlement crosses her face.

"What…?" Kaia looks at me, confused. "You redecorated?"

I fold my arms across my chest, rocking back on my feet. "I did. I thought it would be easier to talk you into moving in if it looked less like an upscale brothel and more like…" I pause, casting my gaze around, searching for the right words. "Well, more like some place that you called home."

Her brow furrows. "You're asking me to move in?"

I nod. "Yes. Well, actually... I have a deed of sale drawn up already with your name on it. I want you to own a space more befitting of my..." I swallow, forcing the word between my lips. "Girlfriend. If that's what you want to call yourself, anyway."

Her eyebrows shoot up. She still looks confused more than anything. "Calum, this is... quite generous... but..."

"There is more." I take the black box from her, setting it on the gray marble kitchen counter. I hold up the key. "This has several functions. It opens the front door, yes..."

I walk over to the wall, motioning to a simple black door. I brandish the key, fitting it into the lock. Then I push the door open and beckon to her.

Glancing nervously at me, Kaia tucks a strand of her hair behind her ear. She walks over and steps through the doorway.

The new room we're in is a simple guest bedroom, nothing fancy. She looks up at me, her puzzlement evident.

"Another bedroom?"

I smirk. "A doorway that leads into my private apartment. No other woman has ever even been invited here, much less been offered a spot next door. Is that enough commitment for you, beauty?"

She seems hesitant, almost stuck in the threshold between my apartment and the one that will hopefully be hers. When she pins me with her green gaze, there is still suspicion in it. "Why?"

Her simple question brings me to a halt. "Why? What do you mean, why?"

I see a flash of anger on her face. She turns away,

wrapping her arms around herself. "Why are you offering this to me, Calum? You could just as easily have any other ballerina in the world. Hell, you could have anyone you wanted. And I'm just wondering… why go to such lengths to have…" She stops, pulling in a deep breath. Emotion blooms on her face, tears misting her eyes. "You've already had me," she whispers. "What do I have to offer you now?"

Her words gut me. I stalk over to her, grabbing her arms and pulling her torso against mine. She swipes at her eyes as she pushes me away.

"Look at me," I command. Kaia shakes her head, still trying to hide though we are pressed together. I give her a shake. "Fucking look at me!"

Her breath halts and her eyes meet mine, shiny with tears. Her little body trembles where I touch it. She seems so tightly strung, as if the simplest touch or word could make her shatter into a thousand pieces.

"I could have anyone I want," I say. Brushing her hair back, I sink my fingers into it, working my fingers under her hair tie and close to her scalp. I grip her hair tightly, angling her head. "Yet I find myself unable to think of anybody else. All day and all night, I fantasize about having you back in my bed. About the way you sound when you come. About the way my cock feels when I'm buried so deep in your pussy that I can't remember anything else. About how I feel when I hold you after we fuck."

I scan her tear stained face, swallowing tightly. She doesn't seem able to speak. But her wide green eyes are glued to my face.

"I thought I could forget about you," I say softly, intensely. "But I was wrong, beauty. I really mean it when I say that I missed you. I've never missed a woman before. Not like I have missed you. I... I crave you."

"Calum..." she whispers. A prayer or maybe a plea.

I take the silver skeleton key and tuck it in her palm, closing her fist around it. "Say yes," I murmur, looking down into her face.

She wipes her eyes then looks at me again. "What about the contract?"

My heart starts thumping against the wall of my chest. "Whatever your terms, I'll sign it. Take the dollar amount you're thinking of and double it, Kaia. Say that one little word so that I can fucking ravage you. Right here, right now."

Her piercing green eyes take in my face. Her hand slides down to my hip. That's the moment I know that she's going to agree. I angle her head back, lowering my lips to her pulse point.

She gasps as my lips part, sucking lightly on her neck. She nods her head. "Yes," she whispers.

A second later, I slide my hands around to her ass and lift her up. She feels so fucking good that I have difficulty thinking. I find her lips and moan at the sweet taste of her. She urges me on, bucking her hips and opening her mouth under mine.

Carrying her out of the guest room, I head for the little bedroom made out of wooden dividers and canopied lace.

7

KAIA

*C*alum is everywhere all at once, his calloused fingers touching my shoulders and my breasts, his hips pinning mine against the bed. I throw my head back as he traces his lips down the column of my neck to the firm lines of my collarbone.

His hands are impatient as he sits me up and readjusts me on the bed. He cups my cheek for a moment and I turn my head, kissing his hand. He rubs his thumb along my lips. I make eye contact with him, letting a mysterious smile flash over my face.

Then I touch his hand, pushing his thumb into my mouth. I suck on it just a little, maintaining eye contact. His brow arches but he also bites his lower lip.

"I like looking at you, sucking on me like that," he says.

I release his thumb from my mouth with a pop. "I want to be good for you. I want to suck your cock. Will you show me how?"

Calum shakes his head. "I don't think you are ready for

it. I like it rough. You understand? You're sweet and delicate—"

I shoot him a glare. "Shut the fuck up. Show me how you like it. Teach me, Calum. *Please*."

Reaching down between our bodies, I find the hard outline of his cock in his pants. I press my hand against it while I moan.

He grits his teeth. "Get on your knees if you want it so bad."

He moves back and I scramble down to the floor. I get on my knees and look up at him, my heart pounding. He smirks as he comes to stand directly in front of me. With one smooth motion, he unzips his pants and pulls out his cock. I take a look at it; it's long, thick, and already hard.

He shifts his hips and runs his hand over his cock, circling it at its base and thrusting. The crown of his cock juts proudly out. "Mmm, beauty," he utters. "I can't wait until I fill up your throat with my come."

Then he runs his thumb over my mouth again.

I part my lips and run my tongue over his thumb. He hisses and pushes his pants and boxers down a few inches. "Open your mouth. Stick out your tongue."

Making eye contact with him, I follow his instructions obediently. He fists his cock and guides it to my lips. I kiss his cock gently, looking up to him for instructions.

"Run your tongue around the head, just here," he motions. "That's where I have a lot of nerve endings so everything is very sensitive."

Tilting my head to the side, I run my tongue against the hot skin of his cock. Calum closes his eyes briefly and exhales softly. He tastes earthy and very male as I keep licking his cock. He motions for me to place my hand at the base of his cock and shows me how to stroke him.

"Just like that," he says, biting his lip as he looks down at me. "Now take my cock in your mouth, beauty. But be careful with your teeth. Cover your teeth with your lips."

I do just as he says, taking the whole crown in my mouth. His gaze is laser focused on me as I bob up and down on it, taking the first few inches into my mouth.

Calum widens his stance and brings his hands up to rest on the back of my head. "I'm going to help you take me deeper. Keep your eyes on mine."

I look up at him and he bites his lip, thrusting into my mouth. For a split second, he slides his cock down my tongue and into the back of my mouth. I tense up, my eyes widening.

His eyes bore into mine. "That's good. Very, very good. Your mouth is so hot, Kaia."

He thrusts again and this time I choke. I try to pull back, but he stops me. "You said you wanted to learn what I like, beauty. I like going deep. I like when you gag on my cock."

My eyebrows jump up. This gagging sensation is normal, I guess. I nod, my mouth full of his dick.

Calum looks me in the eye and thrusts deep. My eyes start watering. I gag a little, my hands automatically coming up to grip his hips and pull him away.

He grabs one of my hands and thrusts into my throat again.

"Ahh," he utters, his eyes sliding shut. "I can't tell you how good it feels. Your throat is almost as good as your pussy, beauty. It's so wet and tight…"

He thrusts one final time, his cock staying in my throat for long enough that I have trouble breathing. I flex with fingers, burying my nails into the sensitive flesh on his hip. He responds automatically, jerking back. His cock leaves my mouth and I gasp.

"Fuck, baby," he mutters. He looks down at me, touching my chin with two fingers. "That was really good. The next time you go down on me, expect more of that."

I nod, still catching my breath. Calum pulls me to my feet, kissing me throughly. Then he pushes me back onto the bed once more.

I'm not wearing a bra, so when he pushes aside the thick pink cotton of my babydoll dress and exposes both my breasts, I'm bare before him.

"Fuck," he mutters again, looking at my breasts. "You look so beautiful right now. You already sucked my cock. Now the rest of your body deserves attention."

My hard pink nipples demand attention. My whole body tingles in anticipation of his mouth on my skin.

He puts his hands on my breasts, pushing them together, licking and kissing them both. My back bows, thrusting my nipples out and pushing my head back. I feel that familiar connection in my body, between my neck and my breasts, my nipples and my pussy. I roll my hips against his, my mouth opening to release a soft moan.

I push eagerly onward, rolling my hips again. Calum has what I lack.

"Fuck. I want you. I want your cock," I gasp.

Burying my fingers in the short hair at his nape, I gasp as he impatiently plucks at my dress. He raises the dress up and I raise my arms to help him get it off over my head.

He groans, looking at me. "Fuck, beauty. I've never wanted anyone like I want you," he grits out. "I need your pussy on my cock. I need you calling out my name."

His gaze is direct and scorching. He is a ravenous fire, threatening to burn me alive. And I am the kindling, stacked and ready, welcoming his spark to my dry tinder. We are so very close to combusting.

"I'm ready," I whisper, writhing against his body. "I'm wet. I'm ready. Come take your reward."

His fingers rip the garment from my body in his hurry to get me naked. I feel so desired, so wanted. I pull up his shirt, exposing his abs and then his chest. He stops and tears his shirt over his head, pressing his kiss down on me like he's drowning and I'm the only oxygen in the world.

Impatient, I slide his pants and his boxer briefs further down his legs. He thrusts towards me and I slip my hands down the strong muscles of his lower back and ass, pulling him against my body again.

Our tongues dance for several beats.

He frames my breasts with his touch, then slips one of his hands down my ribs, down my belly, to run his fingers along the cleft of my pussy. I close my eyes and moan as he probes the folds of my pussy.

I hiss, sucking in a breath. I part my legs as much as I can, moaning his name.

"Calum... oh fuck..." I writhe against him.

"Scoot back," he urges, voice gone to gravel. "Open your legs for me, beauty. Let me see what I bought."

He moves back and I spend my legs wide, eager to feel his touch. I'm so fucking wet right now that I could die.

Dropping my head and moving a couple of inches

further back on the bed, I moan as his clever fingers find my clit.

"That's it," he coaxes, looking down. He puts a little space between our bodies, urging me onward. "Spread your knees wide for me, honey."

I want to be wanton with him, to show him how hungry I am for whatever he will give me.

Calum puts two fingers in his mouth, then drops those fingers down to massage my clit. It feels so damned good, like I'm stretching and reaching for something explosive that is just outside of my grasp. He looks deep in my eyes and controls me with his touch, so that I'm spread open and wet, my heart pounding.

I thrust the tiniest bit and he chuckles. "Easy, beauty. Let me do all the work."

I lean back a little, biting my lip and staring at him like he's a whole damned meal and I'm starving. He rubs my clit with lazy fingers and I quiver, moaning at the sensation.

Calum gets this little smirk on his lips as he looks at me.

"What?" I ask, flushing at his probing gaze.

His smile widens just bit. His fingers dip from my clit to my core, circling and teasing.

"I'm just watching you. Waiting to see you come. I want to memorize every second of it." He slides one finger into my core, lighting me up from the inside.

It feels too damned good.

He sinks down to his knees. My thighs tense and my knees start to close, but he tuts at me. "Stop. You know that you want to feel my tongue pressed against your clit. Don't fight it."

"Fuck," I groan, gripping the sheets. "Hearing your dirty talk is so fucking hot, Calum."

Pulling both hands out to push my knees wide again, Calum starts kissing the inside of my thigh, making a clear path to my pussy. I squirm as I ache for what I know is coming.

I can feel the excitement building, feel myself growing hotter and wetter every second. His nose tickles the inside of my thigh.

I can't help the moan that escapes my lips when he parts my pussy lips with two fingers, blowing delicately on the too-needy flesh he finds there.

My back arches. I feel like I'm already on the edge and he hasn't even touched me yet.

As he slowly kisses my pussy, I hold my breath and bury my fingers in his hair. When his tongue circles my clit, a moan bursts from my throat.

"Oh god," I say. "Calum, your tongue feels like magic."

He sets up a rhythm, licking and sucking, making me as hot as fire. It feels good to rock my hips against his mouth, to whisper *yes* when he hits the right spot, to throw my head back and let soft sounds leave my throat.

All the while, he keeps leading me down a path, driving me wilder and wilder with desire, until…

I climax suddenly, violently. Choking, I feel the vibrations deep within my body ripple out to my breasts, my collarbone, my legs, my fingertips, my toes. Calum seems to know how to help me ride out my orgasm, slowing but not stopping his tongue as I come.

"Fuck!" I say. "Calum…"

He is already kissing his way up my body. I turn my flushed face up to him, offering him my mouth.

He takes it greedily, his breath tasting deep and earthy and charged. My own exotic taste. I recognize it by now.

His hands are everywhere, sliding from my shoulders down to grab my ass, then back up to my breasts. Although I just orgasmed, already I can feel my body preparing for more.

"How?" I ask.

He drops a kiss to my shoulder. "How what, princess?"

I grip his shoulders. "How can I possibly want more? I need more, even though I've just orgasmed."

He laughs against my skin. "That's because you are perfect for me, beauty. Your body just knows what I want."

Kissing him desperately, I try encourage him on with my body. I roll my hips against his, grabbing his ass. I cling to his shoulders with one arm as I fumble with his pants with the other, smoothing my fingers down his back to his bare ass.

Calum leans down and kisses me passionately. He pushes me back on the bed more, then takes his cock from my grip and presses the blunt tip against the inside of my thigh. I pull him in with my legs, making him readjust a little until he settles the tip of his length against my slippery core. We both groan in unison as he pushes inside, stretching me out with each inch.

I grip his shoulders, my nails digging into his flesh. His brow furrows in concentration as he works his length all the way in. We both groan at the sensation of my pussy adjusting to his huge cock; being so snugly fit together feels so fucking right.

"Fuck," he murmurs. "You are so god damn tight, Kaia."

I try to thrust my hips, eager for more. "I swear, if you don't fuck me right this second, I'm going to die."

Calum smirks and starts slow, slowly pumping his cock in and out of me. I start to feel ripples of pleasure as he rocks against me, the sound of his cock filling my wet pussy filtering into the room.

Calum takes my breast in one hand, plucking at the nipple. I start to move in time with him, rolling my hips. Little licks of flame start to unfurl themselves deep inside of me, stealing my breath away.

"Ohh," I moan. Tossing my head back, I meet his cautious thrusts. He's being careful with me, but I don't want that. "I want... *more*. Fuck me harder, Calum."

He looks down at me, a fierce look in his eyes. I'm unsure what I've unleashed in him, more beast than man. But at the same time, I am moving closer to the edge. It won't take much to make me come.

It feels unbelievably good to move my hips in time with each thrust. I focus on that, letting my eyes drift closed, my fingers reaching for my own nipple. Calum groans and pushes my hand aside.

He shifts our positions, creating a little space between our bodies. I hate that, until he slips his hand down between us and finds the cleft of my pussy.

He brushes my clit, the sensation like a live wire. I

suddenly feel electrified, moaning and clutching at his shoulders.

"Fuck!" I cry. "Calum... jesus!"

He rams his cock home, punctuating each thrust by stroking my clit.

"You like this, beauty?" he whispers. "Show me how much of a good girl you can be. Come for me, right now."

"Calum... I..."

Suddenly, I'm falling down a deep, dark crevasse, seizing up, my whole body shaking and clamping down. Feeling a million tiny jolts of sensation overwhelming my entire system, all at once. My pussy convulses, spasming around his cock.

I lose track of time and space for nearly a minute, When I come back down to reality, I open my eyes and keep my hips moving, trying desperately to breathe. He hammers his cock home at a blistering pace, his movement freezes as he approaches his own peak.

"Yes. Look at me!" he says.

Mouth open, eyes glued to his, I can only try to drag in each breath.

"Mine," Calum roars, thrusting into me. "You. Are. Fucking. Mine."

He thrusts unbelievably hard a half dozen times. I feel him coming, feel his cock twitching. The look on his face is one of equal torment and bliss, lasting for half a minute at least. I can only turn my lips up to his once more.

Calum leans down and cups my jaw, kissing me slowly, tenderly. We both struggle for breath as we come down together.

8

CALUM

*I*n the middle of the night, Kaia lays curled up against me, her arm draped across my chest. Her breathing evens out even as the salty sweat on her body cools and dries. She shivers, half awake.

I very carefully extricate myself. She stirs and looks at me through cracked eyelids. Something deep and dark breaks free deep inside the ice cave I call a heart.

I can tell myself whatever I want, but the truth of the matter is that I care about this girl.

Instead of stealing away as I had planned to, I grab the light pink comforter and pull it back onto the bed. Then I take up the same position, tugging the comforter around both our bodies.

Kaia yawns as she finds a comfortable spot against my naked body. She wiggles just a little, sighing as she settles down.

"Thanks, Calum," she murmurs. Her eyes sink closed once more.

My chest tightens as I look down at her. She's so

fucking tiny. I encircle one of her wrists with my fingers, frowning a little.

As a dancer, I spend all day every day that I'm in the studio just looking at bodies. And Kaia looks even thinner than usual. It shows in her wrists, her ankles, the jut of her hipbones from her pelvis.

Kaia has either been exercising too much, eating too little, or both.

My mouth turns down at the corners. I stare up toward the lofted ceiling, trying to decide what I'm going to do about it. Do I just tell her to eat more? Do I add something to her contract?

Ah, the contract. It's a little impersonal. Especially given that I just fucked Kaia's brains out.

But it does give me some latitude to make certain demands. I have a basic need — to never be denied anything sexual, ever. Any time, any place, any thing I want. And while I guarantee that with the contract and a big payday, I might as well get everything I want.

What I want more than anything at this moment is for things to be as if we were never apart for a month. After half an hour or so of thinking about it, I ease myself out of Kaia's bed. I make sure to bury her in the blanket... but she still looks impossibly small on that big bed all alone.

I grab my phone from my pants and start texting my lawyer a list of things that need to be added to Kaia's contract. Biting my lower lip, I pace and text.

The lawyer, for his part, responds right away. For as much as I'm paying the damn guy, he'd better do what I say, no matter what damn time it is.

At length, Kaia stirs sleepily. "Calum?"

I abruptly cut my text conversation off. "Yeah, beauty?"

She pulls back the covers. "Are you going to come back to bed?"

For a second, I think about tossing my phone aside and rejoining her in the warm bed. It seems… peaceful.

But then I shake my head. "No. I'll be back when you wake up though."

Kaia cocks her head and frowns, but I can already see her resistance fading. "If you're sure…"

I stand at the foot of her bed, clenching and relaxing my fists. Her eyes start to close, her resistance to sleep disappearing. "I'm sure," I say quietly.

The desire to stay the night in her bed is very tempting. But once you cross that line, there is no taking it back.

Calling Kaia my girlfriend is the only concession she's getting from me tonight.

I head off through the side door into my apartment, thinking about that word. Paramour. It might be awkward and dated, but it acknowledges a sexual relationship between us. That's all that I can handle at the moment.

I toss and turn in my own bed, that sticky little word following me into my dreams. By the time I actually wake up, it's an hour later than my usual start time.

After showering and briefly checking my email, I print up the signed contract. I dress in my usual dark Armani suit and white button up. Gathering the contract and the deed, I return to her apartment.

Despite the early hour, Kaia is just coming out of the shower. She smiles at me sheepishly, her cheeks darkening. "Hey. You look…" Her mouth twists. "Expensive."

I feel her gaze wander down my torso. My whole body tightens under her examination. Jesus, it's only been a few hours since I've seen her and yet I'm ready to rip that towel off her body and take her on the cold floor.

I arch a brow at her. "I thought you would still be asleep."

She pushes a hand through her wet blonde hair, exhaling. "No. Once you left, I couldn't sleep. About an hour ago I said fuck it and got up to run... And that's when I realized that I'm out of reasonable clothes. Everything that is kept here is all garters and barely-there black dresses."

My lips curve up. "Oh yeah?"

I wander toward her, tracing two fingers up her bare arm. She shivers and looks up at me, a note of hunger rising between us.

"I've missed this," she whispers. Kaia steps forward, pressing her body into mine, biting her lip. I swear, her green gaze pierces me through.

Lifting her chin with my forefinger, I lower my mouth to hers. She still tastes of toothpaste, her minty essence bursting across my tongue when I plumb the depths of her mouth. She makes the softest moan and pushes up onto her tiptoes, her fingers digging into my lapel.

God, I have missed this. Her scent in my nose, the feel of her exquisite bare skin humming under my fingers. The way her quiet moans raise the fine hairs on the back of my neck.

Kaia eventually pulls back, her green eyes gone dark with lust. Her voice is gravel when she speaks. "Is that the contract?"

Looking down, I realize that I still clutch the sheaf of

papers in my grip. For a minute, I almost forgot that I pay her for this arrangement.

My mouth turns down just a hair and I clear my throat. "Yes. If you want to get dressed before you sign these, I can make us some coffee."

She seems to deflate slightly. "Okay. If that's what you want."

She turns away, padding barefoot toward the bedroom. There is a whiff of defeat in her step, as if I've said the wrong thing.

I stare after her for a few seconds and try to parse the things left unsaid. What was it that she hoped to hear?

Shaking my head, I stalk over to the kitchen, tossing the contract onto the big marble island. Damned if I know the answer.

But I can make us both a cup of coffee. So I busy myself for the next few minutes boiling and steeping and pouring.

I look up right as she emerges from the bedroom. There is a cup of coffee in my hand; I forget it as I watch her walk toward me, swinging her hips. It's the dress; with three quarter length sleeves and a modest neckline, it is quite short and made out of ribbed cotton. It fits her like a fucking glove, exalting her natural, near effortless beauty.

Kaia looks at me, grinning a little at my expression. "I told you. Apparently we don't keep anything here but fuck me dresses."

"I am patting myself on the back for that decision right now," I say, my gaze traveling down her taut thighs and chiseled calves.

She saunters up, taking the mug of coffee right out of my hand. "Is this for me?"

She doesn't wait. She takes a large sip and leans her elbows on the marble island. Drawing the contract closer, she starts to read.

I can't do anything but come up behind her, pressing my erect cock against her barely covered ass. She giggles as the cleft of her ass welcomes my hardness.

I've never been more serious about getting my cock out and into the girl in front of me. One hand trails down to unzip my fly. The other tugs the hem of her dress up just a few inches so that her ass is half covered.

"Calum!" she says, glancing back at me. "Let me just read this and sign it. Then you can do whatever you want."

Shaking my head, I grind my cock against her ass. "It's not my fault you walked out wearing that dress, beauty. You sucked all the air from the fucking room."

Her cheeks go pink. "Either I'm really your paramour, in which case you'll cool it while I sign this. Or I'm more than that and you can have me right now."

She looks me dead in the eye and raises her leg, putting her knee on the counter. Exposing her pussy, barely covered by a tiny scrap of lace. I can feel heat radiating off her as I grab her lacy thong and rip it clean off her body. Her perfect little pussy is right there, beckoning me with it's wet pinkness. Her tiny pucker of an ass looks ready to be eaten and filled with my come.

I toss her panties aside as I sink to my knees, burying my face against her exposed flesh. Everything else is forgotten as I feast, exploring her pussy and clit first.

Using two fingertips to massage her clit, I move to kiss around the tight balloon knot of her ass.

She gasps and I can see her contract. God, all I can imagine is how good that's going to feel when my cock is buried to the hilt inside of her ass. Dragging the tip of my tongue around the sensitive skin outside, I rub her clit. All the while moving my tongue closer and closer to her ass.

I finally swipe my tongue over it and she moans, her head falling back. I use a little of her lubrication, gathering it by sliding a thick finger into her pussy.

Then I take that same finger, wet with her own juices, and swirl it around her ass. I see her clench again but she moans too.

Penetrating Kaia's ass with the tip of my finger is slow going. I press my fingertip against her ass lightly, adding in a kiss. I stop for a minute and kiss the outside, leaving the skin wet from my saliva.

Kaia's hips start thrusting. "Do it," she whispers. "Please. Pop my cherry, Calum."

I press my finger against her ass, hissing as it sinks in. In my mind, I'm ready to fuck her, to fill her ass with my cum and watch it drip from her. But I know she needs more finesse than that.

I pause. "Don't move. I need to grab something."

She stiffens. "Calum—"

But I'm already sprinting across the apartment, reaching for lube and a black silicon butt plug. I'm back in a flash, my hands urging her back into position.

"Let me see that pussy," I grate. I pop the cap on the lube, covering the butt plug in it. Then I start rubbing the silicone toy around her ass. "You aren't ready for something as big as my cock in your ass, beauty. Not yet. But this should make you feel so damn full…"

Pushing the tip in her ass, I bite my lip. This is about the hottest thing I'll ever witness, so I am trying to encode this moment on my brain.

"Oh!" she moans, biting her lip as she looks back at me. "Give me more."

I work the head of the toy in and out until she can take the mushroom flared tip of it. It disappears inside her ass, the flat base at the end sticking out. I watch her carefully.

"Tell me how it feels, dirty girl," I murmur.

Kaia bites her lip, closing her eyes. "My clit is aching. I'm so full and my ass is stretched, but…"

I reach around her body with one hand, finding her clit. It only takes a few circles for her to start clenching. She squeezes her eyes tight and starts thrusting against my touch.

I stop, picking her up and carrying her across the apartment to the bedroom. When I put her down on the bed on all fours, I push my pants down to my thighs. I want her to feel my big fucking cock reaming her pussy, to know what it's like to be so full that her orgasm is more of an explosion than anything else.

"Touch yourself," I order as I roll a condom down my cock. "Rub your clit. I love to see you getting wild for me, beauty."

Her eyes are full of impatience and anticipation as she looks me dead in the eye. "Fuck me like you mean it, Calum. Don't hold back. My pussy is ready for you."

In two seconds, I'm burying myself deep in her

wetness, thrusting deep. She hisses, pulling me down for a brutal kiss.

"Fuck, beauty," I gasp. I rock my hips into her, marveling at what a beautiful fucking picture she is right now. "You're so damn tight."

Kaia grips my shoulders and drops her hands down my back, grabbing handfuls of my ass. "Harder! Fuck me like this is the last time."

Holding myself up on one arm, I give her everything I've got. I ram my cock in and out, loving the way her eyes roll up in the back of her head. Her pussy is so tight, so wet, so fucking hot… it pulses as she gets closer to the edge.

She rolls her hips to meet mine. She bares her teeth. I hammer her pussy as fast as I can, rapidly approaching my own peak.

Kaia comes with a scream, her pussy convulsing, her whole body seizing up. "Fuck!"

I let myself go, focusing on how amazing her little body feels underneath mine. She rakes her fingernails up my back; it's the edge of pain that tips me over the edge. I slam my cock into her body as it twitches and pulses. It feels like I'm dying for a moment. Cum drains from my balls and spurts out the tip of my cock.

"*Fuuuuuuuuck,*" I say, thrusting a final time. I still, my heart racing, sucking in deep breaths.

When I collapse on the bed beside Kaia, I pull her close. We lay like that for the longest time, tangled up in each other, unwilling to let go.

9

KAIA

I wake up with sunlight already slanting across my face. Sitting up, I notice that not only has Calum slipped out... he's spent a few seconds to smooth out the comforter on the other side of the bed. As if he was never here.

But as I drag myself up and into the shower, I know that he was. There are faint fingerprints on my hips and several bruises on my tender breasts. Closing my eyes and standing under the shower's spray, my mouth curves up.

Calum was wild early this morning, an unnameable beast. And though I don't like waking alone, I love him for taking me so ruthlessly.

My eyelids snap open. Did I just think that? No. No, it was just an aberrant thought. Just my brain tying itself into knots because I'm in a relationship now. Still, the morning glow is receding, the bubble we built last night contracting and bursting in the cold morning air.

I rush through the rest of my shower and dressing. I will need to be on my A game today when I return to the

New York Ballet Company. Luckily I have several leotards to choose from and tights are plentiful too. After dressing in a pair of sweatpants and an oversized t-shirt, I'm about ready to go. Except… I'm not sure where to go. Who do I ask about getting a ride downtown?

Biting my lip, I search for my phone. The last place I remember having it was the kitchen…

I find it where I remembered, with a handwritten note attached. When I see Calum's precise scrawl, goosebumps break out on my arms.

K — While you live here, Carlos will be at your beck and call. As soon as you're ready to go, text him. He will also make sure that all your personal items are moved over from your apartment.

PS - HERE ARE the contract and the deed. Sign them before you leave.

SETTING THE NOTE ASIDE, I sigh deeply. Calum thoughtfully left a pen atop the documents. I don't even read them. I just dash my name across the dotted lines and leave them for someone else to deal with.

When I text Carlos, he responds almost immediately, saying he's waiting downstairs. Pulling a face, I take the elevator down to the ground floor. The second I step off of the elevator, a Latino man in his twenties greets me.

"Señorita Walker? If you will just come this way…"

He waves me outside and into a waiting limousine.

"Thank you," I say, scooting into the backseat. The door closes and I find my dance bag sitting on the leather seat beside me. Dragging the bag over, I note that it's definitely my bag. KAW is still stitched on the front, the colors both faded so much that the pink and red have long since blended together. I run my fingers over the stitching, feeling a tiny twinge.

My mom added that detail so many years ago. As the limo pulls out, I get my phone out with the intent of calling her.

It's early still. So I settle for text messaging.

Hey mom. Just thinking about you. Are you doing okay?

Nothing in response. Not yet, at least. I tune out for most of the quick ride to the NYB building. Just mulling over all the changes in my life over the last few days. Rejoining the NYB. Taking Calum back. Soon I'll be moving apartments…

It's a lot in one week.

As we pull alongside the enormous cement building, I see a familiar figure heading toward me.

"This is good!" I call to Carlos. Grabbing my duffel, I slide out of the car just in time to catch Ella by surprise.

She does a double take, her mouth falling open. "You… where have you been?"

She runs over to me, hugging me so tightly I can't breathe. I grin and embrace her. She pulls back, shaking her head.

"I thought something had really happened to you," she scolds me. "What…"

The limo pulls away from the curb, catching her eye. She looks at it for a second, her head tilting. "Whose limousine is that?"

My cheeks heat. "You don't have anything you'd rather ask me?"

Her mouth pulls into a frown. "Are you coming inside?"

"Yup." I pat my dance bag. "Come on. We can stretch while we talk."

She lets me pull her along by the hand. I jog up to the building, opening the heavy front door. I suck in a breath; it smells ever so faintly of rosin and perspiration. I shiver; I've missed being here.

When we are in the studio, barefoot and scoring the soles of our pointe shoes with razors, Ella slides me a look. My mouth turns up at the corners.

"What?"

She shrugs. "I took over the role of Aurora. You're not getting it back, either. I think the girl who was The Lilac Fairy just dropped out, though."

She pulls a face, mocking me. "Don't think for one second that I'm just going to stop asking questions. It's a little funny that you think I'm so docile."

I bang one of my shoes, testing how bouncy it is. "That's not the first word I would use to describe you."

She puts her razor aside and starts to pull on her shoes. "Come on. Out with it. And don't even bother trying to lie to me or tell me half the truth. You are a terrible liar."

That gives me pause. Calum and I didn't explicitly talk about what I should tell anybody that is curious about my life. He didn't expressly say that I should keep him a secret.

Our relationship is still forbidden by the ballet, though. And there is the little fact that he first discovered me while I was stripping…

Better not open that can of worms. I clear my throat and start to lace up my shoes.

"I'll make you a deal," I say. "I'll tell you the broad strokes. Okay? But you have to swear not to ask me for the details."

She gives me a sour look. "I can save you a lot of time."

My eyebrows rise. "Oh?"

Ella gets to her feet, pursing her lips. "You're screwing Mr. Fordham. I saw you two together a week before your vanishing act and you were full on kissing." She looks at me pointedly, stretching her ankles. "If you could get pregnant from a kiss, you would be. I hope you're using birth control."

I flush down to my roots. "You didn't say anything?!"

She squints at me. "Neither did you. Now tell me the rest of the damn story before I get cranky and strangle your ass."

As we stretch ourselves out, I tell her about the events from a month ago. How Calum dumped me. How I spent three weeks crying before I decided to apply at another company.

How Calum basically seduced me into taking him back. The only thing I left out is our little contract.

I can't confess that dirty little secret to Ella. Not if I ever want to be able to look her in the eye again, anyway.

Ella puts her hands on her hips, cocking her head at me. "Wait, wait, wait. Let me get this straight. You're sleeping with our boss. You guys... what, get in an argument?"

Blood rushes to my cheeks again. "He says that he has a reason for the breakup. I can't really spell it out for you, but it's... a good enough reason."

"And then he just missed you? He decided that he wanted to have you back?"

I drop my gaze, focusing on my feet. "Apparently."

She makes a sound of displeasure. Ella grabs one of her old pointe shoes from her bag. Then she pads over to me and hurls it at me, hitting me on the shoulder. It didn't hurt, but I still rub the spot.

"Ow!" I protest.

She wags a finger in my face. "Quit letting men tell you what to do, Kaia. You spent your whole damn life trying to get out from under your dad's thumb. And now you are just wrapping yourself around Mr. Fordham's little finger. Show some backbone!"

My mouth opens. "I— I just—"

"Do you need me to get more shoes?" she asks, exasperated. She jerks her thumb over her shoulder. "Really, I will. I have like five pairs and they're ready to go if you want to argue about it."

I shoot her a glare. "Your point is made, Ella."

She looks at me, a little smirk on her lips, and shakes her head. "You're a damn fool, Kaia. A complete and utter fool."

The studio door swings open, punctuating our quiet time. Several other dancers walk in, their eyebrows rising when they see me. Manon is the last in the door and the most taken aback by my presence.

"Look at what the cat dragged in!" she exclaims, dropping her bag by the wall. "I thought you got fired."

I level her with my iciest stare. "Drop dead, bitch."

Manon's brows arch. She starts to retort, but then Calum makes an early entrance. He is dressed in sweats and a loose white tank top, his arms looking more muscular than ever.

"All right!" he calls, clapping his hands. "You're here. I'm here. Let's do some deep tissue stretches."

Ella goes to the barre to our right. Pulled as if by gravity, I fall into line just behind her. Calum starts stretching us all out like a kid playing with taffy.

"Can you hold your pose for five more seconds?" he demands. "Push it a little farther. Go a second longer."

By the time that we reach the hard work, I am noticeably slower. Every step is tougher than I remembered, even lie and pirouette feels awkward.

"Kaia!" Calum shouts. "Keep up! And one, and two, and three—"

I feel like I'm dying. Like I've never taken a pointe class in my whole damned life. I really thought that I had stayed on top of my exercise routine over the last month.

But I guess that just isn't the case.

At the end of class, we are all sweating. I'm gasping and I have a stitch in my side.

"Okay, okay," Calum says, clapping his hands once again. "Enough. Everyone grab a Gatorade and a banana. No excuses. Finish them both before you leave this room."

He points to a tray that has appeared beside the door at some point during the last fifteen minutes. All the dancers look around, puzzled expressions blossoming.

"Move!" Calum's voice booms through the studio. "We haven't got all day!"

I hurry to grab my snack, making wide eyes at Ella as she passes me. When I'm halfway through my banana, she leans over and hisses to me.

"Does this have to do with y'all fucking? What kind of crazy shit do you guys get up to? It'd have to be serious for him to make sure you replenish all these electrolytes…"

I snarf my banana, a combination of surprise, laughter, and denial. Glaring at her with watering eyes, I shove the rest of the banana down my gullet.

It's only then that I catch Calum staring at us out of the corner of my eye. I turn to see what he wants. But just like that, he moves away, coughing into his hand.

Now I really start to blush.

"Creep," I mutter. Shaking my head, I start taking off my shoes. "Hey, Ella. Do you want to walk around the block while we have a break?"

Ella grins at me. "Yeah. Eric should be finishing a morning class in a few minutes… maybe he can join."

Color bursts into my cheeks. I had completely forgotten that Eric even existed. "Oh," I manage.

Her grin intensifies. "Yeah, oh. What are you going to tell him, I wonder?"

Slipping on a pair of flip flops, I shoulder my dance bag. I sigh. "I don't know."

She rolls her eyes, throwing an arm around my shoulders. "I can't wait to find out."

Shaking my head and looking heavenward, I blow out a long stream of breath and start heading out.

CALUM

I stand in the third row of the auditorium, watching the dancers onstage. They fumble their way through a particularly difficult piece of choreography. I cup my hands to my mouth. "Stop! Go back fifteen seconds. We're going to do it over and over again until you can do every step correctly."

There are several low groans as the dancers all run back to stage left, posing. I wave to the pianist, who begins to play once more. It plays out nearly the same way as before; the two male dancers try but do not succeed in a complicated-looking combination. Then, from the wings, emerges Kaia. Before she can pirouette her way over to be swept up in one of the dancer's arms, though... I call cut.

"Stop!" I call. "Let me show you exactly how it should be done."

Kaia looks at me, eyes wide. I shoo her off the stage, chasing the rest of the dancers as I hop over the rows of seats. It's nothing to jump up on the stage and discard my shoes.

I walk swiftly to take one of the dancer's positions, raising my arms. "Remember. There is nothing that I will demand of you that I cannot do myself. I simply cannot do it repeatedly."

I let the moment wash over me, signaling for the music to begin again. "From the top! And one, two, and—"

I execute the combination with extreme grace and a killer muscle memory. In preparation for today, I've spent the last week mastering the trickiest combinations. The only thing I'm not quite ready for is for Kaia to come bounding onto the stage. She's looking at me with those big green eyes, filled with trepidation, anticipation, or some mix of the two.

The very idea of touching her right now, in front of all of these people, starts my heart hammering hard in my chest. The thought that I might get aroused touching her silky skin, thinking about what I'm going to do to her later?

That's definitely a problem.

I finish with a flourish a moment before our characters actually touch. Pulling away, I turn toward the dancers watching from off stage. Essentially giving Kaia the cold shoulder, but it's easier than the other alternative.

One of the male dancers clears his throat. "Do you think you could run it one more time, into the part where Gallifron lifts The Lilac Fairy?"

My heart clatters against my ribs. I slowly nod, knowing that I'm backed into a corner. "Yeah. Let's go."

I move back across the stage, sucking in a deep breath. Posing with one arm raised, I paste a smile on my face.

The music begins. Without overthinking it, I dominate

the stage, performing the pirouettes and jetés flawlessly. I pull out of the final jeté and Kaia appears in my peripheral vision, dancing across like a lively little sprite.

She makes a big, exaggerated leap toward me. I catch her effortlessly, my eyes suddenly glued to her face. Lifting her up along my body and nearly over my head is perfectly natural. Her lithe body presses against mine and I am suddenly looking at her breasts, at the hard little nipples that tease me.

Noticing them is like someone just punched me in the stomach. Suddenly, it's hard to breathe. And when she kicks her leg back, using me as a sort of stretching post to get her leg all the way up… when my hands slide down to hold her thighs so that she can stay en pointe for just a little longer…

When our eyes connect…

There is a perfect moment, a long second where it's just Kaia and me. Everything else fades away. We just float, buoyant, in the green sea of her intense gaze.

The moment recedes, eventually flowing away. Kaia dances away and into the arms of someone else. And I'll admit to a moment of jealousy.

Of anxiety.

What if Kaia doesn't come back? As it turns out, my question isn't answered. Instead, I'm forced back into a semblance of reality.

"Okay," Bas calls, clapping his hands. "Enough. We can't have Calum run through the entire scene, can we? Let's run it back and go through it one more time…"

By the time that rehearsal is over, I'm really ready to get the fuck out of here. I've been pushing Kaia and all the

VIVIAN WOOD

rest of the NYB hard for almost a week. Trying to get her back in fighting form.

While Bas is still lecturing the younger dancers, I grab my stuff and head home. My head is full of angsty mush, something that is not cured by a long hot shower or two electrolyte drinks.

Pulling on a fresh pair of gray sweatpants, I wander over to her doorway. She's only just getting in, sagging a little as she walks to her bedroom. She doesn't seem able to string a sentence together at the moment. She just utters an unintelligible sound and falls face first onto her bed.

"Unfhh."

I saunter after her, a smile playing on my lips. Rounding the screen wall, I fold my arms across my bare chest. Kaia stirs, peeking at me with a groan.

"Was I ever truly in shape?" she moans. "It feels like my muscles are all over-stretched silly putty."

Cocking my head, I look at her, splayed out on the mattress. Brushing my hand up her bare outer thigh, my lips twitch. "I think you would have been worn out today no matter what. But the workout was particularly draining for you. I would guess that your body is adjusting to being an athlete again."

She pushes herself up, turning her head to look at me. "Remind me of this the next time I decide to take a month away from dancing, will you?"

She rubs her shoulder with a groan, eyeing me. She looks so pretty sitting there, her hair thrown into a messy bun, her slender figured still cinched in her simple black leotard. My cock stirs, a reminder that it's been twelve hours since I last got my dick wet. But there is something

76

about Kaia's obviously soreness and exhaustion that calls to me.

I like to think that I just know the feeling all to well. That I, having been a dancer for so many years, just know that she needs a break.

One dancer looking out for another. A teacher caring for his student. A patron showing concern for his mistress.

But there is an undercurrent of something else there, another motive. As much as I am loathe to admit it, as much as I want to bury my cock inside a stranger who is just here for my pleasure…

I know that my feelings do run deeper. My mouth turns down at the corners as I make a decision.

"You should soak your whole body," I say, giving her thigh another squeeze. "I'll run you a bath."

Her eyebrows shoot up. "You will?"

"What, you don't think I know exactly how to care for your dancer's body?"

Her lips thin. "I didn't say that. I'm just… surprised. I thought you would maybe slap me on the ass and tell me not to complain. That's all."

I smirk at her. "Who says I won't? I like to keep you on your toes."

Just to confound her further, I raise my hand and give her a firm slap on the ass.

"Calum!" she squeaks. "You are such a terror."

Turning away, I head to the white marble covered bathroom. This is one room that I really didn't oversee when decorating this apartment. To my surprise, it's light and bright, with a large glass door shower and a separate oversized copper tub. I turn on the taps, noticing that a neat wicker basket of shower essentials has been laid out for Kaia.

In it, I find the usual shampoo, conditioner, and body wash. But I also find a little sachet of bath salts, which I pour into the steaming water as it fills the tub.

When I turn away from the tub, I turn to find Kaia standing in the doorway, watching me with a curious expression. My heart skips a beat because she is standing there completely naked, shivering as she steps on the cool marble tiles.

Her bare nipples beg for my mouth to taste them. The gentle vee between her firm thighs stirs my cock to life once again.

"Jesus," I mutter. "Do you know how beautiful you are?"

Kaia's face flushes but she manages the tiniest smile. "I know that you think so."

I growl at that response. With two fingers, I beckon her over. "Come here."

She sucks her bottom lip into her mouth, her eyes darkening. Her hips sway and her head drops back as she comes up to me, looking so very innocent.

I grab her hand, tugging her along with me. Closing the bathroom door, I pull her in front of me so that both of us are reflected in the mirror's polished surface.

I whisper in her ear. "Look at yourself, beauty. Look at me as I touch you."

I run my hands down her arms, up each both sides of her ribcage, cupping her pouty breasts. As I tease her nipples, pinching them, she quietly gasps.

I grind my erection into her lower back, letting her know I'm hard. "Do you not see what I see?"

My hands flutter down her sides, skating across her lower belly. My fingers dip down to the vee between her legs, just teasing the wetness I'm willing to bet is there.

Kaia hisses, closing her eyes. "Calum…"

I grip her hips hard. "Open your eyes, beauty. Look at yourself. Feel how hard I am. That's for you, Kaia. You do that to me."

Her eyes open a slit, taking us both in. She isn't quite sure what to make of this, I think. So she turns in my arms, reaching up on her tiptoes to brush a kiss against my lips.

As much as I want to, I don't take the bait. Instead I step back with a sigh. Taking her by the hand, I lead her over to the bath.

"Come on," I urge. "Get in."

She pins me with her gaze but leans on me as she steps into the heat. Sinking down slowly, she sighs.

"Ohh. That does feel wonderful…" she murmurs.

Sucking my bottom lip into my mouth, I get an idea. "Open your knees. Let me touch you."

She blushes down to the roots of her hair. "Calum…"

I'm not really interested in whatever her complaint is. Kneeling beside the tub, I run my hand down her inner thigh, plunging it into the water. She parts her thighs for me and looks up at me with an expression of anticipation.

"Don't close your eyes," I say softly. I trail my touch down to the patch of blonde hair at the apex of her thighs.

Her lips part. She squirms a little as I rub my fingertips up and down her slit. Not quite touching her clit or her pussy. Just teasing.

She moans and whines my name. "Calum…"

Just the reaction I was hoping for. I smirk

"Tell me what you want, Kaia."

She gives me a little glare. "I want you to stop teasing me. If you're going to touch me… then touch me."

I raise an eyebrow. "Like this?"

I skate the back of my hand along her outer thigh. She shoots me another glare.

"No."

I slide on digit along the seam of her pussy, challenging her. "Tell me, beauty. I want to hear you beg for it."

Her eyes flicker closed for a moment. I'm worried that she won't actually do it, that she'll demand to get out of the bath.

But I think I underestimated her. Kaia's eyes snap open, burning like twin coals.

"Rub my clit, Calum," she demands. "I want you to make me come."

A feeling of pride swells in my chest. Holding up a finger, I reach into the wicker basket and pull out a little waterproof bullet vibrator. Before she can even say anything, I have the vibe turned on. I stick in down in the water, holding it against the warmth of her inner thigh.

She laughs at the tickling sensation and puts her hands down in the water, moving to block me. I cluck my tongue at her.

"Uh uh. Grab the rim of the tub over your head. Do it now, or I'll get out the handcuffs."

Kaia's eyes widen as she reaches back and grabs on. Her breath seems to come faster now.

"Don't move," I warn her, looking her dead in the eye.

She gulps and nods.

I rub the vibrator across her belly, over the sensitive skin of her inner thighs, up and down the seam of her pussy. She bites her lip and groans softly. She thrusts against my touch once before I even touch her. Encouraged by her response, I slip the vibe between her lips. If I was worried about finding the right spot, I shouldn't have been.

Kaia shifts her hips to just the right spot, hissing when the vibe touches her clit.

"Look at me," I grit out.

Her eyes burn into mine like two green fires. She bites her lower lip, squirming.

"Look at me!" I snarl. "And don't move! Just take what I'm giving you. Take it all!"

Pinning her in place with my gaze, I watch her lovely face as I hold the vibrator in place against her clit. She rocks into my touch and bucks away, unable to control the movement of her hips.

"Oh," she whispers. "Oh, god…"

"That's right, beauty. Hold onto the tub. Try to be still. Keep your eyes trained on me…"

She starts to quiver, her breaths growing labored. "Fuck, Calum. Fuck, that's good."

"Are you going to come for me, beauty?" I ask. My cock is so hard under my sweatpants that I have to stroke it through the gray cotton.

Her whole body bows. She bucks her hips with wild abandon. My cock throbs.

"Oh god. Oh fuck," she whines. "Calum, I'm—"

Before she can finish her sentence, her eyes roll

upward in her head. She pushes against the vibe and convulses, her mouth opening as a low keening sound escapes her.

In this moment, Kaia is more beautiful than ever, more animal than human. The air is saturated with the blossoming scent of her excitement. If I could bottle it and bathe in it later, I probably would.

She pushes my hand away from her clit, her body going limp, her eyelids drooping. The exhalation of breath that forces its way from her chest is very satisfying to me.

Tossing the bullet aside, I reach in the bathtub and pull her out. I get water everywhere as I scoop her up and wrap her in a towel.

She just lets me do it, too. I've never seen her quite like this, her spiky outer shell all worn away, no more resistance to be had.

I carry her out of the bathroom and to the bed, laying her down. It takes a moment to stretch myself out beside her and pull her close, snuggling her naked ass against my cock. Bringing the comforter up around us both, I remind myself that it's okay to just let her sleep, raging erection or not.

There will always be more time when she wakes up. Besides, from the evenness of her breathing, I might have fucked her to sleep.

Content for the moment, I let myself drift.

KAIA

"*W*hat are you going to do on your day off today?" he asks. He rumbles the words into the hair at the base of my neck. Laying in the darkened bedroom, I can barely think.

Somewhere in the apartment, Exupéry meows. I stick my hand down out of the bed and make some kissing noises. Three seconds later, I feel the silky little cat brush against my fingers.

After the longest string of long days, after fucking until I'm so exhausted I could die, he asks this question.

I don't want to answer. I already know that he won't like the answer to my question.

At 10 am, I have a coffee date with my mother. And though I've asked her not to bring my father… I have no idea how that will go.

"Uhhh…" I mumble instead. "What now?"

It feels weird to keep a secret from Calum but I would rather fib a bit than have an argument right now.

I open my eyes a crack, noticing that the sun is just

beginning to bloom in the farthest corner of the horizon. Dawn itself it probably forty minutes away...

"Did you sleep here all night?" I wonder groggily.

There is a pause. I swear, just for a second, I can hear him faintly smelling my neck. Then he throws back the covers on his side of the bed and rolls away suddenly.

I shiver against the sudden absence of his body that has kept me warm. Rolling over, I look at him, confused.

Calum pulls on a pair of sweatpants, looking angry. I have no idea why, though.

"Did you sleep here?" I repeat.

He looks at me, a sneer contorting his face. "I let myself drift off. It won't happen again."

I push myself up on my elbows. "I wish you would just let yourself fall asleep here."

Calum picks up his phone, shaking his head. "The next thing you know, you'll be asking whether we're exclusive and planning weekends away in the Hamptons."

I blink. "Wait, you're sleeping with other women?"

He grabs a pile of his clothes, starting to walk to the door. "Not right now. But that could change any damn time I please. Don't forget it."

With that, he vanishes beyond the screens. A moment later, the door between our apartment opens and slams shut. I just sit there, too tired to go after him, wondering what the hell that was.

The last few days, things have seemed to go really smoothly. Aside from the physical exhaustion, that is...

I lay back down and close my eyes. My tired brain turns over the issue about two times before it fades back into twilight sleep again.

When I wake up again, it's almost nine. I scramble through getting ready and sprint to the little coffee shop just a few blocks away. When I arrive, I stop just outside the shop, running a hand over my hair and straightening my short white dress.

Only now does the conversation from this morning float up to the surface. *I let myself drift off. It won't happen again.*

The whole experience was extremely weird.

Twisting my mouth to the side, I exhale and shove the half-remembered conversation aside. Now is not the time for worrying about Calum.

Not when my whole family might wait inside. Sucking in a deep breath, I head inside. It takes about three seconds of scanning the place to find my mother.

Blonde head bowed, she sits alone at a table for two, staring at her cup of coffee. Maybe it is because she is staring off into space so vacantly, but my mom seems even smaller than usual. As I walk over to greet her, she looks up.

Her eyes light up. She bounds up from the table, hugging me hard. "Kaia! Oh, my sweet girl."

I accept the hug, my gaze sliding around the restaurant. "Are you alone, mom?"

She pulls back, tucking a strand of my hair behind my ear. "You told me to come alone."

I let out a deep breath I didn't even know I was holding. Instead of answering, I slip my arms around my mom and hug her back.

"Thanks for coming to meet me," I whisper.

My mom hangs on for another few seconds and. then

pulls away, reluctant. "I ordered you a mocha. I thought maybe you would let me fatten you up a little bit."

She winks and head around the table, reclaiming her spot. I give her a soft smile as I sit across from her, pulling the mocha towards me.

"Thanks."

She wrinkles her nose. "You look thin, Chickadee."

I shrug. "Okay."

Since I was a kid, every time anyone in my family had anything to say about my weight, I have given them the same response. When my dad gets worked up and digs around in his brain for some way to hurt me, one of the easiest is my physical appearance. After a thousand tiny cuts, the wound has scarred over. I've become so numb to it over time.

My mom reaches across the table, taking my hand. "I don't mean to criticize."

I look up, my eyebrows arching. "What's that?"

A flush blooms in her cheeks. "I've been listening to this self-help podcast and one of the episodes is about being an active listener. I'm trying... to do better."

I swallow, scanning her face. "Well... thanks."

She smiles at me. "It's just so good to see you. After the last time, I thought maybe you would be done with us."

I frown a little bit at that. "I thought about disappearing," I admit, my head bobbing. "But if I go, there won't be anyone else to look after you and Sister."

My mom wrinkles her nose and carefully lets my hand go. She moves to pick up her coffee instead. "Maybe we should change the subject." As usual, my mother is tactful but she definitely has her boundaries in place. She's long since decided what side of the fence she sits on.

I glance around, blowing out a breath. "What have you been up to in the last couple of weeks?"

My mom smiles. "Oh, you know. This and that. Your sister is having her first runway show in a few weeks. So as you can imagine, there are a bunch of mindless tasks to do to set that all up." She gives me a hopeful look. "Actually, Sister gave me an invitation for you. It's not far from the New York Ballet."

I squint as my mom pulls out a dark square of card stock and slides it across to me. I don't examine it; I don't want to give my mom any reason to think I'm going to attend.

"Thanks," I say.

"And what about you? Still not seeing anyone?"

She reaches across and turns my wrist over, showing off a small bruise that looks like a hickey. It did in fact come from Calum's lips. But I'm not about to tell my mom that.

"Nope!" I say, my voice too bright. "There is no one. You know how demanding my ballet career is."

My mom nods her head, her mouth twisting. "Well, maybe you will fare better than I did when I was your age."

That gives me pause. "I'm sorry?"

My mom blushes. "Well. You know. I had a job when I first married your father."

"Oh. Yes, weren't you a teacher?"

My mother rolls her eyes. "That was much later. No, I'm referring to being a dancer. Not a ballerina like you, of course! Nothing so graceful. But I had a job with an off-Broadway musical theater troupe."

My jaw drops. "Wait, you did?"

"Yes." My mom takes a sip of her coffee. "When I met your father, he admired my dancer's legs. He liked to call them my gams."

Her eyes sparkle.

"How did I not know you were a dancer?!" I exclaim.

"I don't know. But I was really something back then. When I had just married your father, I even had admirers. It drove your dad completely insane, the fact that these handsome men - some of whom I worked with - should develop crushes on me."

"Mom!" I say, fanning myself. "I had no idea that you were such an ingenue. What happened to the job?"

My mom's cheeks redden. "You happened, Chickadee. Your father and I... were careful... we took precautions... but I was feeling ill for a while. One thing led to another. I took a pregnancy test and bam! Pregnant. Of course, I had to stop working. And your father thought that I should just stay at home from then on."

I frown. "Did you and dad always have that as a backup plan? You stay home and raise the family, dad goes to work?"

My mom shrugs. "We didn't really talk about it before-hand." She looks off for a moment, seeming a little sad. "Anyway, I got you two girls. So it can hardly be said that I got the bad end of that bargain, can it?"

I smile at her, trying to soak in her story. It's a lot to take in and way more to try to decipher.

Did my father have a hand in my mom's birth control

failing? It definitely sounds like there is more to that story and my mom is only telling me a little bit.

I chat with my mom a bit more, filling her in on the latest goings-on. I talk about my teacher Bas and my good friends Ella and Eric. I'm very careful to pick and choose which stories I tell her. I wonder if other daughters tell their moms as little information about their personal lives as I do.

Is it a broad pattern? Or is my relationship with my mother especially fraught?

My mom, for her part, tells me a very long story about going to her women's only bible study. It occurs to me that the story features other people, only even involving my mother once.

Maybe the secretiveness is a family trait, then.

At the end, we hug for a long time.

"Don't forget this," my mother says, forcing the piece of black card stock into my hands. "It's supposed to be very fancy. Black ties and ball gowns."

I smile a little thinly. "It was great to see you, mom."

"Yes. Maybe we can meet again. I could bring your father and Sister…"

I shake my head. "I don't think that's a good idea. I'm happy to meet with you, but… I just don't think I want to see Dad. Sorry."

My mom's expression sags. "Well, you never know. You may change your mind."

I swallow, giving her another hard hug. "I love you, Mom."

"I love you too, Chickadee."

After that, I bolt from the coffee shop and practically

sprint the next four blocks. My thoughts are in a tumult, memories of my dad banging into reflections from my conversation with my mom. Most jarring is the idea that birth control fails; I just had never thought about what would happen if I ended up pregnant.

Sure, Calum is nowhere near as insane as my father. But still...

I just can't imagine being in such a predicament. Especially not with the man who stormed out of my bedroom earlier.

The one who felt it was important for me to know that he could sleep with anyone, anytime. Gritting my teeth, I pull out my phone and start searching for a family planning clinic.

1 2

CALUM

$\mathcal{I}$ stand at the curb on Saturday morning, waiting impatiently as Lucas pulls his dark Mercedes up to me. I get in, sliding my brother a look.

"You're late," I say, closing the passenger door. "Why on earth didn't you just tell me to pick you up in a limo?"

Lucas pulls into traffic, a smirk on his lips. "Because, Calum. I still like to drive myself occasionally. It keeps me grounded."

That makes me chuckle. "Yeah, you're really grounded. Tell me, how many homes do you own?"

He looks at me, a grin stealing over his face. "I don't know. Are we counting the estates that we own together?"

I roll my eyes. "I feel like you're just making my point for me."

He shrugs, looking forward. "We're going to my place in Greenwich Village. Not that you asked. I know you don't know anything about art, but I have a couple of pieces that I think you would like."

Looking at my fingernails, I purse my lips. "Uh huh. Let's just get this over with."

He seems unfazed. "So where have you been for the last two weeks? You were super active at IndicaTech for about three weeks... and then you just stopped coming in."

"Things picked back up with the ballet."

He slides me a look. "That's it?"

I arch a brow. "What else could it be?"

"A pretty little ballerina. And before you say anything, I already heard all about your dealings with Honor. So don't bullshit me."

I glare at him. "She deserved it."

"Uh huh. My question is, who did you replace her with? Because I dropped by NYB, looking for you. They said you haven't even been at all the rehearsals."

I push out my cheek with my tongue. "I've been spending a lot of time with Kaia. Okay?"

"I knew it!" he says, grinning. "When's the wedding? I assume you're obsessed with her and planning on giving her everything she wants. That's what you did with Honor before she got usurped by Kaia."

I glare at Lucas. "Relax. We don't have that kind of relationship. It's more of a transactional thing."

"What, like she's your hooker?"

I think about Kaia lying in bed, completely naked and ready for me. Only me. The look in her eyes right before I make her come for the thousandth time...

I don't know what she is, but the word hooker is absolutely wrong.

"I've been calling her my paramour."

He scoffs. "What in the fuck is that?"

I grit my teeth. "Look, things with Kaia have been good lately, okay? I've been... not content exactly, but happier. The last thing either of us need right now is you dissecting exactly what we are."

He stares straight ahead, his hands on the steering wheel. "Are you paying her?"

"Is there a woman in the world that wouldn't expect someone as wealthy as I am to drop huge amounts of money on her? This is just... more direct."

He looks away, his hands flexing. "I guess that's true. And you are happy—"

"Happier," I correct him.

He nods. "Fair enough. Contentment must be an adjustment. Usually you're a miserable bastard." He slides a look at me. "No offense, but you can be... rigid."

I blow out a breath. "Rigidity got me pretty far in life."

His head bobs. "My point is, it's probably a good thing that you're letting down some of your walls. I hope you'll remember that in the next few minutes."

My eyebrows jump up. "What? Where are you taking me?"

"Calm down. I already told you, I keep an apartment just up ahead."

I glower at him, but my brother is unmoved.

He pulls into the curved driveway of a tall white building. As soon as he comes to a stop, a valet approaches Lucas's door.

Lucas pops out of the car, smiling at the valet. "We'll probably only be half an hour or so."

I get out of the car with a sigh, following Lucas inside the building's massive oak door. The lobby is luxurious, all

93

marble and sleek stainless steel. Lucas leads me to the elevator and presses a button. I can feel his eyes on me, measuring me as we are ferried upstairs.

I squint into the distance. "What? What aren't you telling me?"

He shrugs a shoulder and doesn't respond. I look at him, trying to parse out what he is hiding. But the elevator stops at our floor and he is quick to step out into the tiled hallway.

I have a bad feeling in the pit of my stomach as my brother leads me to a stainless steel door. He opens it and steps inside. I follow, my eyes burning a hole into his back.

There is nothing much to see when we walk in. It seems like any upscale apartment in the area. There is a small kitchen to the right, an oddly empty living space, a big picture window that looks out onto a terrace.

There is definitely no art here. I narrow my gaze as I swing it around the room.

Lucas turns to me, holding up his hands. "Try to remember what we just talked about in the car. Being less rigid and more flexible only helps things."

I cock a brow, folding my arms across my chest. "What is this, Lucas? Why the secrecy?"

Down a hallway to our left, there is a little hallway. A middle aged woman walks down it, peeking her head in.

"Ah! Mr. Fordham. Anita has been asking when you were going to come."

At the sound of Anita's name, my heart starts pounding. My gaze snaps to my brother.

"What is she talking about?"

She steps out a little further, motioning toward the

bedroom. Lucas puts his hand on my back, stepping toward the bedroom. "Anita's doctor called. Apparently she has some senile dementia."

My brows lift. My heart pounds in my throat. It's funny how even standing here as an adult, knowing that she's in the same building fills my stomach with dread.

"I thought we had talked about this!" I shout. I shake off his touch, angry. "Did I not make myself as clear as a bell when I last saw her?"

He shakes his head. "I know what you said. But she's basically our second mom. She took us in when she didn't have to. It's our turn to care for her now."

A wave of nausea rolls through me. "She's not related to us. She's not a maternal figure. Don't say that."

Lucas turns his head toward the woman, who is clutching a stethoscope. "Could you give us just a minute?"

Shaking my head, I turn around and head out the door. Lucas is right on my heels.

"Calum!"

I stalk down the hall to the elevator, pressing the button. He trots after me, his face red from excitement.

"I can't believe you're still acting like this," he spits. "Maybe Anita isn't our mom, but she's the only parent that we have left. And family is family, whether you like them or not! So whatever petty little fight you two had—"

My hands tremble. I clench them into fists.

"We had sex."

That stops him dead in his tracks. For a second, he just gapes. "What?"

I can't meet his eye, so I just glare straight ahead.

95

"When Anita took us in, right after mom died. That's when I started... we started..." I stop, my jaw clenching. "She didn't take us in out of the goodness of her heart. She did it because then she could have leverage over me."

The elevator dings. The doors slide open. I walk inside, feeling like I'm on autopilot.

I press a button, but Lucas holds the doors open.

"I don't..." He squints. "Are you sure you didn't... sort of embellish what really happened?"

My cheeks burn. I can't make eye contact with him. "Let go of the fucking door, Lucas."

He frowns. "I think we should maybe get some things straight—"

I step forward, shoving him back with all my might. Lucas stumbles backward, only just managing to keep his feet. As he does, the doors glide closed.

As I'm carried downstairs, I can't believe that I actually told my brother what happened. Worse, his reaction wasn't exactly supportive.

Did you maybe embellish what happened?

Rage builds up inside me, filling every inch, pouring out. I lash out, my fist hitting the stainless steel elevator wall so hard that the elevator jolts. I can barely feel the impact.

I can barely feel anything because I'm so fucking angry. At Lucas and his reaction. At Anita, for doggedly popping up in my life again and again.

But mostly at myself. At that little kid, for not realizing that there were other options. And at my current self, for not being able to keep any of this shit under wraps.

I just lose my cool when Anita is involved.

Storming out of the elevator, as I stride through the lobby, I pull out my phone. I start to text my limousine driver.

Then I pause.

Maybe it would be better if I walked. I have all this hateful energy burning through my veins. And if I don't burn a little off before I see Kaia...

My fists flex.

Dropping my phone back in my pocket, I start walking toward Manhattan.

KAIA

I stare at the pink plastic compact, lying open in my hand. Thirty one little pills lie within, each packed in blister wrapping. The doctor I saw was nice but brief when she wrote out the prescription.

"Take the pill at the same time every day," she recommended. "Make it a part of your routine."

Now, in the last minute of my limo ride, I pop one of the tiny yellow pills out and hold it in my hand. I take a sip of water from the open bottle beside me and swallow the pill. It feels like a really big deal to be taking birth control. Like it means something for my relationship.

Not that I plan to tell Calum that I've decided to take the pill. That's kind of the whole point of it. It puts the decision squarely in my hands.

The limo stops. I hurry and tuck the pill pack away in my purse. The door opens and I get out, running a hand down my dress. It's Friday night and I am dressed to kill; my dress is black, strappy, extremely short... and it has a low cut neckline that will turn some heads. Not that I really need to wear anything to get Calum's attention.

But tonight, I want his eyes on me the whole meal. Smiling lightly, I walk up to the front door of Luxe. A younger guy actually trips over his own feet when he looks at me.

I give him a sultry smile and he runs to pull the door open for me.

"Thanks," I say. I head inside, where everything is black with hints of gold. The walls are hung with black fabric threaded through with a gold sparkle. The bar is black with a black and gold counter. The tables are covered in black linen, the plates and silverware are gold.

The hostess walks me over to an empty booth with two gold place settings. At one, I find a little black box with gold ribbon tied around it.

As I sit down, a server comes over with a French 75 already poured. I raise my eyebrows and accept it.

"Thanks," I say. Taking a sip, I sigh at the sharp flavor of lemon and the crisp bubbles of the champagne.

Setting the glass aside, I turn my attention to a little handwritten note on the top of the box.

∽

WAIT UNTIL I ARRIVE. I want to see the look on your face when you open it here in public.

∽

It's unsigned but I know exactly who it's from. What could the box contain? I lift it off the plate briefly, giving it a tiny shake. It's light, whatever it is.

My lips lift at the corners and I sit back, picking up my glass. I sip my drink and watch the servers darting around. The customers here are quite elegant, though it seems like the median age here is about forty. I look at the couples whispering in each other's ears and feeding each other bites of dessert.

What kind of experience is Calum about to subject me to, exactly? Because the vibe in this restaurant is straight up romance and seduction.

I finally see Calum approaching. Tall, muscular, his dark hair set off by a stylish all-black suit. His blue eyes glint. There is a dark humor in his expression that makes him look like the devil himself is making his way to my table.

Calum slides into the booth across from me. A dark energy seems to crackle in the air around him.

"Hello, Kaia," he utters.

I swear, under the table, I press my thighs together. The tone of his voice, the way he's looking at me, the ambiance in here… they're definitely turning me on right now.

I tilt my head to the side, sitting up a little straighter. Biting my lip, I lean forward. "Calum."

As I predicted, his gaze travels down to my breasts. He growls a little.

"Did you wear that dress just for me, beauty?"

I flush and give him a slow nod. "Yes."

He flashes me a smirk. "I appreciate that."

I scrunch my face up. "Are we just not going to talk about the way you spoke to me earlier?"

That gives him pause. His eyes narrow on my face. "Yes. I... I lost my temper."

I arch a brow. "Say you're sorry, Calum."

He squints off into the distance. "I *am* sorry, Kaia."

I put my elbows on the table, resting my chin in my hands. "Mmm. Apology accepted."

Calum pushes his cheek out with his tongue. "Good."

"So? Are you going to tell me what's inside the box?"

His lips twitch. "Open it for yourself and find out."

Giving him a guarded smile, I untie the silky gold ribbon and then lift the lid off. Inside is a silver blob no bigger than two of my fingers, bulbous at one end and tapering to a dull point with a distinct lip between the two. I tilt my head to the side and pick it up. The wide end has a large colorless jewel.

My only clue as to its purpose it a small packet of lube that comes along with it. "Anal pleasures personal lubricant."

I'm completely confused. Raising my eyes to Calum, I shake my head. "I don't get it. What is it?"

He fishes a small remote out of his pocket, pressing a button. At once, the small piece of metal in my palm starts to vibrate. My eyes widen and I hastily drop it back in the box.

"You bought me a..." I pause, glancing around, and drop my voice. "A vibrator?"

He grins. "No. It's a butt plug."

My jaw drops. "A what?"

He wiggles his eyebrows at me. "A butt plug. It does exactly what you think it would."

I can't believe it. "What? Why?"

He gives me a huge smirk. "Because, beauty. It feels good."

"You want me to... to stick something up my..."

He sits back against the booth, his eyes sparkling. "No. I will help you. Pick up the box. Let's go to the restroom."

I shake my head. "You're crazy. I'm not doing it."

Calum cocks his head. "Oh yes you are. You signed a contract. Did you think that I wasn't going to test your boundaries?"

I chew my bottom lip. "Calum—" I start.

"No. Come on." He scoots out of the booth. "Bring the box."

Turning ten different shades of red, I stuff the lid on the box and follow Calum into a darkened hallway. He opens a door to a large bathroom with a black velvet chair in the corner. I swallow and enter, my pulse racing.

I'm pretty sure that I'm going to hate whatever is about to happen.

He locks the door behind us. His eyes are alight with amusement as he takes the box from me and pulls the chair into the middle of the room.

I start to sit in the chair, on autopilot. But he stops me, turning the chair around. "I want you to stand here and hold on to the back. I'll help you put it in for the very first time."

I close my eyes and move to stand where he says, my hands gripping the back of the chair. Behind me, Calum moves close, brushing my hair back from my neck. He places a single burning kiss to my neck and he hikes up my short dress.

I shiver, unsure what to anticipate.

He sucks on the spot on my neck as his hands find my hips and his fingers rake my flesh. I jump when he skims my panties down my thighs.

"Do you know how beautiful you are?" he says against the bare skin of my shoulder. "I almost don't believe it."

I give my head a little shake but say nothing. He shifts the chair, turning it around halfway. Then he lifts one of my legs, resting my foot on the seat.

I'm completely and utterly exposed now, at Calum's mercy. I've been naked in front of him dozens of times but this... this is a whole new level. My breasts tighten and lift, the nipples pebbling. I instinctively suck everything in, a silent prayer leaving my lips.

There is the crinkling of plastic and then I feel the cold ooze of lube above my asshole. I suck in a gasp, surprised.

"Oh!" I squeal.

"Shhh," Calum says. He places another hot kiss against my neck. "Be a good girl, Kaia."

His hand reaches down to ever so briefly touch my pussy. Then two of his fingers work their way back up, lazily circling the balloon knot of my ass.

"Relax for me," he whispers. "I can feel how tense you are. Trust me for just a minute, beauty."

I exhale a ragged breath and try to relax my muscles. One of his thick digits penetrates me, slowly sliding in and out of my ass once, twice, a third time.

It feels so fucking naughty. It also might feel... good.

I let my head fall back. A moan escapes my throat. My

entire body locks up when I make the sound, but Calum is right here to urge me on.

"That's it, beautiful," he hisses. "It feels good, doesn't it?"

As he murmurs into my ear, he introduces a second finger. Long and thick, they slide in and out of my ass, slowly picking up speed. I suck my lower lip into my mouth and groan.

When he shifts and pulls his fingers free, I'm not expecting to feel the coolness of metal. My breath hitches as Calum smears the tip around in the sticky lube, warming it up a little.

"Ready?" he asks quietly.

I can't think, so I just nod. As soon as I do, I feel the pressure of the butt plug's tip on my ass. He works it around and in and out, stretching me and filling me a little more each time.

Then he pushes the butt plug all the way in, tapping it gently. Every time he does, I feel a new ripple of sensation in my tight little ass.

I hiss. His hands slip away from my ass and guide my foot off the chair. I stand here for a moment while he washes his hands, feeling like I'm just stuffed full. How am I supposed to walk?

When I open my eyes, Calum is washing his hands. He comes over to me when he's done, kneeling down and helping me put my panties back on. He smirks at me.

"How does it feel, beauty?"

The corners of my mouth tug down. "It feels... like I'm keeping a dirty secret."

He reaches out, slipping his hands around my waist. Bending my head back, he kisses me.

"You've been such a good girl so far," he says, looking down into my face. "So very compliant. Now let's go enjoy our meal."

I arch a brow. "Like this?"

He smirks. "Yes, princess. Just like that."

I squeeze my ass a few times, trying to adjust to it. It's not painful... just big.

Tossing the gift box in the trash, he offers me his hand. I take it and he sweeps me along, walking quickly through the restaurant. As we approach our table, he whispers in my ear.

"Look at all these people that have no idea that you've got my butt plug in your beautiful ass."

I look around, biting my lip. "Calum?"

He arches a brow. "Yes, beauty?"

I spread my hands across the table. "I don't want to eat. I want..."

His eyes light up. "What do you want, Kaia?"

I smirk, leaning close to him. "I want you to fuck me. You've teased me and played with my ass—"

He stands up, cutting me off and throwing cash on the table. "Let's go."

When Calum offers me a hand up, I take it. He slides his arm around me and escorts me out of the restaurant, patting my ass.

14

KAIA

*C*alum barely gets me inside the elevator before he's all over me. He backs me into a corner and pushes me against the wall, dropping to his knees. He pulls up my designer dress and rips my panties out of the way, lifting my knee. I look up to the ceiling, sure that we are being watched.

"Calum!" I protest. But that's cut short by Calum burying his face against my pussy. His tongue touches my clit. His fingers play with the bejeweled butt plug buries in my ass.

I let out a hiss, burying my fingers in his short dark hair. Too soon, the elevator hits the penthouse. He rises to his feet and takes me by the hand. I grab my panties from the floor and follow him off of the elevator.

Kissing, fondling, and touching each other, we make it into my apartment. He grabs my dress and rends it down the front, hissing at the skin he exposed. I push my dress off, almost as impatient as him.

Calum leans down, cupping one breast and pulling the

nipple to his mouth. I immediately groan at the sensation of his hot, wet mouth on my flesh. He rolls it around with his tongue, then nips it with his teeth.

"God, that feels so good," I moan.

He looks up at me, his eyes full of heat. "Just wait until I have my tongue in your ass."

My eyebrows jump up. "What?"

He bites his lip, grabbing my hand and tugging me to the bed. He turns me around and forces me onto the edge of the bed. "You heard me. I want to see your ass. I want to taste it. I want to put my cock in it."

Calum's words excite me. I can feel a slither of moisture from my hot pussy as I crawl onto the bed and put my ass in the air. He is quick to pull a roll of condoms and a bottle of lube out from under the bed. I didn't even know that he had anything stashed under there.

But in the next second, I'm glad.

He teases my exposed skin, trailing his fingers up toward the butt plug. He pushes in in for the briefest second. I shiver as he removes the metal plug, tossing it aside.

"*Unf*," he says, spreading my legs wider. "Look at your perfect ass. Ready to be kisses and fucked, I think."

"Oh god," I say, biting my lip. "I'm nervous. Your cock is so big…"

He chuckles. "Has my cock ever brought you anything but pleasure, beauty?"

I shake my head, knowing that he is right. "No."

He places his hands directly on my ass cheeks and climbs on the bed behind me. His lips touch my butt cheeks a couple of times, building anticipation. I feel the wet warmth of his tongue near my ass, circling it very slowly. Then he licks directly over my balloon knot, making me tense up. At the very same time, I realize that my pussy is soaking wet.

Yeah, I want this. I grip the sheets, preparing myself.

"Relax, baby," he murmurs. "I can feel you tensing up. Rub your clit for me, Kaia."

Biting my lip, I slip a hand down to my aching pussy and find my clit. All it takes are a couple of the lightest circles with my fingers until I moan. Still, it takes everything in me to force myself to relax.

Calum leans down and I feel his tongue ever so gently behind to work in and out of my asshole. I tense up for a second, then relax again. I focus on rubbing my clit, but my mind keep straying to his tongue in my ass.

I shudder when he pulls me closer, controlling my movements with his hands on my hips.

"Fuck," I whisper. "Calum, that feels so good."

He withdraws his tongue for a long second. "That's good, beauty. That's so fucking hot."

I feel his finger replace his tongue. He slips it in my ass with little resistance and kisses me on my lower back.

"I'm getting you ready. I'm going to bury my entire cock in this tight little asshole." He places another kiss on my lower back.

I rub my clit, feeling naughty. "I trust you, Calum. I know you'll make me feel good."

"*Fuck*. Do you know how turned on I am?"

I blush, slowly shaking my head. "Uh uh."

"Hold on." He pulls his finger out and disappears for a solid minute. I hear the water running into the bathroom and hear the sound of him brushing his teeth. Determined not to get sidetracked, I circle my clit with my fingers lazily.

When he comes back, he taps my ass. "Turn over."

Wriggling, I comply. I'm taken aback for a moment by the image of Calum, completely naked. He's all muscle, his cock juts proudly out... and right now, he's looking at me like he's going to consume me.

He fists his cock, looking down at me. I spread my legs, biting my lower lip, and touch my clit.

His lips twitch as he regards me. "Fuck, Kaia. Do you know how much pleasure you give me?"

He climbs onto the bed, dragging me down to lie beneath him, and he starts kissing my neck again. I wrap my arms and legs around him, pulling him closer. I can feel his hardness against my thigh, long and hot and throbbing. He sucks at my neck, my breasts, and then he moves lower.

I don't know if I can even handle his mouth on my clit, but he passionately kisses my thighs and my knees. His five o'clock shadow tickles me in the best way. I open my legs wide for him, spreading my thighs. He makes a growling sound as he kisses my clit, and my whole body is suddenly alive with electric sensation.

"Oh my god!" I cry out, my hands burying in his hair.

Already, I'm bucking my hips against his mouth, desperate for more. He closes his mouth around my clit and sucks on it in long pulls, each one sending ripples of sensation up my spine. My toes curl as he brings his hand up to my pussy and introduces one thick finger. He ever so slowly pushes his finger inside as he circles my clit with his tongue.

I come suddenly, clenching and crying out. His tongue slows, helping me ride out my orgasm. Soon though, he climbs up my body, kissing me hard. I taste the faint flavor of my own juices on his tongue and shudder.

Calum busies himself rolling on a condom and pouring plenty of lube on his cock. He also swipes his lube covered fingers over my still-sensitive pussy and my asshole. I writhe against his touch.

"Grab your knees," he says. "It'll be easier for the first time I take your ass."

My heart starts pounding. I raise my knees and hold them with a hand on each. I feel so vulnerable right now, more than I've ever been with anyone. But like I said, I trust him.

He pulls back a little bit, grasping his cock and positioning himself just so. The blunt tip of his cock presses against my pussy, and I still for just a second. I'm busy looking at his cock, biting my lip with anticipation of how he's about to stretch me out.

But he repositions his thick cock at my ass and then pushes inside the barest inch. I gasp, feeling so full of his hot cock. It's foreign, this fullness. A little scary.

Calum glances down at me, biting his lip. "You're so tight, Kaia."

I'm honestly not sure if that's a good thing or not, judging by his face alone. He looks like he's trying to defuse a bomb or something.

He closes his eyes and pushes himself inside, inch by slow inch. I feel like he's stretching me out, little by little, filling me up and touching every single part of me. It's uncomfortable, even with the lube. But I'm curious.

He says that I'll like it. When has he ever been wrong?

So I push for more. He works his way in and out, little by little. I gasp, feeling so full that I can't possibly hold any more. And yet he's not all the way in.

"Good girl," he whispers, watching my face. "We're almost there."

When he is finally inside me to the hilt, he opens his eyes, staring down at me with the most intense aquiline gaze I've ever experienced. I don't care that his dick is so big that it hurts a little; I'm too busy being consumed by him, eaten alive.

I reach up to pull his mouth down to mine, tenderly kissing him. He kisses me back, starting to move his body, withdrawing his cock and then thrusting back in. I release my knees as he starts to thrust.

"Fuck," I whisper. It's intense, this kind of fucking. It feels like pleasure and pain mixed together, the volume turned up all the way. "Fuck, fuck, fuck."

"Are you good?" he says, slowing a bit.

I nod, breathless. "Don't stop."

He nods, thrusting again.

"Ahhh, that's so good," he mutters, raising himself up so that he can see our bodies joined together. "Fuck, Kaia. God, you're so damned beautiful."

He grabs my wrists and pulls them up above my head, working his thick cock in and out of my ass. I dig my heels into his upper back as he thrusts into my body. I start to forget the discomfort, focusing instead on the pleasure of the wonderful weight of his body against mine.

I moan as he releases my hands in order to palm my breasts. It feels natural to wrap my arms around him, to lightly rake my fingernails down his back.

Calum suddenly withdraws from me, flipping me over. He rips off the condom, replacing it with another one. Then he guides me to my hands and knees, positioning his cock at the entrance to my pussy before he plunges inside.

"Ohhh!" I cry out, feeling my innermost muscles clench.

"Your pussy feels so good," he grits out. "Just like your ass. So hot. So fucking wet. So tight for me." He takes my hand and guides it down to my clit, rubbing it in gentle circles. "I want to see you come again. Show me what a good girl you are. Make yourself explode for me."

His words send a shudder of pleasure down my spine. He lets go of my hand and grabs my hips, thrusting his cock into me again and again, as hard as he can. I bite my lip as I start to touch myself.

The way he is fucking me now is rougher, coarser than before... but for some reason I like it more. A lot more. I close my eyes, rubbing my clit, and feeling the brutal way he handles me, ramming into me over and over again.

An invisible spring tightens deep inside me with every thrust, feeding my craving. My fingers help me along, but it's really Calum's cock that makes little ripples of pleasure swell and burst across my body.

He's touching some spot deep inside me, a spot that I seem to be able to angle my body just so to encourage him to hit over and over again.

"Yes," I groan desperately. "Yes, right there... I..."

And then I'm calling out his name, screaming it, as I

go over the edge, falling into a deep ocean of pleasure. He stiffens and growls, filling me with three single, brutal thrusts. I can feel his cock pulsing and twitching inside my pussy.

He pulls me down onto the bed, spooning me, and we lie there for a long time, trying to catch our breath.

15

"*A*re you ready?" Calum whispers into my ear. He's behind me, his hands in front of my eyes, his breath tickling my ear.

I scrunch my face up, shivering in the cold air of early morning. "I think so?"

It's a guess more than anything else. All I know is that the entire NYB has the next few days off. And now I'm standing on stained concrete, smelling a pungent scent that reminds me of gasoline.

Is he going to show off a collection of race cars? I can't imagine that, but then again I'm reminded that I really don't know Calum very well.

My mouth twists.

Calum chuckles and pulls his hands away from my face. We are standing on a small tarmac, looking at a very small plane. I blink a few times, my heart rate picking up.

"Are we going somewhere?" I guess. "Is it somewhere that I'll need a passport for? Because I don't have one. I've never been to London. I've never been to Paris. I've never even been to freaking Canada."

"No? You haven't been to Paris?" He smiles.

I smile a little, shaking my head. "No. I want to, obviously. But I haven't had the chance yet."

"You won't need a passport." He grabs my hand as casually as you please, tugging me toward the aircraft. "I thought that we could fly up to my place on the coast of New Hampshire. It's very isolated, on the top of a tall crag that looks out onto the most beautiful seascape."

I give his hand a quick squeeze, my eyes on the plane. "We're flying in that?"

He slows, turning back to look at me. "Yes. It's my favorite private plane. Just enough room for the two of us and our luggage."

As he speaks, two men trundle out with suitcases I've never seen before. Calum arches his brows at the luggage. "I thought you could use a set. It's Louis Vuitton, just like mine."

My brow pulls down. "Two people and a pilot, right?"

He rolls his eyes. "No. I've had my pilot's license for years."

I look up at him, shaking my head. I pull my hand from his grip. "I don't want to fly in such a small plane, Calum."

He moves quickly, grabbing me around the waist. He pulls me close. My hands automatically land on his strong chest. I look up at him, anxiety sloshing around in my stomach.

"I can't," I tell him. "You're asking too much. Flying in a plane that size scares the bejeezus out of me."

Calum scans my face, a note of irritation in his eyes.

"Do you trust me?"

I glance at the plane, licking my lips. He shakes me, causing my gaze to snap back to his face.

"I asked you if you trusted me. Look at me, beauty. Don't look at the plane." He grabs my free hand, bringing it up to cup his jaw.

For a long moment, we stand like that. Our bodies are entwined so intimately that my breath hitches.

How can I say no to those icy blue eyes? Licking my lips again, I nod slowly.

"Yes."

He rewards me with a brief kiss on the lips. Not especially passionate. Just a rather confusing embrace that leaves me blushing for reasons I don't totally comprehend.

As Calum grabs my hand and tows me toward the plane, I touch my lips. Before just now, our kisses were only about the passion between us. But now, it seems like they can also be used for comfort.

I wrap my head around that as we climb into the plane and find our seats in the cockpit. He goes into focus mode for a bit. I'm happy to see him flipping switches and putting on the headset.

But my gaze eventually freezes when I look out the plane's small windshield. I sit back in my seat and buckle myself in. But the whole time, I am thinking of how powerless I will be the second Calum starts to taxi the small aircraft down the runway.

Inside my head, red lights are flashing. Loud alarms are ringing.

Danger! Danger! Get out now!

Calum startles me by leaning over and putting a

headset and headphones over my ears. I look at him, my eyes wide. My fingers are clutching the armrests so hard that it hurts.

"Kaia." His voice comes through the headphones, sounding tinny and far away. "Relax. Trust me."

I gulp. "Okay."

He pats my hand awkwardly. "It'll be great. I've done this a hundred times."

I look away, blinking rapidly. As he starts to taxi the little plane, I focus on trying not to burst into tears. I quickly find out it's better if I close my eyes.

I feel the acceleration of the plane, feel it grow faster and faster. When the wheels of the plane leave the ground, I'm sure we are done for.

But seconds tick by. Then a couple of minutes. Finally I crack my eyelids open and look at him. "Are we... good?"

He casts a quick gaze over me. "Yes, beauty. Everything is exactly as it should be. If you can handle it, you should really watch the city disappearing behind us."

I glance out the windows, swallowing. He's right of course; I look on, the city quickly shrinks and gives way to rolling green hills, broken up here and there by a town.

For his part, Calum seems to take his job as pilot seriously. His eyes are constantly scanning ahead. His hands are on the steering wheel. From what little I know of flying, he seems to be excelling at it.

He shoots me a glance. "You can talk to me if you want."

My mouth twists to one side. "Okay."

He clears his throat. "It's something I've always

wanted to do, you know. Fly my own plane."

I raise my eyebrows. "Oh yeah?"

I'm not sure if Calum is just telling me a story to distract me or whether he's genuinely sharing something about himself.

Either way, I'm listening.

His head bobs. "Ever since I was a kid, I met this really rich guy. And I asked him what his favorite thing he'd ever bought was." He smiles a little at the memory. "He said that he loved flying his own plane. Said he liked being able to look down on the world and feel like he was truly in control."

My lips curve up. "I'm betting that's what you like, too."

"Damn right. I also hate all the red tape that comes with going to the airport." He pulls a face. "That's one of the best parts about having this much money. You can just pay people to deal with all the mundane details. Focus on big picture ideas rather than grunt work."

"That has to be one of the most arrogant things you've ever said."

He lets out a bark of laughter. "Not even close. Don't get me started on the fact that the world needs people like me. Billionaires who are unencumbered by worries over money, who think the sky is the limit."

As he says that, he steers the plane upward, into the clouds. I suck in a breath but we soon break out of the cloud cover, soaring above it.

"Did you just do that on purpose? Time that sentence with the moment when we were going through the clouds?"

He rolls a sly smile at me. "Maybe. My brother Lucas would probably punch me."

"I'm not hitting you while you're steering our plane." I wrinkle my nose. "Maybe after we land."

He chuckles at that. "Fair enough."

I suck in a deep breath. "Are you the older brother or the younger?"

"Older."

"By how much?"

Calum slides me a look. "Four years."

I nod, thinking. "Are you and Lucas close?"

For a few seconds, he's quiet. I turn my head and look at him, trying to determine whether I have crossed some sort of unseen line. Like maybe that's just too personal or something.

But he just squints, looking thoughtful. "We're pretty damn close. We work together at IndicaTech. As a matter of fact, he is the temporary CEO while I'm working at the NYB." He sighs. "I wouldn't trust anybody else to handle the business."

"Do you have other siblings?"

He shakes his head. "No, just us two. Our mom died when I was fourteen and we've essentially been on our own since then."

Tilting my head, I blow out a breath. "That sounds like a pretty tough way to grow up."

Calum raises one shoulder in a Gallic shrug. I sense that I'm digging a little too deep in one particular place, so I skip to another.

"Did you go to college?"

His mouth turns up at the corners. "No. Lucas went to

NYU a few years late. But I never went. I went straight from a dance academy to the NYB."

"A dance academy?" I echo.

"Yes." He licks his lips, looking straight ahead. "Then I got hurt after a few years of dancing. Which was pretty soul crushing at the time... but it did put me on the path to making money."

"You formed IndicaTech?"

He shrugs again. "Eventually."

Several seconds pass. I look at the window beside me. "Why haven't you settled down yet? I mean, you're rich and gorgeous—"

"And I put in eighty hour weeks to keep IndicaTech afloat," he cuts in. "Besides, I don't really want to be tied down. There's too much of the world that I haven't seen yet. How do I know that I'm getting the best of the best if I haven't been everywhere and done everything yet?"

My cheeks heat. "Good point."

He glances over at me, clearing his throat. "I wasn't talking about you."

I force myself to smile at him. "I know."

He narrows his eyes and shakes his head. "Whatever. Let's change the subject."

I sigh. "Uhh... okay. What's your favorite childhood memory?"

His entire face wrinkles. "Hm. I guess... there was this one time that Lucas and I went to one of those little carnivals. I mean, we didn't have enough money for anything. We just walked around a looked at everything. But this guy that sold the funnel cakes threw out a couple just at the right time..." His lips curl. "That was the best thing I think I'd ever tasted. Maybe it still stands."

I twist my mouth to the side. "That's nice. I mean, kind of."

"It was what it was." He shrugs. A few beats pass before he speaks up again. "What about you? Your family, I mean."

I sigh silently, pursing my lips. "Well, you met my dad..."

Calum's expression hardens. "Yes."

"My mom is super nice but..." I bite my lip. "My dad is the final arbiter of what my mom thinks, at the end of the day. And the same goes for my sister Hazel. Only she is missing the niceness." I scrunch up one side of my face. "Actually, she's kind of a bitch and she straight up kisses my dad's ass."

He gives a deep sigh. "They sound pretty awful."

I squint. "They are."

He sneaks a look at me. "You turned out okay, despite them."

I was not expecting that, so I just turn my head away, a flush creeping up into my cheeks. "Are we... uh... close?"

"About ten more minutes, then I start to descend."

I take a full, cleansing breath. "Hey Calum?"

"Yeah, Kaia?"

I steal a look at him. "Thanks for taking me flying."

His lips lift at the corners. "Thanks for trusting me, beauty."

I sit back, spending the rest of the short flight staring out the window. Thinking about the new things I've learned this morning.

16

CALUM

*K*aia is looking out the window as I drive the little convertible up the steep, winding path. Dead ahead is the house. Perched on top of a cliff, it has just four bedrooms and three bathrooms. It also happens to have the best view of the Atlantic Ocean that money could buy.

"Jesus," she says as I navigate around the final turn in the driveway. "You have to be kidding me."

I smirk at her, pulling the car in and opening my door. I shiver as a chilly wind whips around me. Even on this late summer morning, it can't be more than sixty degrees here.

Kaia gets out of the car. She pushes back her sunglasses as she looks up at the house, still looking impressed.

"Well?" I say. "What do you think? You were raised with money. Does this meet with your approval?"

She glances at me with a frown on her lips. "It's beautiful."

The gray house with its traditional white gables almost

blends in with the sea at times. Sitting right on the edge off the cliff, it looks down onto the primordial clash of the waves against the rock. A mist rises off the agitated water, coating everything with its cool slickness.

Just now the sea is a dark, churning blue-green with little whitecaps closer to the cliff. It makes the light colored house and the dark cliffs below stand out.

Grabbing a couple of suitcases from the little convertible, I grin at Kaia. "Come on. You haven't even seen the view from the master bedroom yet."

I push open the heavy front door, stepping back to let her inside. Kaia shivers a little as she enters the house.

"Oh," she says, looking around at the interior. Hardwood floors and polished hardwood walls are everywhere you look. There are also windows in every conceivable spot, looking out into the majesty of the surrounding sea.

Everything has been refinished and refurbished, brought back to its original grandeur. Kaia shakes her head, a grin spreading across her face. "I thought that you would bring me to somewhere that was all modern and sort of impersonal. This is anything but that, though."

I shut the front door with a foot. "Come on. You have to check out the widow's walk."

To our right is a creaky old set of stairs. Mounting them two at a time, I can feel my pulse speed up.

Upstairs is more of the same. Wood ceilings, wood walls, wood floors. I head down the hall and into the master suite.

The king sized bed is tucked in the corner to the right. There is a vanity to the left and a crisp leather armchair beside the doorway to the master bathroom.

But it's hard to even notice any of that because of the views. This room has a jaw-dropping, utterly entrancing piece of the ocean, separated only by thick panes of glass.

I drop the bags, jerking my head toward the door that leads out onto the widow's walk. "Want to walk on the wild side with me?"

Kaia stands in the bedroom doorway, peering out at the sea. "Is it safe?"

"Safe enough." I offer her my hand. She blushes as she takes it, making eye contact with me. I love the way that she pulls her bottom lip into her mouth, biting it with a pearly flash of her top teeth.

I tow her to the door, opening it. The sea winds instantly engulf us and whip around us. Kaia tries is vain to keep her little white dress from blowing up.

I grin at her like an idiot. "There is no need to hide your body from me, beauty. And I'm pretty sure that there is no one around for miles and miles."

Kaia blushes but nods. "I know."

I head out onto the narrow little extension of the roof, gripping her hand. There is a neat little white railing that surrounds us out here. I walk her to the end of the walkway, pulling her against my body.

The sea roars beneath us. Shading my eyes against the sun, I stare into the abyss. White water clashes and churns just seventy five feet from where we stand. The pounding crash and hiss of the water is spine-tingling and lulling all at once.

Kaia squeezes my hand. I glance at her.

"Thank you," she says. She looks at me, then turns her gaze outward once more. "It's insanely beautiful."

My lips twitch. "Funny, I would use almost exactly those words to describe you."

She wrinkles her nose and rolls her eyes. "Yeah right." She looks down at herself, shaking her head. "I'm definitely far from beautiful. I'm clumsy and graceless."

My eyes tighten on her face. "Have you looked at yourself in the mirror lately? Because that description is nothing like you."

She rolls her eyes again. "Stop. You're already sleeping with me. There's no need to massage the truth to get on my good side, Calum."

Pulling her into my arms, I stare down into her heart shaped face. "Why would I lie? I could have anyone in the world, but I choose to have you."

She looks up at me, her lips twisting. "For now."

I suck in a deep breath. "I've been with lots of women, yes. But none of them for more than a couple of weeks. You seem to be the exception to that rule."

Her eyebrows rise. "Oh?"

I cup her cheek and nod. "Yes."

Heat seeps into her cheeks, staining them hot pink. "I keep holding my breath, tiptoeing around. Waiting for you to get sick of me. Waiting for you to decide that our contract has been fulfilled."

Her words are like a hot knife to the gut. I inhale sharply.

She needs something from me. A promise. A vow.

"I am disinclined to advance our relationship further," I say.

Kaia flinches at my words, trying to pull out of my grasp. "I don't really want to talk about this, Calum."

My hands clamp around her wrists, imprisoning her. "You didn't let me finish. I want everything to stay the same forever. I want us to fuck each other's brains out. I like our living arrangement. I like having you close at hand, at my beck and call. I love knowing that I'm the only man you've ever been touched by."

Her lips twist. "Calum—"

I shake my head. "I don't usually use labels like girlfriend. If someone is my girlfriend, I feel like when things end, there has to be... some kind of dissolution. And I don't want that."

"I know," Kaia says, tugging at her wrists. "Can you please let me go now?"

"No. Because while I don't like labels, it seems to mean a hell of a lot more to you to call yourself my girlfriend. So I think you should."

She cocks her head. "I should... what?"

"Be my girlfriend. If it will make you feel... less unsteady, then I'm willing to make that concession."

She looks up at me for several seconds, her eyebrows moving gently. "That isn't what I want, Calum. I want someone to feel proud to call me theirs. I want to feel owned in that particular way."

I consider her words for a moment. "I guess I hadn't ever thought of it like that. I do..." I stop, clearing my throat. My heart starts pounding. "I've always felt that way toward you, Kaia. You've always been mine."

She looks pointedly at me. "Can I go now?"

"That depends. Are you my girlfriend?"

She rolls her eyes. "Do you want me to be? This entire

relationship has basically been on your terms. So you tell me what I am. A call girl? A paramour?"

I release her wrists, catching her around the waist and tugging her against me. "You're mine, beauty. Mine to control, mine to possess. Mine to dominate. I don't want anyone else in my bed. If that makes you my girlfriend… so be it."

She sighs, her lips twitching. "Oh, Calum. What am I going to do with you?"

I grind my hips into her, letting her feel my erect cock. "I can think of where we should start…"

Kaia presses up on her tiptoes, a smile on her lips as she kisses me. Our conversation slips away as I slide my arms around her back, pulling her closer.

KAIA

I let my head fall back, looking up at him. He stares down at me, bringing his hand up to push back a couple pieces of hair that are plastered to my forehead.

I don't dare to breathe. I don't dare to speak. I'm frozen under his beautiful blue gaze, waiting for him to make a move.

Calum cups my cheek, running his thumb roughly along the outline of my lips. He bites his bottom lip; for the first time since I've met him, I know without a doubt what he is thinking.

He wants me.

Suddenly I push up onto my tiptoes, bringing my lips a fraction of an inch from his. His gaze flickers down to my lips. I can feel his breath against my mouth, his warm breath fanning across my skin.

I can't wait. I press my lips against his, impatient. He makes me this way, like a hungry animal. His expressive eyes close and he moans. His mouth presses against mine, warm and soft.

He kisses me with no trace of hesitation. No, his kiss is hard and dominant and full of passion.

He slides up a hand around me, pulling me the last step toward him, my soft body hitting his hardened frame. My hands come up to his chest, clutching his shirt.

His free hand begins unzipping the back of my dress, peeling it off and casting it on the bedroom floor. I shiver with anticipation.

Already, I'm achy, my pussy getting wet just from the simplest touch of his lips against my skin. Without a word, he sweeps me off of my feet, carrying me backward. I wrap my arms around his neck, feeling so small and delicate in his grasp.

But he ignores the bed, heading to the en suite bathroom. With only its clawfoot tub, I don't see what he wants with the bathroom, but he carries me over to the tub anyway.

Calum sets me down, turning on the taps. Then he proceeds to undress me, pulling at the strings of my wrap dress. I step out of my shoes and help him with my dress; soon it falls to the floor, and I am left shivering in my matching white lace bra and panties.

The steam starts to fill the room, its heat very welcome. Calum kneels to take off his shoes, then looks up at me.

"You know what I want, more than anything right now?" he says, reaching out and caressing my hip.

"What?" I say, my voice barely more than a whisper.

"Take off your bra and panties, and sit on the side of the tub for me."

I turn bright pink, but I know I have to do it. I don't have any choice. But more than that, I know that Calum brings me to orgasm over and over and over again.

If he says to sit on the side of the rub naked, I'll do it.

I slowly take off my bra, exposing my breasts to him, my pink nipples pebbling in the steamy air. I see him suck in a breath and then bite his lip.

It's so sexy when he does that. I wish he could see himself in this moment, as I see him. Dark, brooding, hungry.

I'm aware of my pounding heart as I shimmy out of my panties, leaving me completely naked. Vulnerable.

"Sit," he commands, his eyes roving over my naked skin. He may be kneeling still, but his order leaves no doubt of who is in charge here.

I step backwards and sit on the ledge, overwhelmed with self-doubt. Here I am, completely naked, and he's still fully dressed.

Calum moves forward, reaching up to tug my mouth down to his. I bury my fingers in his short, dark hair as he invades my mouth, our tongues dancing together.

I feel his hands on my knees, pushing them open wide. I resist at first, until he stops for a second and murmurs, "Relax, Kaia. Don't you trust me by now?".

I nod, because I do. I let him part my knees, baring my pussy.

I expect him to go right for it, but he doesn't. Instead he moves closer, kissing my jaw, my neck, my shoulder. I run my hands along his strong shoulders, feeling the muscles in his upper back as they move.

He kisses my right breast, cupping my bare flesh and closing his lips over my nipple. I throw my head back and groan as he sucks and licks at it, using his teeth to draw my nipple to a hardened point.

"Fuck," I gasp, beginning to writhe against him. I feel my pussy growing wet, and I am just brazen enough to thrust my pussy against his chest.

"You're so beautiful," he murmurs. "Touch yourself for me. I know you masturbate. Show me how you do it."

Feeling shy, I dip two fingers inside my mouth. I trail my hand down to my exposed slit, touching my clit. I throw my head back, moaning as I circle it.

Calum starts stripping slowly beside me, pushing his pants down and off. He is left in just his striped boxer briefs. He runs his hand down inside of the briefs, grasping his thick cock.

"Look at me, beauty," he orders. "Tell me, which of your holes do you want filled with my cock first?"

I groan at that. "I like surprises…"

He chuckles. "Show me that juicy pussy. Show me how wet you can make yourself while I watch."

Circling my clit with my fingertips, I pinch one of my nipples. He comes closer, stroking his cock. I can see a glistening pearl at the tip, which gives me a thought.

"I don't know how to talk about this exactly…"

He arches a brow, his hand slowing. "What is it, beauty?"

My cheeks flood with color. "I started taking birth

VIVIAN WOOD

control a while ago... so I don't need you to use a condom, if you don't want to."

Calum blinks. "Jesus, Kaia. No barriers between us? Me filling your little pussy with my come?"

I bite my lip, nodding.

He grabs me from the side of the tub, lifting me up and carrying me back into the bedroom. I squeal when he tosses me down on the bed, spreads my legs, and kisses his way up my thighs. He doesn't lay down though.

I need him to either go down on me or fuck me. But he just runs the tip of his tongue up and down my slit, teasing me.

"Calum..." I implore. "Please."

He kisses my thigh instead. "Please what?"

"Fuck me," I beg. "Please, I need you."

He considers me idly, kissing my inner thigh a bit more. When he withdraws, I can't help it.

"Calum!" I whine.

He climbs on the bed and lays beside me, his eyes burning like twin firebrands. I roll onto my side, using my knee to try to hide my nudity a little, but he won't have it.

"Uh uh," he says, pushing my knee back. "There's no reason to hide from me. You are gorgeous, every inch of you."

I flush, nodding a little. He trails his hand from my collarbone to my breast, and down to my hip, giving it a squeeze.

"You're so fucking pretty, Kaia," he tells me, meeting my eyes. "You drive me crazy, almost every day, just by being yourself. I can hardly stand it."

He pushes himself onto his knees, bending down to

132

kiss my collarbone, the top of my breast. He kisses my nipple, then sucks the nipple into his mouth. His mouth is so hot and wet, and my hips raise of the own accord.

My mouth opens, a low groan coming out. He laves my nipple with his tongue, then releases it. I make a disappointed noise, but Calum has other concerns. He kisses his way down to my navel, pushing my knees apart to make room for himself.

He pushes me up the bed as far as possible, then finds a comfortable spot between my legs. He pushes one knee up, trailing kisses along the inner thigh.

I squirm a little, although I know that what is coming will be incredibly hot.

He uses two fingers to find my seam, tracing it lazily up and down, up and down. His fingers get a bit of my juices on them; he stops and pops his fingers in his mouth, making a contented sound as if that's normal.

I blush and lock up, my knees pulling together a little. But then he parts my lower lips with those same two fingers and leans in close, kissing my clit.

"Oh god!" I say, panicked. It feels so good, so wet and so hot, I don't know if I can take much of his teasing. When he kisses my clit again, swirling his tongue around it this time, making loud sucking noises, I bury my fingers in his hair.

He does figure eights with his devilish tongue for a minute, while I moan and try not to buck my hips against his face. After he closes his lips around my clit and sucks, though, I can't help it.

"Oh god, oh god," I repeat over and over again. "I... I'm close, Calum."

133

He shifts a little, teasing the entrance to my core with one single finger. I shiver with excitement and buck against his mouth when he introduces a second thick digit.

And with the third, I think I'm about to boil over. He's sucking on my clit and gently moving his fingers in and out of my pussy, and it's all too much.

I make a throaty sound, almost there…

He slows down, though, and withdraws his fingers. I crack open my eyes, glaring at him.

"What are you doing?" I demand.

"Christ, beauty. Be fucking patient," he says.

I go red at his words. I bite my lip and beckon him. He backs off the bed, stripping of his boxer briefs, laying himself bare. His cock juts proudly out, long and thick and quite beautiful.

He crawls on top of my body, until our hips press together. He's heavy, almost too heavy for me, but his big frame makes up for it. He balances himself on his elbows, taking some of the weight off.

My lips find his, and my hand finds his cock, stroking it gently. He breaks the kiss with a low, needy groan. That sound breaks any plans I had to draw this out.

I position his cock at my entrance, moving my hips a little to encourage him. He doesn't thrust right away, though. He takes a second to look down at me, brushing some of my still damp hair from my face.

"You're beautiful," he tells me. "You have no idea how fucking sexy you are."

He kisses me again, his lips warm and wonderful. Then he slowly sinks in, inch by inch. I grip his shoulders, writhing, trying to encourage him with my body.

Calum withdraws, then thrusts, withdraws, then thrusts. A little deeper, a little faster every time. He sets a rhythm, slow at first. I meet him thrust for thrust, feeling my body warming up, remembering the pleasure that it felt just a few minutes ago.

I wrap my legs around him as he increases the pace. There's a smooth kind of friction happening; it feels amazing, like there is something deep inside me that is on fire, and only he can put it out.

With each thrust I am getting a little closer to ecstasy. I feel a spring winding a little tighter and a little tighter. I just need something a little... more... to be set off.

"Calum," I say, breathless. "Fuck me *harder*. Give me every single thing you've got."

He smirks for a second, then he gives me exactly what I want. He leans over me, fucking me like a jackhammer, sweat beginning to drip from his face and chest. All I can do is hold on, that inner spring growing tighter by the second.

"Fuck," he whispers, his tone reverent. His voice is nearly lost in the melee between us. "God, your pussy is so incredible, beauty."

"Yes," I urge him, my hips clashing with his over and over again. I angle my hips and meet his thrusts. "Yes! Right there... Right there... I'm so close..."

I'm wound so fucking tight. When I start to come, I grip Calum's back with my nails, leaving a raw set of claw marks. He shudders but just fucks me harder, moving like a piston.

When I come, I freeze and start convulsing before I even realize that I'm orgasming.

I topple over a cliff I didn't see coming, and plummet down into the abyss of my own pleasure. A second after I come, I feel the twitch of Calum's cock. As he starts to come, I feel his hot semen spreading inside of me, filling me up. I hear his rugged shout as his body spasms and jerks.

At last, I feel him slow down and then stop.

He rests his forehead against the pillow to my left, breathing openmouthed for a few long seconds. My racing heart begins to slow.

"Fuck," he mutters. "Every goddamned time. I always think that our sex will get bored... or get repetitive... but it's like *that* every fucking time."

I laugh at that. "I'm glad to hear I'm defying expectations."

Calum kisses me then, long and languorous. He tastes like his sweat, but I don't mind it one bit. I sigh into the kiss, bringing my hands up to cup his face.

When at last he pulls out of my body and goes to the bathroom to clean off, I lie still.

He comes out of the bathroom with a washcloth. I raise a brow, but he starts to clean me off in gentle swipes of the cloth. He disappears again, then comes back and sinks on the bed beside me.

He wraps an arm around me, pulling me close and kissing my shoulder. "I'm sorry that was so short. Next time I won't be so trigger happy."

"What, you're not worn out yet?" I ask, turning my head towards him.

"Not a chance in hell. Give me... I don't know, twenty

minutes to reset? Of course, if you're ready, I can always eat your pussy again…"

I have to suppress my look of utter surprise. He grins wickedly.

"Roll over. I want to eat you out from behind this time."

I flush, but a can't hide my grin. "If you insist…"

I roll over, and Calum starts getting up, slapping my ass with a resounding *whack*. His clever fingers find my clit and all other thoughts vanish from existence.

18

KAIA

*I*n the early evening, I wake from a sex-induced nap. Calum is still asleep. His brow is smooth, his breaths deep and even. I would even call his look serene... but I am not fooled by his momentary calmness.

I know that he will eventually open his icy blue eyes; all the turmoil, fierceness, and determination will still be there.

Looking at his face, I marvel at how far he has come in so short a time. Only a month ago he would not fall asleep in my presence. Now he allows himself to fall asleep, one arm curled around me, the other flung wide. I slip out of his hold and quietly lay the comforter over his body.

Walking across the bedroom, I look out over the wildness that is the sea just beyond the dark crag that our house is planted on. Earlier when I looked at the sea, it was gray and whipped to a froth by the wind. But now I see it has calmed somewhat. It's darker, more blue, and it beckons me.

I dress in a soft white tank top, a heavy gray sweater, a

pair of black workout leggings, and a pair of black knee high rainbows. Then I creep down stairs and out of the French doors that face the sea. Despite my precautions, the first tiny step outside is freezing cold. Though the wind is indeed calmer than it was earlier, I am still chilled nearly to the bone.

Venturing further out, I wrap my arms around myself and scrunch my face up against the mist coming off the rocks. I follow a well-worn path cut into the mossy terrain, leading straight to the edge of the cliff.

When I look down, holding a hand up to keep the heavy mist out of my face, I'm in awe. Here the unmovable cliff face meets the forward thrust of the ocean. The way that the sea slams itself into the rock over and over again is primal and entrancing. I watch for a few minutes, noting that the sprays of water have begun to very slowly erode the once-sharp edges of the cliff face. It has probably taken a million years of relentlessly pounding for the sea to make a mark on the rock.

But it's happening just the same. I can't help but feel a sort of kinship with the ocean. I see parallels between its relationship with the stone cliff face and my relationship with Calum. It's hard going, but progress is being made.

But toward what exactly? I don't know. I shiver and stare down at the relentless waves smashing against the rock as if they can foretell my future.

I only feel Calum approaching a second before he steps behind me. He brings a dark parka onto my shoulders without a word. I glance up at him, grateful.

"Thank you," I murmur.

He eyes me for a moment, his lips twitching. "Admiring the view?"

I look out over the sea again. "It's crazy that someone thought to build a house here. I mean, it is so close to being snatched up by the ocean and carried away forever."

He lifts a shoulder. "It's been here since the late 1800s, so I think it's pretty safe."

I frown, looking back at the house. "How long have you been coming here?"

He's quiet for a moment, his expression unreadable. "I bought this place two years ago. But you are the first person other than me to see it. I usually come up here to find solitude."

My lips curve up. "I'm glad you brought me here. It's beautiful."

Calum takes my hand and tugs me back toward the house. "Come on. There is something that I have been meaning to give you."

I follow him back inside the house, shedding the dark parka once we make it inside. Calum turns out the lights, illuminating the open kitchen and brown leather sectional sofa of the seating area.

"I'll be right back." Calum bounds off, heading upstairs.

I'm left to look around the room. The decorating is sparse in this room, maybe done by Calum himself. Other than the leather sectional and a couple of bronze floor lamps, there is a well-stocked bookshelf and a wrought-iron side table.

Definitely a man's taste.

Calum reappears, his hands behind his back. "Take off your sweater."

My eyebrows arch and my cheeks turn pink. "I don't want to dissuade you from whatever you are up to. But if we're going to have sex, could I eat something first?"

He shakes his head, a smile playing on his lips. "Just take off the sweater."

Pursing my lips, I pull the bulky sweater over my head. Calum saunters over, showing me the long black velvet box in his hands. I frown. Try as I might, I can't imagine what sort of toy he's got in there.

"What is it?" I ask.

He gives me a funny look and cracks open the lid. Inside are a dazzling row of emeralds and diamonds, the strand long enough to make my jaw drop. I've received quite a bit of jewelry in my life from my father, but none of it even comes close to the piece Calum holds up. My hands fly to cover my mouth.

"Oh my god!" I croak. I look up at Calum, my gaze pinning him in place. "Is that for me?"

He nods. Pulling the necklace from the box, he beckons. "Come here. Let me put it on you, beauty."

My cheeks flush as I walk over to him, turning around and lifting my hair out of the way. He slides the necklace around my neck, its cool weight against my flushed skin raising goosebumps on my neck.

I touch the necklace delicately as though it might disappear.

"Oh, Kaia," Calum rumbles. "I thought it would bring out the green in your eyes. But next to you, it seems like a cheap bauble."

His words, perhaps meant so casually, nearly undo me. I've never been valued like this before, not ever in my entire life.

I turn and launch myself the short distance into his arms, pressing my mouth against his. I twine my hands into his hair and half climb his body, making him slip his big hands under my ass to pull me up. I kiss him breathlessly for a full minute, only pulling back when a laugh rumbles through his chest.

He looks down at me, his blue eyes filled with amusement. "You approve, then?"

My cheeks are warm, but I grin at him. "How could you tell?"

He laughs, pressing another kiss to my lips. "I don't know that I've ever seen this side of you before, beauty. I like it. If all it takes is a little jewelry, I'll do it all the time."

I wrap my arms around his neck, feeling silly. "It's less about the necklace and more about the sentiment behind it."

"Hey, whatever works," Calum teases. He carries me over to the couch, falling on top of me. I giggle as I kiss him; I groan as he kisses my neck and grinds his cock into me.

I'm soon absorbed in him, my mind and body distracted as the sun slips under the horizon.

19

CALUM

"*A*re you sure you're not going to give me even a hint of where we're going?" Kaia asks.

I look over at her in the back seat of the limo, shaking my head. "No. You look incredible, though. Perfect for our destination."

She blushes, looking down at her dark, clingy dress. I like the dress because it is short and simple... and it shows a daring amount of cleavage. Around her neck she wears the glittering emeralds and diamonds I got for her. "It was hard to know what to wear since you refuse to tell me where we are going. All I had to go on was your tux, really."

I smirk at her, straightening my right cuff link. "It really doesn't matter what you are wearing."

Kaia shoots me an annoyed look. "That only makes me want to know where we're going more."

I look out the window as we turn onto the small town's main drag. A grocery store is on the left. A bank on the right. Ahead, I can just make out the bright lights of the marquee.

"We're almost there," I tell her for the tenth time. "Just be patient."

She wrinkles her nose at me. "You are enjoying keeping me in suspense."

I snort. "You bet I am. I've started to figure you out, beauty. You're impatient anytime that you feel out of control."

She surprises me by scrunching up her face and sticking her tongue out at me. A guffaw bursts from my chest as the limo begins to slow.

"You're ridiculous," I charge.

Kaia makes a big show of straightening her dress and patting her hair. "I don't know what you mean, Calum."

A grin plays about my lips as the vehicle stops. I shoot her a questioning look and then open the door, stepping out. I hold my hand out and she scoots over to take it, following me onto the sidewalk.

Her eyes immediately go to the marquee. "Hallman's Art Gallery Welcomes Calum and Kaia." Her eyes widen. She looks at me, her green eyes impossibly excited and full of questions.

I stick out my elbow, jerking my head toward the gallery's main door. "Come on."

Her eyebrows still arched, she allows me to lead her inside the door. It wasn't hard to find the closest art gallery to my private beach house. Nor was arranging the string quartet that plays in the corner, or the frosty champagne that is offered to us by a middle aged woman.

We both accept a flute. Kaia sips hers nervously as she

stares around at the blank walls. In the corner, the string quartet plays Chopin quietly.

"Welcome to Hallman's, Monsieur Fordham," the middle aged woman says, bowing her head. Her English is heavily inflected with a French accent. Her gray hair is in a neat ponytail, her dress is perfectly fitted. She brows her head. "I'm Louise-Thérése. If you will just begin on your left, you will find your private gallery showing set up there."

Kaia puts her hand in mine, her brow wrinkling. I lead her into the second room of the gallery. The room is an eggshell color, the floors a polished cement. It draws attention to the art itself, two or three paintings per large white wall.

The art was the trickiest and most expensive part of this little date. Kaia moves toward the closest painting, tugging me along.

In the painting, several ballet dancers are seen to warm up in what looks like a dance studio. Dancers wearing old-fashioned ballet dresses warm up at the barre.

A little choked sound leaves Kaia's throat. She whips her head back to me, alarmed. "This is…" She looks again and pulls me forward another step. "Is this…"

"Edgar Degas," I supply. Turning my head, I spot Louise-Thérése. "Which painting is this?"

"It is Ballet Rehearsal," she answers. "All the paintings have small plaques beside them telling which they are."

Turning back to Kaia, I smirk. "There you have it."

Kaia drops my hand and smacks me on the arm. "You had a Degas brought here?"

I give her my most arrogant stare. "No. I had ten of his

works flown in overnight. It was actually tons of work." I narrow my eyes. "Not for me. But for one of my assistants? A huge headache."

She smacks me again, looking either angry or disbelieving. I can't help but laugh.

"Stop trying to injure me," I tell her.

Kaia looks around the room, shaking her head. "These are all... I mean... just..." She sucks in a deep breath. "I can't believe you did this!"

I cock my head. "That's an awfully funny way of showing gratitude."

She looks at me, her eyes misting over. "Thank you, Calum. I just—" She shakes her head, putting her hand to her cheek. "You did this for me?"

Now it's time to act cavalier about doing something nice. I shrug. "For us. Again, all I did is offer the Musee d'Orsay in Paris a rather generous sum for rebuilding one of their galleries. And in exchange, they leant us these paintings and..." I look back at the gray haired woman. "I'm sorry, I've forgotten your name."

She shoots me a tiny glare. "Louise-Therése."

Kaia steps out from behind me, looking apologetic. "Would you give us a moment?"

She bows and steps out of the room. Kaia turns, sauntering toward me. "Is this because I said I'd never been to Paris?"

I watch her hips sway. "It might have something to do with it."

She reaches me, placing a hand on my lapel. She looks up at me, her eyes filled with some tender emotion I cannot quite name.

"You're sweet to me," she says softly.

I roll my eyes. "I'm too demanding to be sweet to anyone."

She grips my lapel, stepping closer to press our bodies together. "No. It's too late to hide, Calum. I'm onto you. You listened to me and you used that little snippet of conversation to surprise me. The paintings are wonderful. But it's the fact that you remembered that really stands out to me." Her lips lift. "Thank you."

It's hard, being thanked so directly. Usually the only times I hear thank you are from employees I'm paying. But right now, this soft, lovely creature is looking me right in the eye. She's pressing herself closer.

And she seems so genuine. For the first time in a long time, for just a few seconds, I am without a snappy retort. "Uh... you're welcome?"

It comes out as a question rather than a statement. She doesn't seem to notice, though. She just lifts onto her tiptoes, brushing a kiss over my lips. I'm struck dumb by her openness and responsiveness.

My hands find her hips, lifting her up another inch to meet my mouth. But too soon, she pulls back and bites her lip.

"We have ten whole Degas paintings to stare at," she says. "Come on."

I put her down with reluctance. She grabs my hand and goes back to the first painting, getting close to the canvas. From less than six inches away, the many fine brush strokes are readily apparent.

"Gosh," Kaia says. "Just look at the level of work that went into this."

But I can barely pay attention to the expensive work of art. Because Kaia tows me around the room, examining paintings, her blonde hair curled just so on her neck, her necklace catching the light.

I know that things with Kaia can't last. We're in a bubble, untouched by the real world.

But just now?

I will let her pull me around the room. I will laugh at her jokes. I will pretend to be the kind of boyfriend a girl like her deserves.

I know I'm an insane, demanding perfectionist. I know that I'm damaged beyond repair. I know I will either drive her away or grow tired of her.

But I can let that all fall away for right now. Can't I?

"This is really amazing," she says. She wrinkles her nose. "I think my father actually has a Degas print in his study."

Her shoulders droop. I frown at the way that that man makes her small, even now. "You should forget about him."

She shakes her head. "I know. I... I went out to lunch with my whole family, when we were still... not together."

My eyebrows rise. "Oh?"

Her mouth twists sourly. "Yes. I..."

Tilting my head to the side, I walk toward her. "What?"

Kaia gives her head a tiny shake. "I'm just embarrassed. My dad asked me for money. A lot of money. I gave him... I gave him two hundred and fifty thousand dollars." She hangs her head, swallowing. "And he turned right around and asked when he was going to get more."

I blink. "You gave most of the money you earned from our arrangement to your father?"

She slowly nods. "Yes."

"Oh, Kaia." I exhale, considering her. She can't even look at me. "It's only money."

She gives a humorless chuckle. "You would say that. You have more money than you could ever spend."

I squint, letting several seconds pass. "Is this a hustle? You know, the part where I'm supposed to offer you more money?"

She looks at me, her eyes widening. "God, no. Don't you dare! I just… I wanted you to know."

I smile a little, crossing my arms. She drifts off toward one of the paintings. I pace around the room, wondering what sort of reaction she was hoping for from me.

Was she just looking for sympathy? Or is there something more going on here that I don't see?

It irks me, leaves a bad taste in my mouth.

"Can I ask you a question?"

I look over at her. She's not even looking at me, but is instead gazing at one of the paintings. Walking over to her, I shrug my shoulders.

"Shoot."

Kaia continues to gaze at the painting. "These girls in the paintings are so young. So innocent, even to my eye. But they grew up. I mean, obviously. This was painted almost a hundred years ago."

I reach out, giving her hand a tug. "None of that was a question for me."

She looks at me, her smile turning a bit embarrassed.

"Sorry. It just got me thinking about the future. Where do you see yourself in ten years?"

I squeeze her fingers then drop her hand. "That's a good question. I guess the best answer for that lies not in where I will be, but where IndicaTech will be. I have a plan for the company that will see us grow much larger. International markets, crypto exchange... the world is my oyster."

A little line of worry forms between her brows. "That's nice. But it isn't what I asked. I asked where you see yourself in ten years. No offense, but I really don't care about your business affairs."

My lips curl up. "You ought to. The business paid for all of this art to be here. It paid for the clothes you're wearing. The apartment you live in, the stage you dance on..."

She gives me a rueful smile. "I didn't say I'm not grateful. I just said I don't really care about the money. It's not important to me."

"You really should care."

She tilts her head, placing her hand on my arm. "The perks of dating you are undeniable. But if you lost it all tomorrow..." She shrugs. "It wouldn't matter in the slightest to me."

I chuckle. "Because you've already been paid for your contract?"

Kaia shakes her head and rolls her eyes. "No. Quit being such a fool. We might have met under strange circumstances—"

I narrow my eyes, an edge in my voice as I cut her off. "In the platinum room at Club X. While I paid you huge amounts of money to dance for me, if I remember correctly."

She squints. "Yes. But in the last three months, I've come to care about you. The money is nice, but that's not why I stay."

My mood is on the edge of turning sour. "You stay because you're contractually obligated."

She pushes at my chest. "No. I stay because I like you."

My heart thuds in my chest. I shake my head, not entirely believing her. "Okay. Well…"

She flushes slightly. "Anyway… what was I saying?" She thinks for a second. "Oh, yes. I was asking about what you want for yourself, ten years from now."

I shrug. "What about you?"

She takes a sip of her champagne while she thinks. "I would like to dance professionally for a long time. Ten or twelve years. Then I hope I can retire and teach ballet. I always looked up to my ballet teachers and thought they were so grand and mysterious. I hope I can inspire that in young dancers someday."

I release a pent-up breath. "I can see that. I will tell you right now, teaching maybe isn't as rewarding as you think."

Her eyes snap to my face, widening. "Oh my god. I… I forgot for a minute that that's how we know each other."

A laugh rumbles deep inside my chest. "It's not how we met. But yes, I do think that we wouldn't have… gotten involved… if you hadn't showed up at an audition."

She presses her hands to her cheeks. "I wonder if we hadn't met, how things would've turned out for me."

VIVIAN WOOD

I slide a hand down her back. "You would still be at the NYB."

She casts her gaze down, frowning. "Or maybe my father would've killed me that day he showed up at the NYB and you chased him off."

I notice that her posture changes as she thinks about her dad. Her shoulders slump, her spine curves, her head bows. I pull her close, wrapping my arms around her. Putting my nose in her fragrant hair and pressing my lips against her head.

My heart aches for her. No one deserves the kind of treatment her father gave her. Especially not Kaia, who is the sweetest, most gentle soul I can imagine.

"You would be fine," I say softly. "You're a survivor."

Her arms slip around my torso. "Thanks for saving me."

I don't say anything. I don't ask anything of her in this moment. I just stand here and hold her.

She pulls back a little, looking into my face. "I have to confess something. I've seen my mother."

My brow draws down. "I'm sorry?"

"Since that day, I mean. I met her downtown for coffee."

I squint at her face a little. More than anyone, I am aware that things get sticky when talking about family. So I decide to go with, "Oh?"

She nods, her mouth twisting to the side. "Yeah. She invited me to my sister's fashion show. No mention of my father. No talk of how he tried to hurt me."

"I hope you told her to shove it," I say.

She gives me a flat look. "I love my mother. But I did

152

tell her that I was probably not going to be in attendance. Not without you at my side."

She says the last line as a sort of joke. But I can see her watching me carefully, trying to see my reaction.

"Are you trying to float the idea of us attending your sister's event as a couple?" I ask, cocking my head. "That's insane."

Her eyes drop. She nods. "Yeah. No, I know. It's just... I don't know. I want to rub you in their faces a little bit."

I scan her face. "I would probably get into a public fight with your father, Kaia. If he even looks at you the wrong way, I would go insane."

Kaia blushes, her eyes pinning me. "That was what I was sort of counting on. Not the part where you get in a fist fight. But the part where you act all growly and protective and possessive of me. I kind of love it when you do that."

I can't help it. Despite the seriousness of our conversation, I am halfway hard at her description of me.

"Yeah?" I slide my hands up from her elbows to her shoulders, my brain flipping a switch. All rational thought flees out the window. In its place is my cave man brain.

And it knows exactly what she's talking about.

"Yeah..." she says. She presses up on her tiptoes, finding my mouth for a searing kiss. "Will you think about it?"

I grind against her lower body. I've completely forgotten whatever we were talking about before.

"That depends," I say. My eyes drop to her cleavage. I bite my lip. "Will you ride my cock the whole way home?"

She blushes down to the roots of her blonde hair. "You know I will, Calum."

Flashing her a grin, I turn her around and start moving toward the exit.

KAIA

"*S*o?"

I glance over at Ella, yawning a little. It's early enough to still be dark outside and yet the two of us are in the dance studio. Other dancers will start to arrive in an hour but right now?

It's my time to shine.

I slide down to the floor, doing splits. "I'm sorry?"

Ella is stretching her right leg out on the barre nearest me. "You promised to tell me all about your weekend away! We're about to finish up the week of dress rehearsals and launch Sleeping Beauty so... Come on, spill the details. All the rest of the dancers will get here for the final dress rehearsal soon."

My cheeks heat faintly. I lean down, pressing my torso into my leg.

"Well, I definitely have a boyfriend now. Even if no one else here at the NYB can know."

I sneak a look at her. Ella's brows rise in mild surprise.

"Wait, really? I always assumed that Calum was

just…" She bites her lip. "Sort of dead inside. No offense. He's just never happy with anything here."

My lips thin. "He's much more complex than that."

She rolls her eyes and drops her leg from the barre. "I know, I know. It's just sort of hard to take in. I'm glad that things are progressing with y'all, though."

I sit up and pull my legs in, standing up. "I'm not sure that progressing is the right word. Progressing in a relationship means that someday he'll marry me and I'll have his babies."

Ella chuckles. "Not for everyone."

I shrug. "For most people, I would think. But I have ten or twelve years before my career is ballet is done. I've worked so fucking hard to get here."

"Except for the man you've been obsessing about for two months."

I arch a brow at her. "I'm sorry?"

"Have you admitted to yourself yet that you're in love with Calum?"

My jaw drops. "I am not! I'm definitely too busy with ballet for… all of that."

She snorts. "So you are in denial. Let me tell you something, Kaia. That shit gets old real quick."

"I wouldn't know."

"You're ten shades of red right now, just talking about how you're not in love with him. If that isn't some kinda infatuation, I don't know what you would call it."

Face burning, I shake my head. "I can't focus on anything else right now, especially not a future with anyone. All I see is ballet."

"Mhm."

"Seriously! Those little girl dreams of the perfect white wedding and the big house? Those are totally off the table. Dance is my life."

Ella kicks her other leg up onto the barre and begins to stretch. "You sound like you're freaking out about something that may never come to pass. Maybe just be present for right now."

Stretching out my arms, I frown. "Ugh, I hate when you give me such poignant advice. When is it going to be my turn to give you my wisdom?"

She cracks up. "What wisdom? You have been so freaking sheltered your whole damn life!"

I shoot her a grin. "I like the idea of it though."

We stretch for a bit in silence. I grab a tennis ball and use it to rub a knot in my shoulder. Ella does some very slow pliés, exercising perfect muscular control as she does it.

I find myself thinking of last night. "I asked Calum to attend my little sister's fashion show with me."

Her movements stop for a second. "Um… you're already pulling the girlfriend card on him?"

My face grows warm. "I don't know. I mean, I know that he doesn't want to go. But I can't face my family alone."

She sighs. "I don't think you should face your family at all. I know you keep saying that you love your mother. But if I were you, I would just try to keep in touch with her when she's by herself. Your dad and your sister sound toxic."

"They are my family, though. You don't just get to decide who is and isn't in your family, Ella."

Ella shoots me some side eye. "You do if your dad tries to maim you."

I scrunch up my face. "I'm sure that he feels bad about that. Deep inside, at least."

She shakes her head. "I think you're wrong. But it's your family, not mine. I'm not the one who keeps opening herself up to get hurt."

I shrug, feeling stubborn. "It's not your situation to deal with."

"Nope. It isn't. Now do you want to try to practice some combinations before everyone else arrives? Or do you want to keep arguing?"

Feeling deflated, I shake my head. "What scene do you want to start with?"

Ella stretches her arms over her head, looking thoughtful. "I'm having some real difficulty with act two, scene three. I want to practice it until my muscle memory kicks in."

In short order, we are bounding across the floor, pirouetting as the sun starts to come up. Dancers slowly begin to show up. Eric and Crispin find their places on either side of us. Bas is about to close the door and start class when Manon slips in, yawning.

Bas lets her in the door, giving her a look. She scurries to the only spot left at the barre. Before I know it, I am swept along into dance class, flowing like a leaf on a current running downhill. With Calum absent, I'm able to really focus and dig in, finally perfecting several hard combinations.

After class, I allow myself a little quiet time. Stretching, watching the dancers as they leave. Ella hurries out of the studio, Eric right behind her.

Still I stay put, trying to train my muscles to allow a greater range of motion while they're still warmed up from class. I find a spot on the floor and go into the splits, lean backward and reaching for my back foot. Crispin is the only person who sticks around with me.

"Mind if I keep you company?" he asks. But before I can even respond, he plops down.

My whole body tightens just a bit at his presumption. I force a smile to my lips and say nothing.

His keen eyes rake over my body.

"I noticed that you are playing The Lilac Fairy. But I can see how pretty and talented you are… What's up with that?"

I flush. "Uhhh… well, I was Aurora originally. Then my spot in the company was in question for a period of time. It fell when the ballet had already been cast, so my understudy got my part. It's sort of complicated."

His eyebrows shoot up. "Why was your spot in question? Obviously if you had such an important role, it wasn't a problem with your dancing."

I squint. "Administrative issues."

A lie, yes. But it's definitely easier than explaining the entire thing to a guy who I barely know.

Crispin narrows his eyes. "What does that mean?"

I sit up straight with a huff. "I don't really want to talk about it, if that's okay with you."

He holds his hands up. "Sure. I don't want to tread on any touchy subjects, I guess."

I repress an eye roll. "Great."

It's quiet for half a minute. I breathe out and try to focus on doing a butterfly stretch, working on my hamstrings. Closing my eyes, I try to find a zen place inside myself.

"I heard you had some drama with your family."

My eyes snap open. My mouth twists with a sour note. "Who told you that?"

He shrugs. "Eric was just filling me in on everyone. It just came up naturally."

I glare at Crispin. "Are you trying to ask really invasive questions? Or is that just a fun bonus?"

Two spots of red appear in his cheeks. "I was just... trying to find some common ground, I guess. I have a difficult family situation too."

He looks down as he says it. Instantly, I feel horrible.

"I'm sorry," I say, unfolding my legs. "I'm just sensitive about my past."

I'm quiet for a beat, waiting to see Crispin's expression. His eyes remain lowered for a few seconds. My anxiety increases, so I get onto my hands and knees, crawling the foot of distance between us.

"Hey," I say. I gently reach out and touch his shoulder.

He looks up, his eyes going wide. I see a moment of calculation slide by in his expression.

"I like you!" he blurts out.

I automatically begin to recoil, surprised. But Crispin lunges toward me, his hands grabbing my shoulders. He kisses me hard on the mouth before I can make a sound of protest.

I freeze, blinking. Then I try to push him away. "What the hell?" I mutter.

He doesn't get the message, apparently. His hands dig into my arms, his kiss turns bruising. I can taste him faintly, like something gone musty and sour.

In the end, I am able to break away by bring my hands up to his wrists, using my fingernails to gouge at his skin, and turning my head to the side. I scramble backward, my hand coming up to my lips.

"Crispin, what the hell?" I cry.

He turns white as a sheet, shooting to his feet. "Sorry! I... I should go..."

I watch, still stunned, as he flees the room. He didn't even take his duffel bag with him.

Heart racing, I sit for a minute, trying to shake off the kiss. But it sticks around for the rest of the day, the memory playing over and over in my mind.

21

CALUM

*W*hen I wake up, the sunlight pouring in through the windows says that I've overslept. I sit up with a yawn, realizing somewhat hazily that I'm alone. Not only that, but I'm in Kaia's side of the apartment.

I've been letting the steel walls of my boundaries slip in the last few days. Sleeping here in her apartment. Letting her curl under my arm as she showed me a video. Sharing a steamy late night shower without anything sexual happening between us. Driven half by inattention and half by distraction, I know I will have to course correct. I don't want to Kaia to think I've gone soft.

Kaia's cat jumps up on the bed and meows at me. I give him an absentminded stroke and he purrs at me.

"You're much easier to please than your mistress," I tell him.

Getting up slowly, I dress myself and then head out of the flimsy screens that shape her bedroom.

"Hey, big brother."

I'm startled to look up and find Lucas sitting in Kaia's kitchenette, drinking a cup of coffee. Looking around, I see the door between the two apartments is wide open.

"What are you doing in here?" I demand. "Kaia could be in here. She could be naked."

He gives me a pointed look. "I saw her leave this morning, actually. It was pretty awkward to have to introduce myself to your little girlfriend. I had no idea that you had her living here, Calum."

I glare at him. "It's just for convenience. Now come on, let's get out of this place. I need a cup of coffee too."

He stands up, his smile rueful as he follows me across the apartment. "Convenience, huh? It's not because you're secretly in love with her?"

I refuse to look at him as I shake my head, showing him through the doorway between our homes. Closing the door firmly behind him, I usher him toward the kitchen.

"I'm not really interested in your baiting me into an argument just now. Is there a reason you're bothering me first thing in the morning?"

Lucas looks back at me as we walk into the kitchen, his light blue eyes narrowing on my face. "It's half past nine. We have a conference call with the realtor from Tokyo in half an hour. Don't tell me you forgot?"

"No." I walk over to the coffee setup in the kitchen, turning on the grinder. "One of my assistants has been leaving me reminders practically hourly. I don't see why I have to be on the call, though."

Lucas gives me a funny look and sets his coffee down on the kitchen island. "Because this is our first international office, Calum. You said that you wanted to be involved with the selection process. Actually, you were a lot more crass than that, but that's what you meant."

I switch the coffeemaker on and put my hands on my face, sighing. "Can you narrow it down to three potential sites for me? Or better yet, use your own judgment and leave me out of the entire process?"

He folds his arms across his chest and leans his hip against the counter. "Not if you're going to nitpick every single flaw."

I shoot him a glare. "No promises. Just try to remember how critical it is that we get a really unique looking space. Spend as much as you think is necessary to really find us or build us the best headquarters possible."

Lucas gives me a skeptical look. "Are you feeling okay?"

My coffee finishes dripping and I inhale, taking a first sip. It's piping hot but so good that I can practically feel it down to my toes.

"Ahh," I murmur. I crack open an eye, looking at my brother. "Why would I not be okay?"

He squints. "First you tell me that you and Anita..." He scrunches his nose up. "Got physical. The next thing I know, you're setting up some dancer to live here and telling me you don't want to work. I'm waiting for you to pull off your face and reveal your true identity, Scooby-Doo style."

I roll my eyes. "Hilarious. You know, it's not too late for you to give up being a CEO and try your hand at stand up comedy instead."

He cocks his head. "You don't want to talk about Anita or Kaia?"

I shake my head and sip my coffee. "Nope. Both of those topics are not really up for discussion right now."

Lucas heaves a sigh. "I think we should have a real talk about Anita. Whether you like it or not, I'm pretty sure that she's on the decline. And it isn't gradual, either."

"I've literally never been less affected by the news of someone's impending demise."

"Yeah, well. She's been asking for you."

"People in hell want ice water. What are you going to do?"

I shrug it off, but all this Anita talk is really starting my morning off on a sour note. Lucas checks his watch.

"I'm going to use your office for this phone call," he says. "But before I forget. I want the chance to meet your girlfriend for real. The three of us, a fancy meal, no room for wiggling out of my relentless interrogations."

I snort. "You make it sound so appealing."

He walks toward my office. "I'm serious. Don't make me go behind your back to ask her to dinner. Make yourself look like an adult. Set it up!"

I roll my eyes and sip my coffee.

As I shower and dress, I find my thoughts returning to Kaia. More specifically, Lucas's little jibe.

You don't want to admit that you're in love with your little pet?

As I pull on my dance clothes and head down to my waiting car, the question stays with me. Am I, as Lucas suggested, a man obsessed?

I don't feel it. Then again, how would I know? The thought gnaws at me, dogs me as I stalk up the stairs on the New York Ballet.

When I arrive, I peek in the back door of the auditorium. I see two of the dancers conferring with Basil. They could probably use my stage direction, honestly.

"No!" one of the dancers shouts. He bursts into tears and flees the stage.

I find myself creeping back and letting the door silently close. It seems like too much to ask me to subject myself to that kind of emotional turmoil. Better just ease myself into the morning.

I take the stairs that lead into the upper balcony. From working in this building for years, I already know that there is a blind spot. A place that no one from the stage can see a person standing and watching from up high.

I cross my arms and lean back against the wall. As I watch, Bas claps his hands. "Okay. Scene three, act one. We will just run it through without Levi. Come on, people. We only have three more rehearsals to get it right."

He turns to the pianist, gesturing that the music should begin. Lively piano music starts. Ballerinas dance out onto the stage, prancing as they go. Some male dancers follow them, setting the scene.

As the dancers all turn, Aurora and her two hand maidens traipse lightly across the stage. One of the hand maidens is Kaia. I know that perfectly well; we've been working on this fucking ballet for over a month. And yet, my stomach still does a flip flop when I see her.

What is this feeling I get when she's around? It's too dark and carnal to be joy. Too heartfelt to be obsession.

Why can't I put a name to this feeling?

Kaia flounces around the stage, executing every pirouette and jet flawlessly. As she dances, I do an inventory. The women in my life are few in number. There was Honor, for whom I felt an obsession bordering on mania. And of course there was Anita. I felt a mixture of gratitude, awe, and deep shame about her.

Then there was my mother. I can barely remember feeling much at all for her, after she left me and Lucas for the hundredth time, assuming that we would just get by somehow.

"There you are, Calum."

I blink, turning my head to see Emma waving me over. Unused to my thoughts being interrupted, I move toward her with a sigh. "What?" I whisper.

She smiles a little thinly, smoothing down her chic black dress. Her eyes turn out toward the stage. She watches Kaia and her two friends dance for a long moment.

"I know about the girl, Calum."

I scowl, but my heart starts beating like a drum. "Come again?"

She pins me with eyes the color of steel. "I know that you're fucking that pretty little ballerina onstage. Don't even try to lie to me. I saw you two kissing in an empty dance studio."

I shrug a shoulder and shake my head. "I don't know what you're talking about."

Emma surveys me. A cool smile plays on her lips. "Kaia's quite talented. Very graceful. When you had me fire and rehire her, I wondered if something was going on between you. Still, I'll admit to some shock when I accidentally stumbled on you two together."

She tilts her head. "She seems so soft and gentle. I wonder if that's why a brute like you likes her so much?"

I shake my head. "I haven't the slightest idea what you're going on about."

She scrunches up her nose. "Yes you do."

I slide her a hard look. "Did you come up here just to fling around wild accusations? Or is there a larger point to be made?"

Emma smirks. "The point is that I have something to hold over your head now. I control Kaia's entire future."

I force myself to look unimpressed. Inside, I want so badly to react. To scream at her, to threaten her.

But I don't.

"Uh huh," I say. Turning my eyes back to the stage, I pretend to be bored.

Emma's fingers grab my arm hard. "I can bench your sweetheart. I have the power. You'd do best to remember that the next time I have a favor to ask."

I shake off her hand, rounding on her. She backs up, trying to find the exit. But I am right on her, looming tall.

"You think you can threaten me?" I hiss, incensed. "I own you. I own this ballet. And I don't take kindly to you thinking that you have power over me."

Emma's silver eyes widen. "I swear, if I have to, I will go to the press about your inappropriate relationship with someone who is basically your student."

I growl at her instead of answering her directly. She finds the door and practically falls out of it in her rush to get away.

I'm left standing here, chest heaving, heart thrumming, acid filling the pit of my stomach.

If I had any doubts before now, I have them no longer. The bubble has burst. Too many people are finding out about my relationship with Kaia.

Turning to look down at the stage, I see Bas glaring up at me. He motions to his wrist, apparently telling me it's time to join him onstage.

My mood gone from charcoal to the deepest black, I storm down the stairs.

22

KAIA

I peek out from the heavy velvet curtain, my stomach churning. The stage is dressed for our ballet and dramatically lit. The theater is empty still, but a few of the dark-jacketed ushers do stand in the back, talking quietly to each other. The fifty-piece symphony orchestra begins warming up.

God, it's really happening.

Backstage, there are a million tiny adjustments happening. Ella is having a seam in her tutu re-sewn. Eric and Crispin are going over some choreography for the hundredth time.

Even Manon is filled with this nervous energy that seems to pervade every single dancer.

I'm so anxious about my performance that I am sick to my stomach. Heading back into the wings, I stretch my ankles and try not to vomit.

"Kaia," a voice hisses.

I look over to find Calum standing thirty feet away,

holding open the door to the costume closet. He jerks his head, inviting me inside.

After scanning my surroundings, I swallow and scamper over to him. He hurries me inside the closet, pulling a long string that hands down between us. The feeble light flickers on.

I suck in a breath and glance up at Calum. I'm in such a state of panic over my first professional performance that I'm worried I may burst into tears, ruining the heavy stage makeup and fake lashes I'm wearing.

Calum touches my arm. "You look nervous, beauty."

My lower lip begins to wobble. "I am nervous!" I whisper.

He tilts his head, his eyes taking in my upper body. "You shouldn't be. You've worked your ass off for the last five weeks. I've seen it. You're ready?"

My eyes mist over. I press my knuckles into the very corners, trying to stave off tears. "You think so?"

He gives me a knowing smirk. "It's my job to stage manage this production. So when I say that you're ready, you'd better fucking believe it."

I laugh a little, although it definitely sounds tearful. "Thanks. I would kiss you right now if I didn't have this crazy makeup on."

Calum pulls my lower body against his. His lips twitch and his eyes sparkle with a hint of amusement. "Same."

Faintly, I hear Basil's voice calling for the dancers. I pull a deep breath into my lungs, looking up into Calum's face. "That's me. Wish me luck."

His hands shape my waist, lifting me ever so briefly. "Break a leg, Kaia."

"Thanks," I whisper.

Opening the closet, I glance around to make sure the coast is clear. Then I hurry deeper backstage to a large circle of my fellow dancers. I squeeze in beside Ella and Eric, glancing at them.

They both look nervous as hell. Well, at least it's not just me.

Basil stands in the middle of the circle. He looks around for a second, searching for something. Calum surprises me by popping up coming from the opposite direction. The circle of dancers part, letting him through.

"Is this everyone?" Basil asks. "Let's all join hands."

I grab Ella and Eric's hands, my heartbeat starting to pound. Glancing at Ella, I pull a quick face and squeeze her hand.

"All right, all right." Bas smiles around at all of us. "The audience is taking their seats now. They've come prepared for a little bit of spectacle. And you have worked so hard over the last two months. You've put in all the hours, all the sweat, all the incredible amount of effort required to put on a ballet. You are going to be great. So go out there and leave it all onstage. Let's give the people their spectacle!"

Everyone cheers softly. Basil arches his eyebrows and looks at Calum. "Anything to add?"

"Go show the public how hard you've worked," Calum says simply. "Break a leg."

We cheer softly again. Then Basil calls us all to our places. I run to my spot behind the curtains, my heart pounding. I can hear blood rushing in my ears as I adjust my tutu ever so slightly.

The symphony begins to play a soft introductory song. My nerves are a bit fried, but now is the time to pull it together. I can hear the babble of the audience; the theatre lights all flash twice, then lower dramatically.

I paste a smile on my face. Lively music starts up, the cue for the first fairies to head onstage. And then something odd happens. From the second that I start moving until we join hands, parading onstage for a curtain call… the whole world is covered in what I call a ballerina's haze. I pirouette to my heart's content. But it's almost as if I'm looking through the lens of some strange camera. Or better yet, that everything is quick and bright and blurred, as if Edgar Degas was painting what was happening in real time.

Time sort of blurs. The next thing I know, we are taking our final bows. I'm out of a little breath without having any memory of what made me that way.

Ella pulls on my hand, squeezing it. "Good job!" she mouths.

A grin bursts across my face. "You too!" I mouth back.

She winks. The dancers all take a bow again, then we run off the stage. My heart is pounding. My endorphins are flooding my body, my brain filled with serotonin. I turn my head, searching for a face in the melee of backstage. In my heart of hearts, I want nothing more than to let Calum wrap me up in a big hug.

But he's nowhere to be found. Which is fine, I tell myself. But I can't help but be a tiny bit let down. Even though a teacher and a student embracing and kissing would be scandalous…

I squeal as I am lifted into the air. Maybe it's Calum. Maybe we are just ignoring the rules today?

My heart beats fast as I turn around. My smile falls a little bit as I find that it's Eric who has me in his grasp. He growls, celebratory, and lifts me high before setting me down.

"Can you believe that?" he exclaims, jubilant. "I would be hard pressed to find a single flaw in that entire production."

I step away from him, a small smile on my face. "Yeah. I mean, it was all a blur for me. I don't remember any of it."

"No?" he says, a tiny frown appearing on his face. "You were brilliant."

He reaches out, gently touching my shoulder. My heart stutters. I lick my lips and glance around, hoping that no one is looking.

"Thanks," I say softly, backing out of his grasp again. "You were too."

Ella comes running up to us, issuing an excited squeal. "Guys! Neal Myer came to the show."

Eric squints. "Who?"

"Um, he's the New Yorker Magazine journalist that reviews ballet, duh," Ella says. She puts a hand on her hip. "He said hi to me and said that the show was one of the best season openers he's seen in a decade!" She fans herself, grinning. "I mean, can you even believe it?"

Manon bursts into the middle of our little group. "Cast party down the street at Nouveau." She looks us up and down. "Don't dress like street trash."

"Fuck you, Manon," Ella says, her tone still cheerful.

Manon rolls her eyes and stalks off to another group of dancers. Ella looks behind me, then makes eye contact with me. She jerks her chin past me, indicating that I should turn around. She pulls Eric away as I look behind me.

Calum stands just two feet behind me, talking to a stocky black man in his 60s, wearing a very neat gray suit. Calum makes eye contact with me, smirking a little, and waves me over.

My cheeks glow hot as I walk to them. "Hello, Calum," I say coolly.

"Kaia Walker," he says, touching my shoulder. "This is Neal Myer. He works for New Yorker Magazine."

I force a smile to my lips and try not to pretend that I can feel heat radiating from Calum's touch. Curtsying slightly, I face Neal. "It's nice to meet you. I'm from the area and I've been reading your work for years."

Neal bows his head. "You are too kind. And you did a fine job with dancing Cinderella. You were sublime."

I blush down to the tips of my hair. "Thank you, sir."

"Please, call me Neal."

"Of course."

Calum leans in. "I was just telling Neal that you have watched the New York Ballet since you were a child. He said he thought there might be something interesting in that, should you choose to write about it."

My eyes go wide. "Me?"

Calum squints at me. "It's just a suggestion."

Neal cocks his head. "The idea has merit. We would have to meet and flesh the story idea out a lot more, of course…"

I bow my head. "I'm at your disposal."

Neal gives me a quick smile. "It was nice to meet you, Kaia. Calum, I just saw someone that I want to talk to. If you will both excuse me?"

Calum watches him go. "He's a good man."

I glance at Calum carefully, taking a step away from him. "What was that? Why did you tell him I could write?"

He waves a hand. "Anyone can write. You have a lot of experience with dance in New York. I was just putting two and two together."

My mouth twitches. "Of course you would think that. Everything you've tried has turned out to be a raging success."

He shrugs a shoulder. "Yeah. So?"

"Kaia!"

I turn my head, trying to locate Ella's voice. Shaking my head, I take another step back from Calum. "So… I'll see you later?"

His smirks. "Oh yes, beauty."

I feel my face turn bright red. There are a million things I want to ask him, but all of them would tip any watchers off to our relationship. So I just start to turn away.

"Until then…" I call over my shoulder.

But I do put a little extra sway in my hips as I walk away, hoping that Calum will notice.

23

CALUM

I look at the extravagantly set table in my dark wood dining room, pursuing my lips. The chandelier spills from the ceiling, the waterfall of crystal emitting a warm glow. Below it, there are places set for two people. Priceless china, expensive platinum utensils, crystal goblets filled with ice water. I lean over and light the white taper candles, adjusting the candelabra that sits on the table by a millimeter.

Behind me, my two employees wait. I cast a final glance over the table. It's perfect.

But there is a nervous part of me, deep down. One that makes himself known no matter how much I try to drown him out.

I take a deep breath and turn to my house maid and my personal chef. "That will be all. Thank you."

Both of them bow, disappearing into the back hallway. Once they are gone, it will be just me and Kaia in this apartment. That's how I prefer it, if I'm honest.

VIVIAN WOOD

Sauntering into the kitchen, I survey the wines left out by the chef. A sauterne. A chablis. A blanc des blancs.

All of them sound delicious. But I want to please Kaia, who still has the palate of a college kid. So I rifle through the fridge, pulling out a bottle of champagne and a basket of lemons.

I'm just pulling a thin strip of lemon peel to garnish our French 75s when I hear her voice.

"Calum?" Kaia calls. "Your note said I would find you here…"

"I'm in the kitchen!" I volley back, finishing the cocktails.

Half a minute later, she appears. She's still wearing her dance sweats and looking around like a skittish newborn fawn. "This is your house?"

I look around at the marble countertops and matching white cabinets. "Home sweet home." I slide her cocktail a few inches toward her. She flushes, hurrying to scoop up the glass.

"I feel like I'm massively underdressed." She looks at me, frowning at my jeans and a t-shirt. "I'm sorry, but how is it that you seem to blend in seamlessly?"

I smirk, raising my glass. "I don't know. But I'll toast you anyway."

She smiles, tilting her head at me and resting her hip against the counter. "Cheers, Calum."

I take a sip of my drink, chuckling. "Did you have fun at the cast party?"

She sets her glass down with a tiny smirk. "No."

I trail my hand down her shoulder and her arm, stopping at her hand. She takes my hand, lacing my fingers with hers.

"You didn't enjoy yourself?"

Kaia smiles, pushing her mane of hair back. "No. The only thing I wanted was to be with my boyfriend. But... that's not allowed. So I went through the motions until I could come back here to be with you."

It's only a small step until our bodies are all but touching. She looks up at me with a small smile. Expecting, I think, that I will kiss her or initiate something physical.

Instead, I surprise her by looking down into her eyes and murmuring words that she probably never thought she would hear out of my mouth.

"Do you like lasagne?"

For a second, she frowns. "Uhh... sure. I mean, I don't really eat a lot of carbs and cheese and tomato sauce..."

I raise a brow at her. "It's important to indulge today. You just had the best opening night one could have. Come on."

I grab my drink and Kaia's hand, tugging her toward the still-warm oven. Grabbing oven mitts, I open the oven. The kitchen immediately fills with the scent of garlic, tomato, and bubbly cheese. I pull out two perfect individual dishes of lasagne.

"What?" She looks completely surprised. "You didn't cook for me, did you?"

I shrug a shoulder. "Yes. But I definitely had help from my personal chef. She prepped everything and made the salad."

She laughs a little. "Still! You definitely did not have

to make me food. I would've been happy with anything at all."

I give her a long look.

"You earned it. Now grab our glasses," I say, closing the oven with a foot. "Follow me."

I lead her into the dining room. Anticipation didn't quite tell me what to expect her face to look like when she walks in. Her eyes go wide as she takes in the table.

As I set the food down at our places, she trails after me. "Calum, I had no idea that you even owned a dish, much less a table setup like this."

I smirk at her a little. "I'm multifaceted."

"I see that now," she admits. She puts the champagne flutes down by our designated places and starts to sit in one of the high backed chairs.

"I haven't shown you the best part yet."

I pull her to her feet again and guide her over to the wall, which is heavily curtained. When I open the curtains to reveal a jaw-dropping view of Central Park, one hand flies to her mouth. She hits me with the other hand, seemingly unable to believe her eyes.

Before us, the entire park is splayed out, street lamps providing most of the light. There are a few blocks of buildings in between us and the park itself, but none so high as this lofty perch.

It's the entire reason I bought this penthouse.

Kaia looks up at me, shock apparent on her face. "I can't believe how beautiful it is!"

I put my hands on her shoulders, massaging her muscles for a moment. "Believe it."

I move away, leaving her to stare at the view while I

grab the huge salad from the refrigerator. Then I bring the big bowl back to the table and take a seat.

"Come eat," I beckon. "The view will still be there when you're full."

Kaia turns to me, her cheeks flushed. "How do you do that?"

She heads over as I help myself to some salad. I arch a brow as she sits.

"Do what?"

"Just act like it's no big deal that we're sitting in a penthouse, in Manhattan, with an amazing view." She frowns, helping herself to a large helping of salad.

"I don't know. I guess I'm used to it." I point my fork at her plate. "Try some lasagne. Don't go nuts with the salad first. Remember, I know all the diet tricks."

Her cheeks redden and she shoots me a glare. "You're awfully bossy."

I shrug a shoulder, focusing on my own food. "Just trying to force you to enjoy my food, beauty."

She purses her lips, smirking a little, and digs into her steaming dish of lasagne. The second the forkful of pasta, meat, cheese, and tomato sauce is in her mouth, she moans quietly. "Oh my god," she mumbles. She looks up at me, chewing for a moment. "This is so fucking good, Calum."

I grin at her reaction. "Good."

We eat in silence for a few moments. Kaia gets a faraway look on her face as she zones out and chews. I allow my gaze to drift off to the view, thinking of how strangely pleasant it is to simply be right now. This feeling, this contentment, is very weird to me. But I'm trying not to overthink it.

For once, I want to just revel in the feeling of satisfaction I feel.

"Do you want to have kids?"

I blink, looking back at Kaia. "What?"

She pauses, a forkful of salad alway to her lips. "Do you want to have kids? And get married?"

Her question is so out of the blue that I'm a little taken aback by it. "Are you... proposing to me?"

Kaia flushes down to the roots of her hair. She shakes her head. "No! I didn't mean that! I just mean more generally. I guess I am just asking if those are items on your bucket list or not."

Pushing out a long breath, I crinkle up my face. "I don't know. I mean... maybe someday. Statistically speaking, men who are very wealthy usually marry a few times in their lives."

She rolls her eyes. "Okay, I'm not talking about what other people do. I'm talking about you."

I squint. "I guess when I think about my future, I do see myself as the head of a family. So yes, I guess. Although that's all pretty abstract to me at the moment."

She nods her head, slowly taking another bite of her lasagne. I narrow my eyes at her.

"What about you?"

She looks up, surprised. "Me? Oh. Uhhh... Yeah, I guess. Eventually. After I spend the next decade of my life dancing, I would settle down and start a family. Sure."

My lips tip up as I picture Kaia holding a toddler version of herself. That seems to suit her pretty well.

Her mouth puckers into a frown. "I'm a little worried about passing on some of my family's... tendencies."

My eyebrows jump up. "You're worried about being a pigheaded narcissist piece of shit?"

Her cheeks color faintly. "Maybe."

I chuckle, pushing my plate away. "I wouldn't give it a second thought, beauty. Honestly. If anything, you care about other people too much."

She frowns. "Well, maybe my father was normal until he had children."

I snort. "No. Definitely not."

"You don't know that. And besides, what if I turn into my mom? What if I meet some total asshole who thinks he is the greatest thing since sliced bread? And then for some reason that I can't explain, pheromones or something, I just hang on his every word and act totally brainwashed by him?"

I give her a cool smile. "If that was your tendency, Kaia, I think we would have already figured that out by now. After all, I'm only a step or two away from your father. An egomaniac. A perfectionist. A man who wants to own the world."

Kaia scrunches up her face, laughing. "You are nothing like my father."

I raise my hands in a sign of surrender. "Far be it for me to argue with you."

Her expression sobers and she looks at me, her gaze narrowing on my face. "What are your parents like?" she asks softly.

"Dead," I say matter-of-factly. "My mom was a junkie. She died before I made it to high school. My dad left when I was really little. It's always been me and Lucas fighting against everyone else in the world."

Her eyebrows furrow. "It was just you two? Nobody stepped in to try to help?"

Anita's face flashes in my mind. Suddenly I feel a rising crest of anger inside my chest. I feel like I'm helpless to stop it.

I jerk to my feet suddenly, my mood gone pitch black. "That's it for question and answer time, Kaia."

Her expression is perplexed. She cocks her head. "Sure, Calum."

Yanking her dishes off the table, I stack them with my own and carry them into the kitchen. I set them in the sink and try to breathe, my fists flexing and relaxing again and again.

I close my eyes and lean against the counter, trying to stave off the ticking time bomb inside. I feel Kaia's small hand touch my back.

"Are you all right?" she asks, her voice small.

I suck in a deep breath, rounding on her. She looks small and afraid. I reach out and brush the back of my knuckles along her pretty face.

When I speak, my voice has gone to gravel. "Are you ready for dessert, beauty?"

She sucks her full bottom lip in, her face going pale. When she speaks, it comes out as a breathy whisper. "Yes. Whatever you want, I'll do."

I lean down and press my lips to hers with a growl.

24

KAIA

I lean into the kiss, my heart pounding. He picks me up and I wrap my legs around his body. Calum carries me to a room I've never really spent any time in. His bedroom.

He looks me deep in my eyes. "How much do you trust me?"

My body tenses. "What do you mean?"

His eyes are steady on me. "I want to fuck you roughly. But I need to know that you trust me not to actually hurt you."

My eyes widen. "I... I trust you, Calum."

His hand cups my chin and controls my head. With my head lifted towards him, his lips are on mine. I can taste nothing but the flavor of him, clean and masculine and raw.

His hand slips down to my neck, gripping the front gently. He puts a little pressure on it and I can't breathe. My eyes meet his. My mouth opens. I almost start to panic.

And then he realizes his grip, petting my neck. "That's

good. You may not like it now, but when I'm fucking you, you will. I promise."

Nodding, I touch my neck, feeling the imprint of his fingers. "I believe you."

Calum kisses me slowly. When his tongue slips between my lips, I let out a moan, meeting it with my own. My back arches, my chest pressing up against him.

He explores the stretch of silky skin at my hip, and slowly moves lower, lower. He drags out every moment, an exquisite torture. He grabs my thigh and drapes it across his lap, leaving me exposed. His hand travels up toward my center, kneading and squeezing my thigh as he goes.

When his fingers brush my core, he finds me already wet.

"Your pussy is already so damn wet," he murmurs, his voice gone to gravel. He teases my crevice again with the lightest of touches. "And it's all for me. Isn't that right, beauty?"

I can do nothing but gasp and nod. "You turn me on," I whisper.

"Tell me who owns this pussy, Kaia."

He keeps teasing me, brushing his touch just the barest inch from my clit and my pussy. I gasp against, writhing.

"You do, Calum," I tell him. "It's all yours."

He grins and squeezes my ass as he pulls me on top of his lap. As I straddle him, I can feel his cock between my legs through the cotton of my panties and the silky material of his pants. I'm already wet, but can't help grinding against him.

He nips at my ear, letting out a soft groan. "Fuck, baby.

You're killing me. I want you so fucking bad and we've only just started."

I rock my hips against his, making a needy sound. Even through his pants, I feel his heated weight, and I'm ready for him to tear off the rest of our clothes and fuck me right this second.

It's never that easy or fast with Calum, though. He likes to take it slow, to tease and torture me. He likes to pull every last ounce of satisfaction from my body until I'm nothing more than a husk of a person.

His mouth moves from my lips to my jaw and then down to my neck. The light cotton of my dress stops him, and he growls. With one hand, he pulls the entire dress off over my head. I'm left in my bra and panties, bare skin heating under his gaze.

A part of me feels suddenly shy, even though this is far from our first time together. Calum smirks at my shyness.

"You're blushing, beauty. I love it when I make you fucking blush."

I shoot him a tiny glare. "You're terrible."

"And yet, you stay with me." He grins wickedly. He very slowly unhooks my bra and draws it down my arms. My bare breasts jut proudly out and Calum gives them their due.

He lifts me up by my waist so my nipples meet his mouth. The warmth of his mouth consumes one nipple, and the other. I feel the strange connection between my pussy and my nipples. Teasing one makes the other starts tingling.

I whimper as I feel my nipples harden under his tongue and teeth. I want desperately to be lower, to be able to rub myself against his cock again, but he keeps me firmly poised inches above his lap.

I squirm. He shifts his hands down to cup my ass. His hands that clutch my ass shift closer to my center. His fingers slowly, slowly spread me apart. I still have my panties on, but Calum doesn't pay any attention. The ache of emptiness is unbearable.

"Tell me how wet you are," he tells me. He never stops sucking on my nipples. "Hmm? Slide your hand down to your pussy and tell me if you're ready for me, beauty."

"Stop teasing me," I say, frustrated.

Calum pulls back, cocking a brow. "I told you to do something, little girl. Don't make me tell you again."

Pushing my lower lip out in a pout, I trail my hand down between my legs. Closing my eyes, I press my fingers against the white cotton, feeling the wetness he's caused. A little huff of breath leaves my lips.

"I'm ready," I say, still pouting. "I'm just waiting for you, Calum."

"Hm," is his only response. "Take off your panties, Kaia."

Yes.

My lips part. I can't take my eyes off of Calum as I quickly get rid of the piece of cotton.

"Straddle my lap," he orders. When I hurry to comply, he smirks. "My beauty is thirsty, I see."

I blush, but there is no hiding it. So I nod and settle against his lap.

He slides a finger inside my pussy and pushes his thumb against my clit. I shudder at the surprise of it. I wasn't ready for it, exactly. But it still feels good.

I move against his hand eagerly. His hands are deft, with practiced flicks against my G-spot and just enough pressure on my clit to get me halfway to orgasm. I throw my head back and moan, writhing against his hand.

"Easy, baby," he says. "I'm trying to be gentle with you."

"Who said I want gentle?" I kiss him deeply, squeezing my eyes closed. "I want fast and furious."

"Slow down," he tells me. "Enjoy the ride, beauty."

There is a part of me that thought maybe he'll just stop. Maybe it is all just a game, a power trip. I ride his hand harder, lifting my head, and offer my breasts to his lips again.

He spanks me once once on my ass, hard.

"I said slow down," he growls. "I want to watch you fall apart."

The slap surprises me, but even as the sting fades and I feel my ass turning red, I also feel a new gush of wetness between my thighs. My pussy is on fire for him.

I need him like I've never needed him before.

Calum slips his finger out of my pussy and lifts me off his lap. He pushes me down onto my back. He kneels and spreads my legs wide, his eyes glinting as he takes me in.

"Fuck, Kaia. You're so goddamned beautiful when you're naked and wet for me."

I let my head fall back as he kisses his way down my thighs. When he reaches my mound, he kisses his way across it, trailing his tongue against my sweat-slicked skin. I dig my fingers into his hair, moaning at the thought of what is to come.

He comes so close to tasting me, really tasting my pussy, and yet he pulls back.

I shake my head back and forth, ready to burst.

"Fuck! Calum, come on!" I cry, pounding my fists.

"What do you want?" he asks me, smirking.

"Calum, *please*," I say, arching my back as far as I can. "Taste me."

"Taste you where?" he asks. "Here?"

He kisses my inner thigh. I make a frustrated sound.

"Eat my pussy," I demand. "Eat my ass. Quit being gentle with me."

He makes a satisfied sound. "Good girl."

His tongue runs across my clit, firm and slow, before it dips down into the deepest of my folds. I cry out and dig my fingers into his hair to hold him closer to me.

"Oh god. Oh, Calum!!" As he works his tongue faster, I can't stop calling out his name. When he slides a finger into me again, I reach for my breasts and pinch my nipples.

But this is too easy. I don't want to come, not like this.

Not without giving him a taste of his own medicine.

"I want to taste you," I moan, breathless. "Let me suck your cock, baby."

Apparently I've said the right things, because he immediately stops. He pulls his finger from my body and leaves a flutter of kisses on my clit.

"What about you? Don't you want to come?"

But even as he says it, he's unzipping his pants.

"Yes. But I want to give you a little payback. I want to suck your cock but not let you come."

He gives me a look. "That doesn't sound as terrible as you think it does."

When he shows me his cock, I bite my lip. I know I've seen it all before, but his cock is so perfect, so thick and long, so perfectly pink. That ache that throbbing deep inside of me doesn't have a chance of stopping.

I reach for him, but he stops me. "Let's flip the script. Lie down and prop your head up with a pillow."

I'm not sure what he means, but I eagerly do just that. He straddles my chest, leaning on the headboard, and thrusts forward. I don't have the use of my hands so I just open my mouth.

Calum bites his lower lip and uses his hand to guide his cock into my mouth. His mouth falls open on the very first stroke. "Fuck, beauty."

He tastes salty and earthy. I can't move, can't set the pace. I'm helpless.

Which is probably exactly what Calum wants.

He keeps one hand loosely on my head and caresses my cheek while he watches me take him deeper and deeper into my mouth. Because of the way I'm laying, even the mildest thrust makes me gag. My eyes water. I try to relax my throat and breathe through my nose.

His gaze goes from intense to nearly black in only a few minutes. "Fuck, beauty. If I don't stop, I'm going to come in your pretty little throat. I like the idea, but I really want to fuck you."

He rises up, letting me sit up a little. I pant for a second as he brushes my hands away from my breasts, gently twisting my nipples until I cry out. He leans down and kisses me.

VIVIAN WOOD

"I thought you wanted me to stop being gentle with you," he whispers.

I look at him, issuing a challenge. "If you don't fuck me right now, you're a dead man."

Calum climbs on the bed, looming over me. His eyes blaze with amusement.

"Dead man, hmm?" He grabs me, roughly pulling me into position beneath his body.

When he penetrates me, I feel every bit of his thick cock. It feels so fucking good. I feel every single inch of him as he thrusts his long, proud cock inside my body.

"Oh fuck," I moan. "More! Give me more."

He rams his body into mine, his groin and thighs slapping my naked flesh. I squeal, eliciting a chuckle from him. He rocks his hips into my body a dozen times at lightning speed.

He buries his face in my neck and breathes me in. He fucks me fast for a couple of minutes before slowing down, going painfully slow.

"Calum…"

He shushes me. "Be quiet, Kaia. I'll make sure that you get what's coming to you."

He teases me, lingering with barely his tip inside me. I writhe against him, lifting my hips. "Calum!"

He responds by going deep, fucking me so hard that I almost cry out.

Almost.

Every time he slides against my g-spot, I scratch at his back and call out his name.

"Oh, god. Calum… please! Please…"

He kisses me, slowing even though I just told him

192

not to.

"Not so fast. I want you to slow it all down. Get on top," he tells me. "I want to watch you."

I bite my lip as he pulls out, laying down. On his back, he watches me straddle him. My hair has come undone and hangs in knotted waves over my breasts. He reaches up, pushes the hair aside, and pulls my nipples. I look down and grasp his cock to bring him to my opening.

He moves his hands to my hips.

"Slowly," he tells me. "Remember what I said."

I let my weight fall onto him, but he holds me up. I blush again. He seems to want to watch me take his cock into my pussy.

"Please," I whisper when he is halfway in. He pulls me down onto him as hard as he can. I throw my head back and call out. It's pleasure on the verge of pain, so complete and perfect that I can't complain.

I want him too much.

My nails dig into his chest and he clutches my ass as I ride him. For a moment, the two of us move as one, our breathing harsh. All I know is the slap of flesh, the quiet groans pulled from his chest.

My breasts bounce wildly. Every part of his skin feels like hot silk underneath my fingertips.

"God damn," he utters. "You are so tight, beauty. So wet."

My wetness is so intense it drips down between his thighs.

My eyes close tight and I grind hard against him.

"Look at me," he tells me. "Tell me whose pussy this is. Tell me that it belongs to me."

"It's yours. Only yours, baby." I flutter my eyes open, breathing hard. "I'm close. I'm so fucking close."

He pushes himself up and wraps my legs around his back. From here, he is in complete control.

He lifts me and lowers me onto his cock, while he covers my breasts in marks that I know will darken to hickeys by the next day. I score his back with my nails, marking him in my own way.

My legs are locked around him. His cock is soaked with my wetness.

"Fuck! I'm going to come…" I gasp out.

I can feel my orgasm start to wash over me as my innermost muscles clench.

"Fuck!" he roars. "Christ, Kaia—"

We both barrel over the edge together. When he explodes inside of me, I cry out.

"Fuck!"

"Fuck! Kaia, fuck," he whispers.

I shudder against him as I ride out the last of my orgasm. He kisses my neck gently and makes his way to my lips.

Calum lies beside me, lining our bodies up and holding me close as I struggle for breath. He's breathing hard too, but he kisses my neck, my shoulder, the curve of my breast. Each kiss is a burning brand, causing a shudder to ripple across my exhausted body.

I want to beg him to stop, but I also want to have him again, right now. There's something about him that just makes me insatiable. He looks up at me, then presses a kiss to my lips.

I smush my face into his shoulder and try to breathe.

25

CALUM

"*A*re we almost there?" I grouse. The air smells like fried food. In the background, I can hear the swell of excited voices and the clang of metal on metal.

This is really not how I wanted to spend my birthday. Blindfolded, guided by Kaia's hands into my limo and driven… somewhere.

"Okay, we're going down a step. And then we're home free." Kaia's hands stay on my arm as she leads me to a mystery location.

The blindfold over my eyes doesn't allow any peeking. But I can smell salty food in the air and hear a little girl squealing with glee.

"Where the fuck are you taking me?" I demand to know.

Kaia pulls me to a stop. "Relax. We're here."

She pulls the fabric from my eyes. I squint into the bright mid-morning sun. We are standing in the middle of a carnival. A giant ferris wheel turns slowly to my right, along with a tilt-a-whirl and a small roller coaster. In front of us are a whole bunch of fair-style food booths. People are walking around eating corn dogs, cotton candy, deep-fried Snickers, and funnel cakes. To the my left there are a handful of games booths; behind that are more rides.

"Ohhh," I say, my lips twitching. "Now the sounds make sense." My brow furrows. "Why are we here, though?"

Kaia smiles nervously. "I didn't know what to get for the man that can literally buy anything he wants. So I decided to recreate one of your experiences. The picture of you and your brother at the carnival?" She spreads her arms wide, as if showcasing the whole fair. "Happy birthday."

My eyebrows rise. She really put some thought into this, apparently.

"Uh…" I rub the back of my neck, looking around. "How did you know today's my birthday?"

"Lucas." She smirks. "When I told him what I had planned, said not to bother. That you don't like anybody making a big deal out of your birthday."

Releasing a long sigh, I shrug. "He's not wrong."

Kaia links her arm with mine, smiling timidly at me. "I didn't buy you anything. I certainly won't tell anybody that there is a reason we are celebrating. But I hope you will prove him wrong, Calum."

She squeezes my arm and peers up at me with a hopeful expression. How exactly am I supposed to say no to that?

I roll my eyes. "Usually I like to be alone today. But I'll make an exception… for one hour."

Her face lights up. "Oh good. What should we do first,

then? What's your favorite thing?"

Sliding my arm around her waist, I look around for a second. Everything is done in neon and brass; every single booth or ride emits some kind of sound. It's overwhelming, trying to pick one place to start when the whole carnival is in constant motion.

Finally I shrug. "Let's start on easy mode. How about we play a game?"

Excitement shines in her green eyes. "Okay! Let's see…"

She pulls me over to the games, putting a wristband on me as we look them over. I end up choosing the ring toss game, which is basically a bunch of statues of varying heights and thick rubber rings to try to land on top of them. Above our heads hang the prizes we are trying to win, mostly brightly colored stuffed animals.

When the young guy walks over to us, I start to pull out my wallet. But Kaia tuts me, showing off her wristband.

"We're both wearing these," she says. She sneaks a look at me and after a second, I flash mine too.

The teenager looks like he doesn't care in the slightest. He plunks down a stack of neon colored rings.

"Go nuts," he says, pacing to the end of the booth again.

Kaia picks up one of the rubber rings with a grin. "I'm going to be horrible at this."

I select a ring, feeling the weight of it and the rubber texture. Squinting at the statues, my mouth turns down.

"This is definitely going to be hard."

She grins. "Ready?"

"Yep. Might as well."

We both throw our rings. Mine hits the statue right in front of me and bounces to the floor. Kaia's ring flies to the side and bounces off the wall.

Kaia's reaction is to take a deep breath, narrow her eyes at the statues, and glare. "Let's do it again."

I hand her a ring, watching with amusement. She aims and throws like she's bowling. This time, her ring lands on the stage where the statues stand. She lets out a hair raising yowl of displeasure.

I can help but laugh. "Are you always this competitive?"

She slides me a hard look and picks up another ring. "I don't like to lose."

For the next ten minutes, I half-heartedly attempt to toss rings onto the statues. All the while, I keep watching Kaia throw rings from high and low, harder and softer, from one side of the booth to the other. None of it works, but she's just taking the game so damn serious.

It's not nice to laugh at someone playing a game. Especially not when the person is supposed to be your girlfriend. But Kaia eventually gets fed up and throws a ring onto the concrete at her feet.

Without even thinking about it, I reach out and snatch the rubber ring as it rebounds. Kaia looks at me, her cheeks turning red.

"The stupid game isn't fair," she insists.

My lips tip up. "It's a carnival. The games are all rigged to be super hard."

She screws her face up, pouting. "Stupid ring toss."

My lips twitch. "Which prize do you want?"

Kaia's brow furrows. "Honestly? At this point I can't be choosy."

Turning back to the pile of rings, I throw thirteen quick shots. On shot fourteen, one of the rings makes it onto the statue and settles about halfway down.

I turn to Kaia. "Not bad, huh?"

She smiles at me, wrinkling her nose. "That was a lucky shot."

"Want me to throw another fourteen shots?" I ask, casually picking up a ring.

She plucks the ring from my fingers, tossing it back into the pile. "No. How about a kiss instead?"

I swoop in and pull her up off her feet for a second. She squeals but when our lips brush, she blushes and kisses me back. I step back, pointing to the biggest, most vividly green stuff frog.

"That one," I tell the teenaged boy.

He pulls it down with a stick without a word. I present it to Kaia, who shakes her head. "I can't believe you're so much better than me at this dumb game."

"I really am, though." I grin.

She smacks my arm. "You are the literal worst. Do you realize that?"

I shrug a shoulder, pretending not to care. "Maybe."

Scanning the area, I decide that what we need is a change of scenery. I thrust my hand out, catching hers. "Come on. Let's ride some rides and then eat some junk."

Kaia goes on every single ride that I suggest, even the HairRazr. It's basically a roller coaster on a single circuitous track that goes upside down approximately half the time.

By the time we get off that ride, I throw and arm around her shoulders. "What do you say we chill out for a bit and grab something to eat?"

She nods quickly. "Yes. Yes please. That last ride used up the last of my adrenaline, I'm pretty sure."

She gets a corn dog and some cotton candy. I get a deep fried turkey leg, a funnel cake, and two bright pink slashes. We plunk our haul down at one of the picnic tables and I dig in.

"I'll be right back," Kaia says. "Don't eat my corn dog, okay?"

Assuming that she's going to the bathroom, I sip my slushy and nod gravely. "You got it, boss."

She dashes away, returning in a couple minutes with a plain white box about the size of a softball. It's totally undecorated, but she puts it down on the table beside me.

Funny, until this moment, I'd forgotten that it is my birthday. Giving her a hard look, I put my turkey leg down.

"Kaia, I really don't want anything. What can you buy me that I can't buy for myself?"

She crosses her arms, shooting me a look. "You are such a tyrant. You know that? Just open the frigging box, Calum."

Glaring at her, I lean over and brush the box open with a flick. I'm expecting a watch, maybe. Or even a set of car keys.

But instead, I find a cupcake. There are two ballet dancers on top made of fondant icing. One lifts the other up over his head in a pas de deux, the other looks dainty and delicate as if she is flying. Under their feet is chocolate frosting and chocolate cake.

There's a plaque, too. Sorry You Hate Your Birthday.

I arch a brow, looking up at Kaia. She's smirking and looking at me, unapologetic.

"You can say you're sorry any time now," she says, her eyes glinting.

My lips curve upward. "Have I been badly behaved?"

Her eyes scan my face. She uncrosses her arms and shrugs. "Has there ever been a situation in which you've reacted normally? No. So on a scale from one to ten... your bad behavior is at about a five right now."

I blow out a long breath. "I am, for what it's worth. Sorry, that is."

Her lips twitch. "Come apologize to me properly, then."

I surprise her by lunging across the table and stealing a kiss. She kisses me back and I can feel her smiling. Heedless of the food in my way, I crawl across the table, deepening the kiss. I hear something hit the ground, but I don't care.

Cupping her cheek, I slip my hand into her hair as I kiss her. Tugging her gently toward me, I control her movements ever so briefly.

When we pull back, Kaia's lovely green eyes pop open. And then words rush out of her mouth.

"I love you."

I freeze. "What?"

She turns so red that she puts beets to shame. "I didn't... I mean... I didn't mean to say that. It just popped out."

"Oh." I finally release a pent up breath, although I'm keyed up now. "Okay."

"I do love you, though." She wrinkles her nose. "God knows why."

I disentangle myself from her with a frown. "Kaia…" I sigh.

She tucks her hair behind her ears, looking down. "How about we just pretend that I didn't say anything at all?"

I look at her for several seconds, my heart pounding. "Does that mean you take it back?"

She slowly shakes her head. "Nope."

My hands form fists, squeezing tightly. "Do we need to talk about what our relationship is and why we shouldn't use words like love?"

She looks up at me fiercely, her green eyes piercing me through. "No."

"Good." I sit back down in my own seat. Covering the cupcake, I look at her frankly. "Maybe we should go."

I notice that she swallows tightly when she nods in agreement. "Sure, Calum."

I start gathering the remnants of our lunch together, tossing everything in the garbage. I realize maybe a half second too late that I've thrown her cupcake away.

I just… I don't want it.

The sugary fondant ballet dancers. The rich, thick chocolate cake. The sappy note. The whole damn thing is just too much.

Kaia notices that I've thrown it away, but she makes no move to save it. Instead, she just heads for the parking lot, not saying a word.

And I stalk after her, reminding myself that this birthday is just as weird and awful as the rest.

26

KAIA

*W*hile I am sitting alone in the back of a limo, on the way to a mysterious dinner, my phone begins to buzz. A quick check of the screen says it's Ella and it's a video call. I look up at the partition of the limo, checking that it's raised.

I try to make myself seem serene when I answer. "Hello?"

Ella's face pops up; she's all dressed up and seems to be inside a very fancy building. "Where are you?"

I look over at the city passing by my window. "I'm on my way to dinner with Calum. He left a cocktail dress and a note that I should not be late." I purse my lips. "He's a twit. But anyway… where are you?"

"At The Ritz-Carlton! Like you should be. I just walked down the hall to call you. Anybody who is anybody in the dance world is at this gala," she says.

I grimace. "Oh. I think I remember you inviting me to that."

After a second, she sighs. "Does this mean I shouldn't

be saving you a seat, then?"

"I'm afraid not." I shake my head.

Ella gives an aggravated sigh. "Kaia! We just finished a whirlwind week of performances! And yet you weren't at the cast party…"

I'm quick to interrupt. "Yeah, sorry. That was my fault. I went home and crashed for like a full day. We did eight performances, including two on Sunday! That was enough Sleeping Beauty for me."

Ella's gaze narrows on my face. "You have been super weird all week. I don't think it was just being hyper-focused on your part, either. What's up with you?"

I twist my mouth to the side and heave a sigh. "You're going to laugh at me."

Her eyebrows rise. "Yeah?"

I roll my eyes, reliving a little of my shame. "I accidentally told Calum that I loved him."

Her eyes go wide. "You said what now?"

I scrunch up my face. "That was pretty much his reaction, too."

"What did he say?"

I suck my lower lip into my mouth, pausing. "He told me not to say that again. And I just had to sit there, anxious and smothered and unheard. It was bad, Ella."

She blows out a breath. "Oh, Kaia. What are you going to do?"

I shrug. "I don't know. This last week has been tense. We've barely seen each other at home. And now he asks me to come to dinner…" My eyes well up. "Ella, I think Calum is about to break up with me."

"Because of what you said?" She shakes her head. "I

hope he's not that stupid."

My voice sounds watery when I speak. "This is making me have flashbacks to my dad. All my life, I worked so hard to get on his good side—"

"Okay, wait," she interrupts. "Sorry, but are we talking about the same dad? Because your dad doesn't have a good side. He's terrible through and through."

I blot at my eyes. "What if Calum is secretly a narcissist too?"

Ella pulls a face. "Calum is moody and rough and demanding as hell. But... he doesn't seem insane. Talking to your dad for five minutes was enough to let me know that he was crazy. They aren't the same."

I exhale a long stream of breath. "I guess you're right. If only that made me less anxious for the dinner I'm heading to. All I can think is that I'm walking into the last meal we'll share together."

She winces. "I love you, Kaia. I'm not scared to say it. And if your man is dumb enough to leave you, you get in a cab and you come here. Okay?"

I blot my eyes again with my fingertips. "Okay."

"Text me and let me know what the dinner is about," she orders, pointing a finger at her screen.

"Okay," I say, giving her a shaky smile. "I will. We are pulling up now, I think..."

"Good luck. Or break a leg, I guess..." Ella flashes a smile and then disconnects the call.

The limo stops, right on cue. I step out and adjust my white silk dress, low cut in the back and front and perfectly draped across my body. Before me is a very fancy sushi restaurant in the bottom floor of yet another skyscraper.

My heartbeat picks up as I move toward the front door. I look at the floor when I get inside; the designers made an interesting choice in floor covering, choosing thousands in intricate tiles that spill out across the floor. As I tell the hostess my name and I'm escorted to my table, I keep looking at the tiles. Trying to coerce the patterns into making some type of sense.

All the while, I can't hear anything over the beating drum of my heart.

"Kaia?"

I look up, realizing that I stand before a table that is protected from prying eyes by screens. Calum is also standing up, pulling out a chair. His face is impatient and expectant at once.

My eyes dart to the other person, who only now stands up. Dark hair, blue eyes, an impeccable suit. He reaches over to me, stretching out his hand.

"Lucas," he reminds me. "We met briefly."

My cheeks go pink. I shake his hand, feeling a little ambushed. "Oh! Lucas, of course. You're Calum's brother."

He unbuttons his jacket with a flourish and sits. "The one and only."

I move toward Calum, looking at him with wide eyes. He wanted me to meet his brother? God, why didn't he tell me that?

He gives me a funny little smile, greeting me with a kiss on the lips. It feels a bit hollow. But then again, maybe everything is performative, all to give Lucas a certain impression.

I let Calum guide me into a seat and push in my chair.

He sits down beside me, throwing an arm casually around my shoulders.

Lucas scans both of our faces, as if trying to decide what to think of us. Calum clears his throat, opening a drinks menu.

"Will you have the usual?" he asks, not looking up. "A French 75?"

I blush. "Whatever you think."

Lucas gives me a small smile. "Aren't you under the drinking age?"

Calum shoots his brother a glare. "Fuck off, Lucas. You wanted a dinner. Here we are. Now act civilized."

Lucas arches a brow but lets the matter drop. The waitress comes to take our orders and I let Calum choose. Somehow, I am entirely certain that he has great taste in sushi... just like every other expensive thing we've encountered.

As soon as she is gone, Lucas leans forward. "How is your ballet season going, Kaia?"

I'm a little surprised that he should ask. "Fine. We just finished our first production, actually."

His lips twitch. "I was there on opening night. You danced beautifully, I should say."

My head tilts to the side. "I didn't know you had an interest in the ballet."

He sits back with a laugh. "I'm pretty sure that there are tons of things you don't know about me. Calum and I came up together as dancers. But I let it fall to the wayside when Calum got hurt."

My eyebrows jump up. I look to Calum. "You got hurt?"

Calum shrugs. "Yes. I thought my career on the stage would last many, many years. But then I tore my ACL. That's a death sentence to dancing."

My brow furrows. "But I've seen you dance."

Lucas cuts in. "He can fake it for a short while. Isn't that right, Calum?"

Calum nods but doesn't give me any more information. I want to ask him a million questions, but I squirrel them away for now. I focus on Lucas instead.

"So I gather that you two were alone for your teenage years? That must have made you exceptionally close."

Lucas frowns at Calum. "Yes and no. Our parents were out of the picture. We were raised by a family friend. And more often than not, we were competing with one another. You know, trying to be the next Baryshnikov."

Calum's glaring at his brother so intensely that I'm worried that a fight is about to break out. I slide my hand under the table, resting it gently on Calum's leg. He actually jumps, startled.

I keep talking, as if that's normal behavior. "And now you two run IndicaTech together. Pretty damn impressive!"

Lucas gives me a toothy grin. "Wait till you find out what it is supposed to IPO for."

My forehead wrinkles. I look to Calum for help. "Is what he said even in English?"

That brings a tiny smirk to Calum's lips. "It's just how the stock market might rate our business should we decide to sell stocks publicly."

I nod my head. "Oh, I see. So you got a good... er... rating?"

The waitress bring our drinks over. Calum and Lucas

smirk at each other.

"It'll do," Lucas says.

Calum grins and sips his drink. Under the table, I feel his warm hand find mine and hold it.

I don't want to jinx it, but this seems to actually be going pretty well. I keep up the conversation, asking Lucas about his life and details about Calum's background.

Our food arrives. Perfectly plated rolls of sushi and nigiri, plus some edamame and miso soup. Calum and Lucas argue about nearly everything; nitpicking every single thing seems to be a part of their relationship.

"You're using chopsticks the wrong way," Lucas says. "In Japan, they use them like this."

He demonstrates a very elegant technique, arching a brow.

Calum rolls his eyes. "Says the man who douses his entire meal with enough soy sauce to drown out the flavor of the fish. Soy sauce should be used sparingly."

Lucas glares at him. "You are such a prick."

Calum raises his chopsticks, smirking. "You only say that when I've bested you."

As they go back and forth, I can't help but imagine them as little boys. Entertaining each other, keeping each other afloat. It's actually pretty endearing.

"So Lucas... do you have a romantic partner?" I ask.

He shoots me a look. "A girlfriend? No. I'm way too busy."

I nod slowly. "I can see that being true. Since Calum has temporarily stepped down from IndicaTech, I imagine your schedule is pretty packed."

He nods. "Yeah. I'm opening a new office in Japan,

actually. So I have been back and forth to Tokyo a dozen times in the last two months. It's exhausting."

"I thought you mentioned a girl in Japan," Calum says.

Lucas shrugs. "Girls come and go. Making money is more important to me right now."

Calum sits back in his seat, glancing at me. "My brother is a bit of a man whore. He always has been, even when we were dancing. He almost got kicked out of the New York Ballet for it, as a matter of fact."

Lucas's lips twitch. "My brother may have had the superior dance technique, but he was always terrible with women."

Calum shoots him a glare. Before he can fire back an insult, I spread my hands on the table and cut him off.

"Wait, what was the situation that almost got you kicked out of NYB?"

"Pff. We were doing Romeo and Juliet. I was sleeping with the ballerina who danced Juliet... and two other lesser dancers, too. These three girls found out that I was sleeping with all of them. Hysterics ensued. It was really nothing."

Calum corrects him. "Actually, Lucas caused all three of the lead ballerinas to fight over him. It was impressive to me. Not so much to the people stage managing and directing the ballet we were working on, though."

I can't help but grin at that. "Sounds like you were a handful."

"I was, but I was nowhere near a dramatic as Calum. He thought that his talent meant that he walked on water."

I raise my brows, looking to Calum for confirmation. "Is that so?"

He surpasses an eye roll. "You never saw me dance when I was in my prime, beauty. You would've swooned at the sight of me."

I shake my head. "You're so cocky."

Calum slips his hand onto my thigh, smirking. "And yet, I'm not wrong."

That pulls a genuine laugh from me. I grin at him, feeling an insane connection between us. He leans over and gives me a brief yet deep kiss.

It's obvious that he feels the connection too.

After we say goodbye to Lucas, we head outside into the dark. Calum takes my hand and pulls me away from his waiting limousine. "Why don't we walk a little?"

I'm surprised, but I just agree. "Sure."

He sets a very laid back pace, strolling along. I wait for him to announce something. But it seems he has nothing to say.

I clear my throat. "Thanks for introducing me to Lucas."

He shrugs. "It's nothing."

I stop, which forces him to halt. "It's not nothing. Introducing me to your brother felt like a step."

Calum looks distinctly uncomfortable. "You are reading into things too much. Can we just… enjoy the rest of our night? Why ruin everything by talking it to death?"

I give him a small smile. "Come on. I think there is a place around the corner that sells macaroons. I'm buying."

I start to walk away. But Calum tugs my hand, pulling me into his arms for a kiss. And I let him do it, because I crave every single touch he has to offer. And all I have to do is pretend I never said those three little words…

27

CALUM

*S*tepping out of my limo in front of the NYB, I groan. Lucas is waiting at the top of the concrete steps. He shades his eyes, spots me, and bounds down to meet me.

"Two visits in two days?" I say, eyeing him. "You must want something."

He flashes me a tight smile. "I was actually just having a meeting at the restaurant across the street. I just saw Kaia, who told me you'd be here shortly." He pulls a face. "Actually, I think asking her your whereabouts in front of her friends was not the smartest move. I guess I hadn't put much thought into how you guys are trying to keep your relationship a secret."

I pinch the bridge of my nose. "Lucas…"

He shrugs. "Sorry. Kaia covered pretty well if it makes a difference to you."

I make a face at him. "If word gets out, I won't be hurt. I'll just go back to my career. Kaia has a lot more to lose."

Lucas turns his head, looking at the looming building behind him. "Let's go for a walk."

I fall into step with him easily as we head down the block. "So what's up? You could have just video called me."

He smirks. "What, you don't like seeing my handsome face?" He sees my eye roll and shrugs. "I just wanted to talk about yesterday."

"What about it?"

"She's into you. You know that, right?"

I narrow my gaze. "Yeah. Kaia accidentally told me that she loves me the other day. I've been trying to convince her otherwise."

Lucas slows, his hand shooting out to grab my arm. "Why?"

I scrunch up my face. "Why does she feel like she loves me? Good question. I honestly don't think there is much to love."

He shoves my shoulder. "You are an idiot. You know that?"

I arch my eyebrows. "Me?"

He shoves my shoulder again, his expression aggravated. "Yes, you. It's clear to me that you guys are on the path to being together-"

"Uh uh," I interrupt. "No. We're not on the path to anything. I'm perfectly happy with having her sleeping next door. There is no need to blow this out of proportion."

He shakes his head at me, starting to walk again. "I saw you two together yesterday. You two were all over each other. If that's not love-"

"It's not," I insist.

He gives me a sharp look. "What is it, then? Because whatever it is, it's a lot more than friendship. And it goes both ways, no matter what you have to say for yourself."

I stop in my tracks. "Did you just stop by to give me a hard time?"

Lucas looks at me. "You are so bull headed. No, I came here to tell you that I like Kaia. I like her for you, man."

I glance at my watch, sighing. "Well, I like her too. Not as much as you do, maybe..."

"You're a fool," he interjects. "And a total fucking moron. Girls like when you tell them your feelings. Tell that girl you care about her before she gets some sense and leaves you."

I raise my hands, backing away. "I said it before and I'll say it again. I am broken. The part of me that is supposed to feel those things? It's missing."

Lucas rolls his eyes. "I'm telling you, Calum. Don't keep going down this path. I know Kaia took you back once. If she leaves you because of this, there is no winning her over again. And I don't want to see you moping around like last time."

I shake my head at him, turning away and raising a hand to say goodbye. "I'm done with this conversation. Later, Lucas."

On the few blocks walk back though, I start to think about what Lucas was saying. Is he right? Do I stand to lose Kaia over something stupid like not saying I love you?

I pull back. Wait a second. I am looking at the situation like suddenly there is a permanent structure housing my relationship with Kaia. My brother's influence, surely.

I need to go back to thinking of my relationship with Kaia as having a definite ending point. Maybe the summer's end?

I look up at the sky and feel the breeze as I walk. It's already nearly autumn. Just a couple of weeks from now the leaves will begin to change and there will be a chill in the air.

Two weeks is not enough time. Maybe I should set the end of the year as the end of our relationship. That should give me enough time to enjoy Kaia… right?

There is a sinking feeling in the pit of my stomach just thinking about breaking things off. God, have I gone soft?

My mood sours further as I stalk up the steps outside of the NYB. By the time I make it inside, my temper is curdling inside, festering.

And that's the moment that I spot Emma standing at the top of the marble staircase. She smiles demurely at me as I thunder up, a glare already on my face.

"What?" I snap.

She doesn't move out of the way, forcing me to stop a step down from the landing. She tilts her head at me. "I heard that IndicaTech is expanding globally. Starting with an office in Tokyo."

I force my way up to the landing with a soft growl. "What does that have to do with anything?" Looking around, I realize that I have no idea where the ballet dancers are.

"Where is Bas?" I ask coolly.

Emma puts a hand on my forearm. "If I were you, I would focus on the conversation between us. Otherwise, I'll have to use this."

She produces a simple black thumb drive, holding it up for me to see.

I squint at her. "Am I supposed to magically know what that is?"

Her lips curl upward but there is a malevolent tint to her eyes. "It's evidence."

Pulling out my phone, I start to fire off a text to Bas asking where he is. "You have ten seconds to say something important instead of fucking around and playing games."

Her cheeks color. "I have video of you kissing and intimately embracing one of our youngest ballerinas. So assuming that you don't want the whole world to know your secret—"

I look up at her with a frown. "Is this blackmail? I thought we had already talked about this, Emma."

Her lips thin. "I have the email already set up to send to every single newspaper in the world. Oh, and it's copied to the personal emails of every member of every board of every dance company in the world. I understand that it won't do that much damage to you... but it'll crush Kaia."

It takes all my strength not to bellow with rage. Again, I'm being blackmailed. And again, the antagonist is gunning for Kaia instead of attacking me directly.

Is Kaia such an obvious weakness?

Instead of voicing all the things I'm feeling, namely rage I don't move a muscle for a count of ten beats. It's long enough to bring myself to heel and keep me from doing some kind of physical violence.

"Do you just want me to release this, then?" Emma asks.

"You haven't even told me what it is that you want." I fold my arms across my chest, willing my heartbeat to slow. It is a feat to relax my hands so that they aren't balled up fists.

She smiles at me. "I'm so glad you asked. I want to provide you with an opportunity. You're going to a lot of trouble, trying to forge all new connections in Japan. I want to help with that."

I gesture angrily. "Emma, I swear to god. You have a genuine gift for using a lot of words but saying exactly nothing. What did any of what you just said mean?"

Her smile deflates slightly. "I own the majority share of a tech business in Japan. I want you to run your new business through my existing firm."

I cough out a laugh. "I'm sorry, what now? Do you even know anything about what my company does? There are a million different niche specialties under the umbrella of tech."

She falters for a second. "We can do anything you need us to do."

"I don't need you to do anything. I don't even want to be having this conversation!"

Emma clenches the thumb drive in her palm. "If you won't have even the most basic discussion, I'll send out the email today. Your little ballerina girlfriend's dreams will all be burned to cinders."

Rubbing the back of my neck, I look at her and shake my head. "You are really terrible at this. Maybe blackmailing isn't your thing."

She arches a brow. "If that's true, then I should sell the information. I bet there are a ton of people that you have ticked off who would love to have it. Rival CEOs, for starters..."

I stretch my neck. The second she said that, four names flashed in my head. So called rival CEOs, people that would love to have dirt on me. I purse my lips.

"What about a fair trade?" I offer. "You give me the flash drive and delete all the copies. I give you money. Seriously, I would rather not stand here for another second."

Emma lifts her chin, her expression hardening. "No. I have thought this through."

"Seriously?" I ask. "Come on. What's your number? Five million?"

She crosses her arms. "This would net me around one hundred and eighty five million in the next five years. So now, I don't accept your pitiful offering."

"You have no idea if our companies are even compatible!" I bellow. "For fuck's sake! Just because they are both international and in tech does not mean fuck all!"

She leans close to me, reaching out her hand and prodding two fingers into my chest. "Figure out a way to make it work. You hear me? You figure it out or I email the file out to every place I can think of. Your little plaything will never dance again!"

With that pronouncement, Emma spins on her designer heels and begins marching to her office.

I start walking toward the dance studios, my thoughts a mess. All I can picture is Kaia's pretty face when she hears the news. No one cries quite like Kaia.

But how do I keep that from happening? That's the question...

KAIA

*C*alum looks over at me as we cross the street in Soho.

"You talked me into coming to this," he says, narrowing his eyes on my face. "If you are having second thoughts about being here—"

I shake my head, smiling tightly. "No. We're here now. I'm just trying to be calm about seeing my family."

He gives me a long look and then shrugs. With his dark hair pushed back, his cheekbones carved from granite, and his elegant black suit, he could easily be mistaken for a model. There are several men who look just like him crossing the street with us, all heading into the large brick building lying directly in front of us.

A huge banner with *Soho Fashion Festival* written on it is draped over the entrance. I look at it, blinking rapidly.

I'm so out of my element here it's not even funny. Everyone is taller than me. There are a hundred waif-like models who are thinner than I could ever be.

I am dressed to kill in a black maxi dress with a very

low neckline and a slit in the hem. Add a pair of towering strappy sandals and I am pretty much bulletproof. But no matter how polished I look, I can't keep the anxiety off of my face.

"We can turn around right now," Calum reminds me.

I give my head a tiny shake. "No. I'm here to show my family that I'm doing fine. Since I already told them I'm coming, it would look bad to bail at the last possible second."

Calum reaches out to me, grabbing my hand. "Who are you trying to impress? Because you shouldn't feel beholden to your father."

My expression hardens. "I'm not beholden. I just... I need him to see me be successful without him."

Calum arches a brow but I pull him toward the beckoning doors. There are two women with clipboards at the doors, checking names.

"Your name?" one of the stylish young women asks Calum and I.

I open my mouth to respond. But Calum stops them asking questions when he whips out a stack of hundred dollar bills. He drops them on the young woman's clipboard and breezes past her without a word.

He grips my hand and pulls me up the stairs, into a large airy space. A runway is situated at one end of the room. Hundreds of people mill around the surrounding seats. Everyone in this room looks terribly chic, bright red lipstick and dark sunglasses everywhere I look. Black dresses, charcoal gray suits. It looks like a very expensive funeral in here.

"Kaia!"

I turn to find my mother weaving her way through the crowd. She looks out of place with her white pantsuit and her sunny smile.

"Hi, Mom," I say, letting go of Calum's hand. I give my mom a tight hug.

My mom's eyes are already on Calum. She inspects him curiously. "Kaia, who did you bring?"

A wrinkle of worry appears between Calum's eyebrows. "Calum Fordham. You must be Mrs. Walker."

He extends his hand. My mother shakes it, blushing a little. Ah, so Calum's intensely good looks affect someone other than me.

"Call me Serena," my mother insists. "Are you here as Kaia's date?"

He steps back, putting his arm around my waist. "I'm just here to support Kaia."

For a long second, my mom's expression freezes in confusion. But then she manages to compose herself. "Right. Well, Mr. Walker and Hazel are just this way."

She turns and starts winding her way through the crowd. I glance up at Calum, wishing I could cling to his side forever.

His ice blue eyes bore into my face.

"It'll be okay," he says simply.

I give him a tight nod of my head. He grips my hand and turns to follow my mother. Calum weaves his way through the crowd. It's not long before I hear my father's booming voice.

"And that's when I told Mr. Gingrich that if he didn't like what I was telling him, he could take his business elsewhere!"

A step further and I see my father standing in a circle of hip-looking people. My dad is doing what he loves best, commanding his audience. And these people do titter at the punchline he's just delivered, as expected.

One woman speaks up. "Mr. Walker, it's a bit of a surprise to that Hazel should come from such a charming father! I always just assumed that she came from somewhere... well, humorless."

The crowd titters. My dad looks around the circle with a smirk. "Hazel only takes her talent from me. The rest is surely from her mother."

The whole group laughs again. I can tell by the brief look of confusion on my father's face that he wasn't kidding, though.

"Robert!" my mother calls, cutting into the circle. "Look who I just found."

My dad turns to look at us. When he sees me, his expression hardens. Then he looks at Calum and his entire expression darkens.

"I'll be right back," he says to his little circle. Half of the people are already distracted by their phones and talking to each other but I don't think my father notices.

No, his gaze is firmly set on me and Calum. He runs a hand down the front of his white button up as he stalks toward us. I reach out a hand to Calum and he smiles at me tightly before taking it.

Calum's smile tells me that he thinks that coming here was a mistake. He still grips my fingers tightly though. I swallow against the lump that forms in my throat, glad that he's on my side.

My dad stops a few feet away, his eyes narrowing on me. "We should go talk in the hall."

He spins on his heel and threads through the crowd, just assuming that we will follow him. My mother gives me a half shrug and goes after my father. Calum follows her, pulling me along.

We exit the main hall through a set of side doors, stepping into a quiet hallway. My dad is waiting impatiently, his gaze focused on me.

"Your friend should leave us," he says. He ignores Calum entirely. "We have family business to discuss."

Calum pulls me close and slides an arm around me. "I'll leave when Kaia asks me to."

I glance at him gratefully. "I think Calum can hear whatever you have to say, dad."

My mother settles against the wall, nearly unnoticed. "Robert, I think Kaia and her friend have come here to make amends."

My eyebrows jump up. "Make amends? For what? Dad asked for more money. I said no. He choked me so violently that if Calum hadn't intervened, I think he would have killed me. What do I have to make amends for in that situation?"

My dad scowls at me. "You provoked me. You purposely goaded me—"

"Hey!" Calum says, raising his voice. "No. It's not her fault. Kaia is the kid here. You're supposed to be a fucking adult. You laid your hands on her. You were in the wrong. End of discussion."

My heart thuds in my chest. I lean into Calum's body more, unabashedly needing his strength.

"This is why I said that this is a family affair," my dad spits back.

"Really?" Calum asks. "Because it just seems like you want the bully pulpit all to yourself."

I squeeze Calum's hand and clear my throat. "I'm willing to let the past go if you are, dad."

Calum shoots me a hard look but says nothing. My dad smirks.

"You still haven't repaid me in full."

Mom pipes up. "Robert, we talked about this—"

"Shut the hell up, Serena." He fixes me and Calum with a glare. "If you two think for a second that I don't know what's going on, you're crazy. There is a lot of cash exchanging hands between you two. Isn't that right? And I just want my cut."

A surprised laugh leaves Calum's chest. "What in the world are you talking about? What money? And in what reality does the father get a portion of his daughter's earnings, anyway?"

My father jabs a finger at both of us. "I'm going to get paid. I'm going to keep getting paid for as long as Kaia is spreading her legs for you—"

"I think we should leave," I cut in. "This was a bad idea."

Calum drops my hand, digging inside his jacket. "How much? How much will it cost for you to fuck off and never bother Kaia again?"

I frown at Calum. "Hey. Will you stop? Put your checkbook away."

"Ten million," my dad says stonily, crossing his arms. "Ten million dollars and you will never hear from my family again."

My jaw drops. "Dad!"

My mom steps in between the two men, frowning at my dad. "Robert, that's out of line."

My father goes off like a nuclear bomb. "No it isn't! What I say goes!" He takes a step toward Calum, ignoring my mother's hand on his chest.

I don't make any move to hold Calum back. He glowers at my father.

"You're not in charge of anything anymore," Calum grits out. "Now that Kaia is out of your house, you will never have that kind of power over her again. You hear me? You are through!"

My father jostles my mother aside, teeth bared. "You're not going to take my place. No one ever will. You won't take Kaia from me."

Calum's hands ball into fists. "I don't have to. You already drove her away, you fucking monster."

"That isn't true!" my father howls. "Kaia, tell him. Tell him that you will always pick your family over some prick you barely know."

My eyes widen. I'm already shaking my head by the time he finishes the sentence. "No. That's crazy. If I have to make the choice—"

"You don't," Calum growls.

"There has to be some middle ground here that we can find…" my mom tries.

"Mom, seriously! If you can't stand with me right now, you're against me!" I lash out.

My mom's eyes widen. "Oh, Chickadee…"

My eyes fill with tears. I grab Calum's hand and give

him a hard look. "We should go. I don't know why I even bothered coming here in the first place."

"You can't leave!" my father rages. "We haven't finished talking money."

"Yes, we have," Calum says. "Come on, Kaia. Tell your mom goodbye."

My mom and I glance at each other helplessly. I swallow, wiping away the first tear that rolls down my face.

"Bye, mom," I whisper.

"You're all worthless," my father seethes. "Kaia, I never want to lay eyes on you again. As far as I am concerned, I only have one child now."

My heart wrenches in my chest. Calum starts to pull me away, heading down the hall. I look at my mom, who is openly crying. Her eyes are glued to my face, her mouth balled up.

Calum puts his arm around me and hurries me down the hall. We go around a corner. My mom disappears from sight.

"It'll be okay, beauty," Calum says. His expression is fierce, his eyes fixed on the exit door ahead. I let him rush me down the emergency stairs and out onto the busy Soho street.

And that's when I burst into tears as Calum flags down his limo.

29

KAIA

"*I* didn't come all the way down to lower Manhattan for brunch just to hear you crow over how you're dancing a solo in the next ballet." Eric points his fork across the table at Ella.

"Um, I'm dancing a *featured* solo, thank you. It's basically one step away from being the company's best dancer." Ella looks down at her plate of poached eggs and mixed greens with a smirk. "Kaia is my main competition these days. Right Kaia?"

I'm staring down the long table that's filled with dancers from our company, completely spacing out. When Ella nudges me a second time, I blink rapidly.

"Huh?"

Ella pulls a face at me. "I was just telling Eric that I feel like you're my main competition for the best dancer in the company. Keep up."

I flash a timid smile at Eric, Ella, and Crispin, who are all sitting closest. "Sorry. I am just massively tired right now. I took yesterday off and just slept... but I'm still exhausted."

Crispin leans in. "You're not pregnant, are you?"

Ella huffs. "Crispin, that is so rude. I hate when people suggest pregnancy as the cause for like every fucking ailment I have. It's like, dude. Sometimes I'm just tired."

Crispin shoots her a hard look. "Sorry for asking about her well being."

I screw my face up, pushing my omelette around my plate. "I'm just emotionally drained, I think."

Ella gives me a sympathy look. "Is your boyfriend being a jerk again?"

That pulls a chuckle from my lips. "Hah! No. Quite the opposite. He has actually been really sweet for the last few days."

"Wait, wait. Hold on," Eric interjects. "What boyfriend?"

Crispin chimes in. "Who do you even have the time to see other than us?"

I roll my eyes. "Guys, chill. I've been seeing the same person for months. It's very..." I pause, trying to find a word to sum up my relationship with Calum. "We both prefer to keep things low key, I guess."

Ella huffs a laugh. "That is one way to put it."

"So you've met this mystery man?" Crispin asks.

She smiles slyly at me. "I have. He's older than us. More worldly. And if you would believe it, Kaia hooked herself a rich man."

Eric wrinkles his face. "I thought... I mean, Kaia, you were so dedicated to ballet..."

"I can be dedicated and still have a boyfriend. People do it all the time," I say.

Crispin pushes his plate away. "Sure, people do lots of things. But if you're in a serious relationship, you kind of have to choose. Ballet or some dusty old dude."

Ella gives him a pointed look. "Both of you can just shut up. You both wish you were dating someone as hot as Kaia. Or someone at all, come to think of it."

I pinch the bridge of my nose. "You guys are actually zapping my energy as we speak. So way to go on that."

Ella shakes her head. "You can thank your family for that. Going through a break up with your own family has got to be so hard."

I clear my throat, widening my eyes at her. "Can you not tell everyone my business?"

She blushes and pulls a face. "Sorry."

Eric looks at his watch with a frown. "If we want to make it to the movie theater for the one o'clock showing of Rent, we'd better get moving."

I ball up my napkin, putting it next to my plate. "I think I'm actually going to bail. I feel like I'm fighting off a cold or something."

Eric frowns. "Do you need a walk home?"

My cheeks turn pink. He doesn't even know where I live now... or that I share the penthouse floor with Calum. I shake my head. "Nah. Thanks though. You guys enjoy the movie."

Ella grabs my hand and gives it a squeeze. "See you in the studio tomorrow. Okay?"

I give her a hug, then grab a twenty from my wallet and leave it on the table. As I step outside of the restaurant,

I straighten my dress and pull my sunglasses on. Today is the last day that I'll be able to wear a sundress without a jacket, I'm pretty sure.

I walk down the busy New York City sidewalk, thinking to myself about how the summer has flown by. The next thing I know, it will be fall. Will that signal a change for the ballet?

More to the point, what about Calum? I can only imagine that he'll soon lose interest in stage directing. And when he's not hanging around all day... what does that mean for me?

Our relationship is a fragile enough thing without putting another single thing on top of the already colossal towering pile. My brows pull down as I try to work it out in my head.

"Kaia!"

I slow, turning my head. Crispin is running to catch up to me, his blond hair getting in his eyes. My mouth pulls to the side. I don't have the energy for Crispin right now. But I stop anyway, cursing the social niceties that dictate I wait for him. He jogs up to me, smiling broadly.

"I thought I could walk with you while you head back to Manhattan. Are you going to take the train?"

"Uhh... I actually hadn't gotten that far. I was still just sort of walking and thinking. It's good for me to be alone and just work out my thoughts—"

He totally isn't listening to me, because he perks up at my statement. "Great! I don't mind walking a few miles! Isn't it so beautiful outside?"

Wrinkling my nose and sighing, I start walking again. "Yep."

"So…" Crispin says. "This guy that you've been dating. How long have you been seeing each other?"

My mouth pulls down into a frown. I glance over at him, noticing how he pulls at the pockets of his casual slacks. He does it every minute or so, like a nervous tic.

"Um… a few months," I say. "I really don't want to talk about him, if that's okay with you."

Crispin stares straight ahead. "Sure. I mean, I guess I just wish that you'd told me that you were with somebody when we kissed."

Stopping dead in my tracks, I cock my head. "You mean when you kissed me and I asked you not to?"

He frowns. He's. stopped walking but he's still just looking straight ahead, not at me. "If that's what you think happened, sure."

An uneasy sensation slides through my gut. "Crispin, I shouldn't have to have said that I had a boyfriend. Having a boyfriend was not the issue. The problem with that kiss was that it was unwanted."

His mouth balls up. He keeps staring at something in the distance. "Let me buy you a drink. You know, to say that I'm sorry."

"I don't think so. As a matter of fact, don't feel like walking home anymore. I'll just grab a Lyft."

Crispin finally looks at me, his expression dead-eyed. "I know that you're fucking Calum."

My eyebrows fly up. "What?"

He scowls, jabbing a finger toward a bar at the end of the block. "I need a drink. Come have one with me."

I take a step back, raising my hands. "No. I don't think so."

He lunges forward, catching my elbow. His expression is a grimace. "It's the least you can do after you've led me on so many times."

I try to shake him off. My eyes rove around, looking for help. On such a busy street, no one even notices him gripping my arm painfully.

"Get away from me," I warn, raising my voice. "Let me go. I'm not going anywhere with you. I swear, if you don't let go, I'll scream."

His upper lip twists. "She said you were going to be easy."

Shaking my head, I try to wrench myself out of his grasp. "I don't know what you are talking about."

"Honor. She said that if I just got you alone, you would fall right into my arms." He gives me a violent shake. "That's what I get for trusting a female to give me directions. All of you are just vultures. Looking for the man with the most money and the biggest dick to spread your legs and pose for."

I inhale a huge breath and scream. "FIRE! FIRE! I DON'T KNOW THIS MAN! FIRE! HELP!"

As soon as I start, Crispin loosen his grip on my arm. I slip out of his grasp and stumble backward.

"You are supposed to come home with me!" he growls. "She said that this would be the easiest thing I'd ever done!"

Turning away, I sprint toward the nearest intersection. There is a woman just stepping out of a yellow taxi and I dive in the backseat, slamming the door.

"Drive!" I beg the cab driver. "Anywhere! I'll pay you triple your normal rate…"

The driver doesn't ask questions. He pulls off with a squeal of tires. I glance back to find Crispin glowering at me from the curb, his expression menacing.

My hands shake as I pull out my phone and dial Calum. I start tearing up when he answers.

"Hello?"

"Calum?" I ask. "I need you. I… I'm in a cab and… I need you right now!"

I burst into incoherent tears. Calum asks me to pass my phone to the driver. Ten minutes later, I pull out outside Calum's address.

He's waiting for me on the curb with a sheaf of money for the driver.

I get out and bury myself in his arms, feeling very foolish. Calum lets me cry, pushing my hair back out of my face and walking me inside our building.

When he is finally able to coax the details out of me though, he goes practically incandescent with rage.

"That puny little dancer from the NYB did what?!" he yells.

"It gets worse," I sniffle. "I think Honor has been coaching him. He kept saying that. Honor said I would be easy. Honor said I would just fall into his arms."

Calum's look turns black. He walks me into my apartment, pulling out his phone. "I need to make some calls. First, I need to terminate Crispin. Second, Honor promised me that she was done with New York. Since she's apparently stuck around, I think the Russian mob would love to know where to find her. They'll probably sweep up your boy Crispin too."

My mouth twists to the side. "That sounds like you are

saying that they'll kill him. I... I don't want anybody to be harmed."

Calum sucks his teeth and shrugs. "I'll pass that on to the Russians."

He deposits me on my bed and starts to leave, but I don't want him to go.

"Calum? Will you stay with me? I don't want to be alone right now."

His gaze lands on my face, expression tightening. Then he softens and sighs. "Okay. How about I hang out with you for twenty minutes first?"

I nod, exhaling a shaky breath. "That would be good."

He sits down on the bed beside me and slips his arm around me. With his free hand, he sends a number of texts. But after a minute, Calum puts his phone away and just embraces me.

I feel warm and safe in his arms. Letting my eyes close, I exhale what feels like the first full breath I've taken since I was at brunch.

And to my surprise, Calum seems to lean into his new role as caretaker. His fingers rake slowly through my hair. His big size compared to my small one seems to be perfect, at this moment in time.

"It's okay, beauty," he murmurs. "No one will ever hurt you. I promise you that."

I lean my head against his shoulder. I'm unable to believe what has happened today, but still comforted by Calum's touch.

30

CALUM

*A*s we near the ballet, I look over to Kaia. She's looking out the window with a faraway stare. It gives me a moment to take her in unobserved.

Pale blonde hair, tousled and braided so that it is out of her heart shaped face. A scattering of freckles across her cheeks and nose. Wide green eyes, a full mouth with lips that smile too easily. She's wearing an oversized hoodie, one of mine I think.

God, how quickly this girl has gotten under my skin. How deeply she's made me care for her. And how badly I feel the need to protect her.

When the limo stops, she opens her door and glances back. Waiting for me, since I told her I would take her to work today.

I motion for her to come back and then kiss her lips briefly. "Go ahead. I have some business outside the NYB." I pause. "I think it would be wise to give you a security detail."

Kaia's eyebrows arch. "For me? No… thanks, but I'll just be extra safe."

As she's backing out of the limo, I shoot her a cool smile. "It wasn't really a request. The guards are already here. It's just to make you feel safe while I track down that little weasel and his puppet master."

Kaia huffs. "It's been a couple of days, Calum. They have gone to ground or cleared out of the city. Either way, a security detail is going to be super obvious. Where would I even get a security detail of my own accord?"

"It'll be fine. You'll see." I flap a hand.

She just makes a strangled sound. "Goodbye, Calum."

The car door slams. I watch her stomp up the cement steps. It takes about half a minute before I see a lady jogger sprint up the same steps, hot on Kaia's trail.

My mouth curves up. I recognize that lady from her photo. She works for me now. She was passed in front of my face by my private investigator and I selected her for being closest to Kaia's age.

Another half a minute and I see the other half of Kaia's detail, a big burly guy with a newspaper. He sits on the cement steps, surreptitiously watching all the passersby.

"Head to Lucas's place on the upper east side," I call to my driver.

He pulls out, giving me a few minutes to think while we navigate traffic. I spend the entire time brooding about Kaia's brush with danger… and how I'm going to crush the two perpetrators. Once I find them, that is.

I get out of the limousine at my brother's penthouse, heading up to his floor. When I get to his door, it's opened by an older man in tails.

"Good morning, sir," he greets me. "Come in. Mister Fordham is in the kitchen."

"Thanks," I say, trying not to roll my eyes. I walk through my brother's place, sighing at how every single piece of furniture is antique, every wall hanging and rug with its own story. Lucas likes old, heavy wood and has a penchant for finding very expensive pieces.

I shed my jacket as I walk into the airy kitchen, putting it on a coat rack in the corner. The butler comes right behind me and sweeps my jacket away.

When I look at Lucas with a puzzled expression, he just smirks. "That coat rack is from the fifteen hundreds. Winston doesn't like anything to hang on it."

I suppress an eye roll. "Why did I agree to meet you here again? I hate your house. I feel like I'm in a museum, constantly being scolded for touching things."

He gives a half a shrug. "Come on. Come into the breakfast nook. There is coffee waiting for us."

I follow him to a large terrace. Tucked away on one side is a booth, the red and white striped laminated seats and white formica table shielded from the elements by a wall of thin glass.

"Do you like?" Lucas says as we slide in. "It's one of the booths from Seinfeld."

I look down at the cup of coffee in front of me. "You have too much money."

"Or just no one to spend it on. No terribly attractive girlfriend that attracts stalkers. So there is no reason to spend a hundred thousand dollars on security and on upgrades to my apartment for her…"

Eyeing him, I shake my head. "I would spend more on

it if I could. Kaia was already pretty unhappy about the two guards that I had to tell her about…"

"And how many did you book?"

I look up into the sky above. "Ten. Then I scaled it back to four, just because she would definitely catch on if I had all the guys I wanted."

Lucas slides me a cool look. "Still convinced that you're totally not in love with this girl?"

I glare at him. "I can leave if you're going to start questioning my motives again."

He waves a hand. "Chill. I want to hear about what happened to Kaia."

Acid swirls around in the pit of my stomach. "Do you have cream? I shouldn't drink any more straight black coffee today."

He leans over and presses a hidden button. "Winston? My brother would like some cream, please."

A minute later, I'm stirring my coffee, trying to decide how to start.

"Honor is back."

He arches a brow. "How do you know?"

"Because the little shit that almost hurt my girlfriend kept saying her name. Apparently this kid caught up with Kaia on the street and tried to force her into a bar with him. She kept saying no and even screamed. That's when he started saying that Honor had told him how easy it would be to… I don't know, abduct Kaia or…" I pause, grinding my teeth. "Or worse, I guess."

"And Honor and this kid are where, exactly?"

Slamming my hand on the table, I grimace. "I'll be

damned if I know. I've got everybody out looking for them. So far, I've got nothing."

I stare down at my hands, feeling useless.

Lucas sips his coffee. "I'm sure they'll turn up at some point."

I look up at him, pinning him with my gaze. "She didn't tell me. Kaia, I mean. She didn't tell me that this kid, this fucking Crispin, already tried to kiss her. He used force on her. And she didn't tell me." I suck in a breath, feeling nothing but a white hot rage. "How the fuck am I supposed to protect her if she doesn't even tell me stuff like that? Huh?"

Lucas squints at me. He reaches over and pulls my coffee out of my clutches. "No more caffeine for you today. And to your question... I don't know. Maybe Kaia didn't think it was that big of a deal."

I scrub a hand over my mouth. "I don't know, man. I'm falling apart over this. I have to find those two fucking idiots. Honor... I mean, it's my fault that she's still walking around. If I'd just given her to the Russians—"

"Stop," my brother says, waving his hands at me. "That's not helpful." He looks at me, pursing his lips.

After a few seconds of his inspection, I glance at him. "What?"

"I don't want to say anything if it means you're just going to yell at me again."

"And yet you're staring at me like a creep. So just spit it out already."

Lucas smirks. "You're protective of Kaia."

"I've been telling you that since I got here."

"You like to watch her dance, presumably. You think you are infatuated with her."

I glare at him. "Don't say it. If you say I'm in love one more time-"

"Even if you may not think you love her, I've never seen you act like this over a woman. It's really interesting to watch."

I shake my head. "I'm so glad I can provide some entertainment for you, Lucas."

His lips curve up. "That Mercedes-Maybach I showed you? The one that even I am on the wait list for?"

Squinting, I nod. "Yeah, I remember. You showed me. I'll admit, it is a nice looking car. Very futuristic."

"That's a cool half million. And I'll wager it, right here, right now."

I pull a face. "On what?"

"I'll bet you are engaged by New Years' Eve. Because I'm telling you right now, you feel something for her. And you would be an idiot if you were to let Kaia dance her way into someone else's arms."

"You're just stuck on this."

He gives me a cool smile. "I'm trying to help you, you incredible moron."

"I don't need help."

Lucas glares at me. "Yes, you do. I don't know what fucked you up so much, but you have a real problem with your emotions. Namely the idea that you could be in love. What's so bad about it?"

I flex my fists. "Not that it's really any of your fucking business, Lucas. But I am broken. Okay? I've been broken for years. And because of that, it's only a matter of time before things between Kaia and me end."

He pushes out his cheek with his tongue. "Why do you think that?"

I lose my temper. "Because, Lucas! Because every woman who I have loved in my life, be it Mom or Anita or Honor, has used my love against me. No one has ever loved me for me! Kaia is the same as the rest of them. Hell, even now, I'm paying her! Just give her the time to prove that she's no better than Mom and Anita and Honor."

Lucas puts his hands up. "Slow down. Have you talked to Kaia about this?"

"No," I spit. "She told me that she loved me weeks ago. But I won't fall for it. I can't."

"Wait, she already told you that she loves you?" His eyes widen. "And you stonewalled her? You fucking goon. For someone so smart, you are really fucking stupid."

I give him my iciest glare. "I am not."

"You are! Kaia's not Mom or Anita. And she sure as hell isn't a creepy narcissist like Honor. You need to get that through your head. I honestly cannot believe that Kaia has stuck around. I would have left you high and dry by now."

"I pay her, you clown."

"Yeah, so you said. But if she's already been paid... and she's financially solvent..." He flicks his fingers. "My point is that she doesn't have to stay. She can walk away whenever she has had enough. And either you love her, or she'll leave you when she figures out that you lack the emotional depth that she does."

I fold my arms across my chest. "I don't want to have this conversation again."

"I don't care. Kaia has chosen to stay. Because apparently she loves you. I think you had better figure out pretty damn quick that you love her too. Or else one day you'll wake up and find her gone."

I roll my eyes. "Are you done?"

"I don't know. Are you really listening to me?"

Favoring him with a glare, I get up. "I always enjoy our little chats."

Lucas shakes his head at me. "Sit back down. We need to talk about the plans for Japan. I promise, sibling gossip hour is over."

Enticed by the lure of Japan, I sit down and listen. But if I'm honest, I don't hear a word Lucas has to say after that. Because I'm too in my own head, too busy turning over what Lucas said to me.

She doesn't have to stay. She can walk away whenever she has had enough.

The question is, when will that be? My heart hurts in the strangest way when I consider that the end could be sooner than I planned for...

KAIA

*T*he limo drops us off at the address I requested. Or at least as close to it as we can get. I shade my eyes against the sun as I peer down the alley sandwiched between two tall buildings.

I look at Calum, who is glaring at me.

"What?" I say, looking down at my body. "Seriously, Calum. Are my panties tucked into my dress?" I run my hand over my butt, frowning.

"I told you, it's nothing to do with you."

"I keep catching you glaring at me when you think I'm not paying attention. And then when I call you out for it, you scowl at me!"

He gives me that same brooding, moody look. "Can we just get this over with? Whatever this big surprise is…"

I give him side eye. "You've been grumpy all day. No, scratch that. You've been off kilter for three days. Whatever this funk you're going through is, you need to snap out of it already."

He bristles. "I'm not in a funk."

I pull a face. "Okay. Who would be a better judge of that? You, who always insist you're okay no matter what? Or me, the one who has to put up with this black mood?"

He looks dour. "Maybe you should just get a clue and leave me alone."

"Mm... no. I don't think so. I tried that on the first day. I had dinner with my friends and then I came back to find you drunk as a skunk. So today, you're sticking with me. Besides, I think you will like this place."

I head toward the unassuming back door entrance to the marketplace. He follows, grumbling to himself.

"I think it's the door on the left," I said, pointing it out.

He slides me a look. "You don't know for sure?"

Grabbing his hand and rolling my eyes, I drag him the last few steps to the pair of double doors. To the left of the doorway is a simple if dusty plaque. *Carney & Sons Background, Set, and Costume Design. By Appointment Only.*

And above it is a small, well-worn white button. I press the button and then look at Calum. He's glowering at me. My response is to act more cheerful because it seems to get on his nerves so damn much.

After a half a minute, a loud buzzer sounds and the doors unlock. The door opens and an honest to god Keebler elf pokes his head out. White blond hair, a green sweater and knit cap all coupled with his slenderness and diminutive size. His dark gaze slides from me to Calum, narrowing.

"Kaia?"

I smile at him. "That's me. This is Calum." I reach back, putting my hand on Calum's broad chest.

The elfin man sighs and steps back to allow us to enter. "I'm Fred. Come in, please."

I step into a wide room filled with old, dinged up looking shelves. The lighting in here isn't very good, but I can see that the shelves are stuffed from the ceiling to the floor with different fabrics. One wall is entirely devoted to used tulle and elastic tutus, meticulously divided by color.

I glance back at Calum, who has stepped inside the room. His eyes travel around the room as he takes the tutus in.

"What is this place?" he asks.

Fred glances at him sharply. "We specialize in set and costume design. We've done customer and sets for practically every single ballet you can name. And a lot of famous movies and musicals, too."

I grab Calum's elbow, arching my eyebrows. "They keep a lot of old costumes and props. I thought we might spend the morning seeing what Hollywood starlets wore in the roles that made them famous. Plus there are a ton of old ballet sets here."

He lips tip up. "This is the weirdest date anybody has ever taken me on."

"I'm taking that as a compliment." Giving him my most dazzling smile, I squeeze his hand and turn my attention to Fred. "Do we just… wander?"

Fred nods. "We don't get that many visitors in here. Anything that is really special - such as a pair of Dorothy's red shoes from The Wizard of Oz - will be encased in plexiglass. Other than that, have at it. We only ask that you be respectful and cautious. Some of these things are quite old."

"Is there any organization we should know about?"

Fred shrugs. "The collection started off very tidy. Then thirty years passed and things were wedged in wherever they would fit. You'll see."

"Sounds hectic," Calum interjects.

"Honey, you have no idea," Fred says. "I'll be upstairs if you need anything."

"Thanks!" I call after him. I let my eyes rove around the room, wandering into the aisle that leads to the next collection.

Calum walks over and touches a stack of dark purple tutus. "These look old."

I tilt my head, staring at a stack of extremely worn black pointe shoes. "I mean, this place does dozens of ballets a year. I wonder when they just stopped stockpiling this stuff?"

"That's a very good question." He shakes his head and then walks into the next room. "Jesus."

I follow him and find racks and racks of costumes, screwed into the walls and five rows high. The rack closest to me is labeled Romeo and Juliet, with a bewildering variety Shakespearean robes. "Jesus," I say, sorting through the rack. "I can't even tell if these are new costumes or really old ones. I don't think this is for a ballet, though... there aren't enough sequins."

Calum chuckles and pulls out an all-black robe with a hood. "This rack is just labeled miscellaneous."

I turn to look, but a bright white suit with gold filagree splashed across the front catches my eye. "Is that from The Music Man?"

He shrugs. "Don't know. I haven't ever seen it. Actually, I haven't really seen any musicals. I don't particularly like them."

My jaw drops and I turn to him. "What?"

He glances at me, rolling his eyes. "I don't like musicals. I don't really even like movies that much."

"I don't even know how I'm supposed to respond to that information," I say. I shake my head. "Who doesn't like movies?"

"Me. I would rather see a play. Or a ballet, obviously. Usually people in movies have to talk about everything. And in musicals, they have to sing about it." He shudders. "No thanks."

"Oh, of course. You hate talking about your feelings."

Calum shrugs a shoulder. "Is it my fault if I don't want to watch other people have feelings?"

"You are emotionally stunted, I think." My lips curl up and I start to meander toward the next room.

He follows me, sounding a little defensive. "I prefer to think that I'm just more evolved than everyone else."

"Hah!" I look at him, giggling a little. "No offense, but not being connected to your emotions is probably holding you back, if anything. Emotions are another layer on top of literally everything that humans do. Not being able to parse them does not make you more evolved, Calum."

Calum shoots me a look. "Is this your way of telling me I'm not as smart as I think I am?"

"No. I just... I'm honestly trying here."

He frowns. "Trying what?"

"To shake you out of your slump. I was sort of casting around for an activity to break you out of the weird mood you've been in for days. And I thought about you and the things you like to do. Ella was telling me a story about this place and I thought about you." I squint. "Actually, I thought about how you said the costumes were uninspired. And I felt if I brought you here, maybe you would feel more creative again."

Cocking his head, he looks faintly puzzled. "You brought me here to help me solve a problem?"

I give him an odd look. "Yes. I have trouble watching you struggle. I think that's normal girlfriend stuff."

He doesn't answer right away. Turning toward the doorway, I start moving into the next room.

Calum surprises me by grabbing me from behind. He won't let me turn around. Instead he just growls in my ear. "You drive me crazy. Do you know that? Absolutely fucking insane."

I huff a laugh. "Is that a good thing or a bad thing?"

His grip eases on me and he turns me around. The second I'm facing him though, his mouth comes down, finding mine with a punishing kiss. He lifts me up and carries me over to the closest rack of clothing, pinning me against it. His lips are brutal, the lash of his tongue swift.

But I open my arms to him, part my lips for him. Wrap my legs around his body, pulling him closer. His mouth leaves mine as he kisses a scorching trail down my neck.

"Beauty," he groans. "My beauty…"

My eyes close as he presses against me, showing me his need. As long as Calum needs me like this, as long as he desires me physically, I will be here for him.

I turn my head up as a gentle moan escapes my lips.

32

KAIA

*W*hen we get back to my house, at my door, he's undressing me even before I get the door unlocked. The second we're inside, he picks me up and carries me into my bedroom. Calum sets me down and sits back on my bed.

He looks me up and down, his icy blue gaze piercing. It seems like he sees right into my very soul. I feel almost shy, like I should have worn more than this skimpy dress, but it doesn't matter.

The way he's looking at me, our clothes are only going to be decorating the floor soon.

"Do you have any idea how fucking hot you are?" he growls into my ear. I moan and shift to straddle his big body, moving closer any way I can.

I flush hot all over. Straddling him like this, it's impossible not to feel his hardened cock through his pants. It feels long and thick and perfect. I get a flash of how good it will feel inside my pussy, stretching me out and making me writhe in ecstasy.

"Maybe," I whisper. The air in the room feels too hot on my skin, too heavy.

"You definitely don't," he says, sliding his hand into my hair and bringing me down to meet his lips. I enjoy the little bit of pain as he grips my hair, controlling me.

I kiss him, enjoying the warmth rising up from his body. He moves down to kiss my neck, which makes me shudder with pleasure. He squeezes one of my breasts, his movements lazy and slow. My body burns for his, the fire spreading first between my breasts and then down between my legs.

"Fuck, Calum," I whisper. "I'm so hot for you. My pussy is already soaking wet."

I rock my hips against his, craving his touch. My breasts, my ass, my pussy... I slide my hand down my belly. He sucks in a breath as my hand creeps down between our bodies.

"Not so fast," he says, using his grip on my hair to pull my head back. "I want you to get off my lap and get naked."

I bite my lip, pushing off of him. He releases my hair and gets up.

"Good girl," he says. "Now get naked and sit on the edge of the bed. Wait right here."

He disappears, leaving me to strip down. I take off my dress, shimmying out of it and dropping it to the floor. I hesitate, then unhook my bra and slip my panties off.

I sit on the very edge of the bed. He comes back in the room, brandishing a few toys.

"Ladies' choice," he says. He lays them down, naming

them. "A butt plug for your beautiful ass. A clitoral vibrator to tease you with. Or a dildo…"

"A dildo?" I say. The very idea of him using that on me makes me squirm. "What would you do with that?"

Calum looks at me for a second and then grins. "I think you'll enjoy finding out, beauty."

He tosses the dildo on the bed, pulling his t-shirt off over his head. He looks appreciatively at my naked body, at my perky nipples. He runs a hand down my hip.

I can't stop looking at the dildo on the bed. It's girthy and long and black. Completely intimidating.

"You're getting in your head. Just kiss me, Kaia."

I kiss him, desperately trying not to worry. After a minute, he pulls back and kneels down on the floor between my knees. He starts teasing me, placing heated kisses all over my inner thighs and along the length of my seam.

"Fuck," I whisper. "*Yes*, Calum."

I moan, vaguely aware of how needy he's making me, and thrust my chest out. He sweeps his tongue over the top of my clit, barely brushing it. I cry out and my back arches. He pushes me back on the bed. I buck once and make a frustrated sound.

He stops and looks up at me. "Be a good girl, Kaia. Don't move. Don't make a sound. Do you understand?"

My mouth opens. It takes me a few seconds just to nod.

"Good. We're about to test your limits," he says, pushing me back down.

He kisses my inner thigh and the top of my slit again. A little sound of need leaves my lips.

Calum stops, looking up at me. "That's not being very quiet."

I nod. He drops lazy kisses to my knees and thighs for a minute. When he returns his mouth to my pussy, I have to grip the sheets, trying desperately not to squirm or moan.

Fuck. It's a sweet kind of torture, that's for sure.

He kisses my clit but makes no move to spread my pussy lips or use his tongue. Instead, he moves to retrieve the dildo. I see it briefly as he settles between my legs again.

"Stop overthinking it," he murmurs against my flesh.

I freeze up a little. But he returns to lick my clit in slow, lazy circles, which makes me forget that we were even talking about anything at all.

I am desperate for him, clenching my hands into fists in the sheets and repressing a moan. He takes full advantage, easing the dildo against my lower lips. I am so wet and excited that I don't need any lube. As he presses the dildo against my pussy I make a sound, a kind of whimper, and he takes his mouth away again.

I moan, frustrated. He clicks his tongue.

"Bad girl," he says. I feel him nip my inner thigh softly, making me squirm. I hold the sound of complaint that bubbles to my lips in. I can feel my body weeping for him, feel the sheets beneath my body growing damp, clinging to my ass cheeks. I want him to put his tongue against my clit again *so* badly.

"Shhhh," he murmurs against my bare flesh. "I really want to put this dildo up your ass and fuck you. But it's a process. Are you going to let me do my work?"

I nod, feeling my face grow red. I shut my mouth and go still, willing him to continue.

He presses against my pussy lips again with the dildo. I am so wet, it slides in partially with no resistance. God, the pressure of the dildo does feel good, almost like his cock.

He withdraws it, kissing my clit hard. I writhe, struggling to be silent. He doesn't pause this time, though. He just moves the dildo to my pussy again, licking my clit.

Oh god. My lower body lifts off the bed. I grab the sheets and he starts licking and sucking. I feel my innermost muscles start to clench. My toes curl.

"You're close, aren't you?"

I nod, feverish. He gently pulls the dildo out of my pussy and moves it to my ass instead. There is a pause as he adds some lube to the dildo, but then he French kisses my clit again.

I am shocked enough by the contact between the dildo and my ass to make a noise, but luckily this time he doesn't stop licking. He turns up the intensity of his French kiss as he gently presses the dildo against my ass.

I bite my lower lip and close my eyes. It feels so naughty but so fucking good. He works it into my ass very carefully, kissing my clit the entire time. The sensation of being very full and very fucking ready to come washes over me.

A strangled noise leaves my chest.

He chuckles. "I think you're ready. Don't you?"

He leaves the dildo right where it is, stretching out my ass. I shift uncomfortably as he sheds his pants, his expression intense. Flipping me over on my hands and knees, he smacks my ass once. A chill runs down my spine, unbidden.

"Fuck!" I bark.

Calum actually growls his excitement, which only increases my sense of anticipation.

"You like that dildo in your ass, beauty?" His hands caress my ass cheeks. "God, I can't wait to fucking stretch you out."

He pushes my thighs apart and presses his thick cock against the entrance to my pussy. He feels so huge from this angle, impossibly big. It's almost certainly too much, considering how full I am already.

I grip the sheets, trying to prepare my body for the invasion. Calum stops to add some more lube to my entrance and then fits the blunt tip of his cock to my pussy.

He presses himself in using slow thrusting movements. I groan with every thrust. But to my surprise, it doesn't hurt. It just feels *intense* as fuck.

We both groan as Calum grips my hips and finally thrusts all the way in. His cock is buried in my pussy; the dildo is filling my ass. He withdraws slightly, and then hammers himself home.

"Fuck!" I cry out, the pleasure bordering on pain. He is so big, filling every single inch of me, touching every secret spot inside. I've never felt so goddamn full.

"Kaia?" he asks.

I shake my head, moving my hips. "Calum, if you don't fuck me—"

I don't even finish my sentence before Calum rams his cock into my body again. He growls and does it again and again, slowly building momentum.

I shudder as he withdraws and then fills me completely, again and again. Calum increases his speed, fucking me harder and faster.

I moan, feeling him filling every inch of my pussy. He shifts a little, and suddenly he is hitting my g-spot. I tighten and clench instinctively around his cock.

"Oh fuck!" I cry out. "Oh fuck, Calum! Don't stop!"

"Ahh, beauty. I love hearing you scream my name. Tell me who your pussy belongs to, little girl." He keeps up his pace even as he talks dirty to me and I fucking love it.

"Yours, Calum. My pussy is yours. My ass is yours…"

"I want you to cum so hard. I want to feel you cream all over my cock."

I groan as he hits my g-spot over and over, his thrusts as rapid as gunfire. Everything inside my body tightens. I feel like I am exploding, my eyes rolling back in my head.

He groans as he comes, finishing with a final thrust. I can actually feel the hot spurts of cum as he releases them deep inside my body.

I sag forward, completely losing the willpower to move.

"Fuck," he mumbles, struggling for breath.

Calum pulls himself free of my body. He very, very gently slides the dildo from my ass, throwing it on the floor. Then he leans forward to kiss my lower back.

I collapse on the bed, giving a breathless chuckle.

He falls onto the bed beside me. I sweep my hair over my shoulder and roll over, facing him. He grabs my hand and kisses my knuckles.

As he lies there next to me, trying to control his breathing, I can't help the way my heart squeezes. I love him so, so much.

But he doesn't want to hear that. So I just close my eyes and let him touch me, trying not to think too much.

33

CALUM

I stand in the ballet studio, glaring at everyone. My mood is shitty. If anything, the visit to the set and costume shop only twisted me up more inside. Because I can't get my brother's voice out of my head.

Either you love her, or she'll leave you when she figures out that you lack the emotional depth that she does.

That's undoubtedly true. At the moment, I watch Kaia practice pas de deux lifts. That means that I have to watch as she holds onto Eric, the male partner she chose. She gracefully walks to him, goes en pointe, and then he tenderly grips her waist and spins her. Then he lifts her high in the air for half a second as Kaia raises her arms. The entire dance seems effortless.

There is an ease between them that I just don't like. When Eric puts her down, she laughs. They break up the whole routine by teasing each other. Eric flashes a million dollar smile and says something to her. And Kaia blushes faintly as she laughs.

If I were functioning on all cylinders as opposed to

thinking with my dick, I would realize that everyone in the studio is doing exactly the same thing. But I'm unable to stop staring at her. Jealousy blooms deep in my heart, little poisoned blossoms sprouting everywhere.

Basil swans over to me, his lips twitching with humor. He leans close. "It is quite obvious that you've been glaring at Kaia for twenty minutes. If you don't want to spread gossip about you two sleeping together, this is not the way."

"Fuck off." I scowl at him. I clap my hands loudly, calling to the class. "That's enough! We are done for the day."

All the dancers look at me, a little startled. I stare stony at everyone because I've found that it doesn't exactly invite questions. Rushing out of the room, I wait a ways down the hall, leaning against a pillar.

Kaia takes her time, exiting the dance studio next to last. Her eyes dart around and connect with mine. I casually look to my right, indicating that I'll be in the empty studio.

She looks away and tells her friends that she'll catch up to them. I move across the hallway just as she has bent down and is tying her shoe. The flimsy dance skirt she's wearing rides up as she does, showing her ass in her tights and leotard.

It's a sight I see every day, hundreds of times. But damn if that doesn't make me hard. I grip my duffel bag as I step in the room, throwing it to the side.

I'm walking on the edge right now. Clasping and unclasping my fists. Feeling tense. Needing to claim Kaia as my own. For the next minute, I try to cool my engines.

But my efforts are all wasted the second that Kaia strolls into the studio. She shakes her hair, lifting her chin. She tosses her bag by the door. Her eye rove around.

"We've already almost been caught in here," she notes. She turns to me, arching a brow. "Why are we in this room?"

I pin her with my gaze. "You were awfully flirtatious with Eric today."

Her eyebrows lower and she looks mystified. "I was *friendly* with him, if that is what you mean."

Crossing my arms, I start to pace. "The laughing after every attempt? The touching each other's bodies even when you didn't have to?"

"Are you serious? I can't believe you're acting jealous. It was your frigging direction for the class to do it!"

Squaring my jaw, I shake my head. "No, it was Basil's idea, actually. And you took it to the next level. Anyone watching you would have thought that you were a couple."

Kaia makes an angry noise. "It's called acting, Calum." Her voice turns mocking. "See, when a ballerina goes on stage, she has to pretend to be someone she's not…"

I thump my chest with a fist. "Do you think you need to explain that to me?"

She tosses her hands in the air. "It would seem so. Just because I get along with Eric and enjoy having him as a pas de deux parter doesn't mean anything."

The next words out of my mouth cross the line. But I just blurt them out without thinking. "I would just think that after having such a close call with Crispin that you would be more careful with the people you cozy up to. You can't exactly afford any more stalkers."

Her hands drop to her sides. She studies me carefully. "Are you saying that I encouraged Crispin? That he attacked me because I was nice to him?"

I'm wrong. I know it. But I just shrug. "That's one way it could be interpreted."

"You are being such an asshole right now."

"I'm just telling you what it seems like from the outside."

She waves her hands at me. "Heads up, Calum. You're not on the outside, looking in. You are very much on the inside. Plus, you know that I didn't invite Crispin to assault me. I'm offended that you're acting like I did."

"I didn't say that."

"You did!" she says, her voice rising. "And speaking of Crispin, where is he? Why haven't you found him yet?"

I blink. "I told you. He's pulled a vanishing act. Him and Honor both."

Her mouth twists to the side. "Which is why I still have a security detail twenty four hours a day?"

My eyes tighten on her face. "Yes."

She releases an exaggerated sigh. "Agggh. You... This isn't what I should be doing right now. I shouldn't be in here fighting with you. I should be off living my life, hanging out with my friends. Yet you're basically picking a fight over nothing. Why?"

I glare at her. Anger simmers in my stomach, threatening to boil up up and explode.

"I'm not doing anything like that. Maybe you just miss being around your dysfunctional family so much that you are spoiling for a fight."

She throws her arms wide, looking straight up at the ceiling. "That's it! Calum, you're in time out."

Giving her a glare, I walk to the wall and lean against it. "What does that mean?"

"I don't know exactly!" she shouts. "You drag me in here. You play the blame game with me. You are being a huge asshole for no reason…" She grits her teeth. "I don't deserve this, Calum. So you get the rest of the day to stop playing these crappy mind games."

Her words sting. "Or what?"

Kaia storms over to her bag, scraping it up and hoisting it onto her shoulder. "Don't. You're trying to get an ultimatum out of me. I can feel it. I don't know why you are freaking out right now. But until you can talk to me like an adult, I don't want to see your face."

I glower at her while she storms over to the door. "Where are you going?"

"I don't know." She opens the door. "But I want an apology the next time we see each other."

She sails out the door, letting it shut silently behind her. I swallow against the lump that forms in my throat. My anger just simmers inside me, filling up every nook and cranny inside my body until I want to scream.

I don't know what to do. So I stalk over to the spindly metal stool, raising it over my head. And then I swiftly send it arcing through the air, heading right into a section of floor to ceiling mirror. There is a giant crash as the mirror splinter. But it's safety glass, so it doesn't fall out. My chest heaves as I stare into the broken mirror, looking at the twisted and cracked version of myself.

It's about the truest representation I've ever seen.

I spin on my heel, grabbing my bag. I burst out of the door, finding the long hallway empty. It's after six on a Friday evening. No one should be here by now.

Yet there is one person waiting for me as I walk down the hall. Emma spots me and makes a beeline for me, oblivious to the fact that I'm not in the headspace to deal with her right now.

She smoothes the front of her white pantsuit, smiling at me like a shark at her next meal. "There you are, Calum. I was starting to think you had slipped out another way to avoid me."

I walk right by her, giving her a glance. "Why would I do that?"

She hurries to keep up with me. "Well, as you may know, my partners in Japan—"

I stop dead in my tracks. "I thought I told you no."

Emma stops, pushing back a strand of her stick straight hair. "I thought that I would sweeten my offer a little." She gives me a saccharine smile. "I think we got off on the wrong foot last time."

"We've never been on the right one. Not about business. Not about anything, come to think of it." I stare at her, tilting my head. "Emma, I think it would be a smart maneuver for you to find a new job. Because the board of trustees meets in a couple of weeks... and I don't think I will have a single nice thing to say about you."

Emma's mouth opens and shuts, making her look like nothing so much as a gaping trout. "Calum, I don't think you've put enough thought into this. I mean, I know so much about your affair with that little ballerina—"

I put my hand up to stop her. "I'm giving you two

weeks. That's enough time to find somewhere else. In the meantime, I'm going to have my personal army of private investigators combing through your life. I'll have a forensic accountant go through every single financial disclosure form you've ever filed. They will talk to former coworkers. They'll talk to neighbors. They'll buy your fucking garbage. Simply put, I will dig up some kind of dirt on you. And then I will use it to silence you. Do you understand me?"

Her cheeks turn a dusky red. "You're not going to find anything. I haven't done anything worth blackmailing me for."

I start walking again. "Yes. You have. It's just a matter of time before I find it. So if I were you, I would really focus on brushing up my resume and putting out feelers. Because Emma?" I slow and turn around, but don't stop walking. "I will not have this conversation again. Seriously, don't even talk to me unless it's to tell me what your new position is."

Emma looks completely shocked. "Calum!"

I raise a hand over my head, turning and walking toward the exit. "Goodbye, Emma."

I trot out of the building, feeling less victorious than I should. Normally I would do a victory lap. Maybe even go to the bar in my building, pick up a girl.

But the only girl I want is nowhere to be found when I get home. So I retreat to my study with a bottle of whiskey and my age-old rage.

KAIA

I stretch my neck on the elevator ride up to my penthouse. The elevator is crowded with two bodyguards; their presence at brunch with Ella this morning was a reminder that Crispin still hasn't been caught. When we get to the top floor, I step off the elevator and wait for two minutes while they make sure that no one is lurking in my apartment.

Then I shut the door in their faces, sagging against the wall. Exupéry comes running up, loudly purring and demanding to be petted. I sigh and give in, but my mind is elsewhere.

It's been a tense couple of days. And the bodyguards are only slowing everything down, making even simple things just that much harder. Dogging me at work, while I run errands, while I hang out at home.

The whole thing is pretty tiresome.

"Kaia?"

Calum's voice filters through the doorway between our apartments. My mouth twists to the side when I hear it.

He's been acting like a lion with a thorn in his paw for the last ten days. And he won't let me sneak in to remove it, even a tiny sliver. What does he want from me, then?

I push myself upright with a sigh and head to the door connecting my apartment with his. I wander into the spare bedroom and then into the hallway, looking for him.

I find him drinking a cup of coffee in his pristine white kitchen. He's dressed in workout clothes and he smells like sweat. He looks up at me, his eyebrows rising. "Ah. You're home."

"Yep." I lean against the doorway, wrinkling my nose. "You smell… interesting. Kind of sweaty. Actually, you smell like you usually do after we fuck."

His eyes crinkle. "I just finished a really great session with my personal trainer. We spent two hours working on my core."

"That would do it."

He looks at me, his eyes tightening on my face. "Where have you been?"

I push off of the door frame, my hands sliding onto my hips. "I went to brunch with Ella. I'm sure one of your flying monkeys could have told you that, though. They have to report every single move I make to you, don't they?"

Calum sets his coffee cup down with a clink. "They are just a temporary measure, Kaia. Meant only to keep you safe while Crispin is still at large."

I pin him in place with my eyes. "I don't want them any more. They are more trouble than they're worth. Besides, I feel conspicuous with them hovering right behind me. I feel like they draw unwanted attention to me."

Calum's icy blue gaze studies me. "I was thinking of hiring them on a more permanent basis. You know, to keep you safe. Often men like me are targeted in kidnapping schemes. And if you were... my girlfriend, more openly, that is..."

I squint. "It's unclear to me what are you trying to say, Calum."

He clears his throat. "I'm trying to say... you know... that I care about you."

I give him a quizzical look. "Okay?"

It comes out as a question more than an answer.

He frowns. "I don't want to use cliched phrases. I don't want to be trite. But you know..."

He slides a long, flat box out of his pocket. "This is for you."

He opens it, revealing a sapphire and diamond tennis bracelet. Then he glances up at me.

My mouth puckers. I shake my head. "Wait. Wait a second. Are you trying to give me jewelry instead of just expressing that you have feelings for me?"

He gives me a one sided shrug. "I said that I care about you."

My mouth flattens. "Calum..." I walk over to him, closing the bracelet's box. I peer up into his eyes. "Ever since I told you that I love you, you've been twisting yourself into knots. Trying to prove that you're not emotionally stunted, I guess. But this? The jewelry? This is nice. But this is not the way that you tell me." I rap his chest with my hand. "Just open your mouth and say what you feel."

His expression hardens. "I'm trying."

"You're going about it the wrong way. I know that you don't like making yourself vulnerable—"

Calum kisses me, putting a stop to my words. I allow it for a second, then push him away with gentle hands. "Again. I already know that you like my body. That's not what I'm asking for. Money isn't the problem. Physical attractiveness isn't the problem. I already know that you're gorgeous and rich."

"I don't see what the fuss is about."

I flatten my hands over his chest, looking up into his face. "Do you really not love me?"

Pain flashes through his eyes. He looks away. "Just say it. Say that we're through. I've been waiting for you to call a spade a spade this entire time. Just say that we're not connecting—"

My heart thuds dully against my ribs. "You are so fucking stubborn, Calum. Seriously."

He looks back at me, emotion flickering in his eyes. "I just have to say the phrase? That's it? Then you'll stop hounding me?"

I push him away, shaking my head. "I'm not hounding you! I've never once made an ultimatum or tried to make you feel bad about this. If anything, *you* are the one who won't quit asking *me* to make some grand declaration."

Calum exhales loudly. "I just hate this tension."

"You are the one making it, though!"

He looks at me for a half a minute, his mouth twisting. "You'll end things with me."

I clench my jaw. "Calum—"

He shakes his head, cutting me off. "You will. You

267

think you won't. You say you'll be tolerant. But at some point, you will get tired of it."

He very clearly means that I will tire of him. Calum seems so broken down. I can't stand to watch him hurting.

"Why do you have to live so far in the future?" I murmur. "Hmm?"

"Why do you need me to say what is in my heart?" he fires back. "Why does everyone need me to do things and say things according to their established patterns?"

I cross my arms, pacing a little bit. "I only want honesty from you. Okay? That's all I've ever wanted. Just... you know, give me a sign."

He narrows his eyes. "That's not true. That's not how all of this started. It started with you dancing for me at a fucking private club."

Heat rushes to my face. I hesitate, trying to get the words right. "That's true. But I think we both knew what we were signing up for when we decided to take our relationship out of the club."

Calum chuckles humorlessly. "Beauty, I can assure you that I had no idea. I just knew that I wanted to sleep with you. And I didn't want anyone else to even look at you."

"Things change. Circumstances change. But what's in my heart doesn't change." I touch my chest briefly. "I can't always be the one taking all the risk."

His phone starts buzzing on the table behind him. His brows draw down and he turns to check it. "Fuck." He glances up at me, his eyes pinning me in place. "It's Lucas. He never calls, so I had better answer."

I can't help but be a little bit crestfallen. I sweep my

hand out, turning away. "Get it. I need to decompress anyway."

I start moving down the hall, back to my apartment. He calls after me. "This conversation isn't over…"

But for me, it's done. We've talked this subject to death. The idea of what love is like a swift moving river. We are on one side, struggling to get across. And more and more, it's looking like our relationship will not make it to the other side.

35

CALUM

J'm nervous. It's making me fidget, which in itself is unusual. I run a finger under my bowtie and try to breathe.

I can't help but feel like I'm drowning.

Looking around the black tie gala, I swirl the whisky that is in my tumbler. The ice cubes in my drink clink together quietly. This restaurant is impressively high end but their whisky for this affair is pretty basic.

How disappointing.

I'm leaning against a wall, trying not to look as tense as I feel. All around me, well-dressed people gather in groups around dancers. Waiters circle with *h'ors d'oeuvres* and glasses of champagne.

There is a small but lively four-piece band playing uptempo music. A few people are drunk enough to dance. Downing a gulp of whisky, I am trying to get there.

Lucas is right beside me, in a matching tuxedo. He keeps glancing at me as if he can parse what is in my expression.

"We don't have to be here, you know." He leans against the wall and casts a look over me. "This event allows the obscenely wealthy donors to hobnob with the ballet dancers. You are both a dancer and a wealthy son of a bitch, but you already have something that no one else here has."

I squint. "What's that?"

He levels a smirk at me. "You have a dainty little ballerina waiting patiently for you at home."

I shake my head softly. "I left a note at Kaia's apartment asking her to meet me here."

Lucas narrows his eyes. "You look like you're worried. What do you have to worry about?"

Tossing back the rest of my whisky, I make a face. "Nothing new. I think I figured out the solution to my little issue with Kaia."

He sucks in a breath. "God, you're not going to propose, are you?"

"Jesus. No. She said that she wanted to know how I feel about her. So I'm going to tell her tonight. I just have to get the words right."

"Ohh." Lucas claps me on the shoulder. "That sounds better. I'm glad that you figured it out."

"Yeah." I check the time, my mouth twisting. "Kaia's running on dancer's time today, apparently. She was supposed to be here ten minutes ago."

As I say it, she appears. She's wearing a gorgeous pure white ball gown, her hair pinned up to show off her stunning neck and shoulders. Diamond earrings wink at her ears. And to finish the look off, hanging around her neck is the diamond and sapphire necklace I gave her.

271

It's enough to make me breathless. As she floats through the room, her eyes roam around, searching. When her eyes land on me, she lights up. Her smile is just for me.

My chest tightens. Pushing off the wall, I discard my glass on a table as I walk toward her. When she reaches me, she pulls up short. I look down at her, smirking.

"It's hard not to kiss you when you look at me like that," I say, my voice gone to gravel.

Her hands clench. "Do you have to be so tall and handsome? It's not fair to the rest of the world."

I give her a sly smile. "Don't forget that I'm rich, too."

Kaia flaps a hand. "As if I care about that."

"You really don't do you?" I look her up and down, pursing my lips. "It surely doesn't hurt, though."

She flushes. "Why am I here, Calum?"

Tilting my head at her, I notice that she hasn't grabbed a glass of champagne. "Let's get you a drink. Come on, I could use another one."

I walk her over to the bar and order our drinks. As we wait, I put my hand on the small of her back. A possessive gesture, to be sure.

She squirms, stepping back. She gives me a hard look. "Calum, watch your hands."

My lips curl up. I sip my drink, smiling over the rim. "Yes, Miss Walker."

Kaia gets a French 75 in a champagne flute and takes a small taste. "Mm. This tastes… off. Heavier, somehow."

I arch a brow. "I think that means you've developed a palette. The drinks you usually get are made with the finest champagne and top shelf gin. The ones at this gala… well, they're intended to get you drunk, but they are not guaranteed to be the best liquor."

She wrinkles her nose. "I see."

After one more sip, she hands the glass off to a waiter with a gleaming silver tray. She looks at me for a long moment. "Do you think you can behave yourself enough so that we can dance?"

I give her my most mischievous grin. "Oh, I think I can manage."

Draining the contents of my glass, I set it down on a table. And then I give her a tiny bow. "Ladies first."

Kaia's brow wrinkles. "You're in an awfully strange mood, Calum. It's nice to see you smile, but it's a little weird. Just yesterday, you were begging me to break up with you."

"Come on."

I put my hand on her lower back and guide her to the dance floor. I take her hand in mine and pull her small waist against the wall of my torso. Leading Kaia makes perfect sense. As a couple, we glide effortlessly around the dance floor. She looks up at me, a laugh bubbling up to her lips.

"What?" I murmur.

She shrugs a shoulder, amused. "I just forgot how it could be between us. For the last two weeks, it's been a little like pushing a very large boulder up an impossibly angled hill. But tonight... I don't feel any of that tension. It was weighing me down, I think. I didn't even realize it."

I pull her closer still. She's magnetic right now.

"I think I figured out how to tell you what I feel."

Her eyebrows jump up. She looks around, her cheeks

coloring. When she speaks, her voice has lowered to a whisper. "Should we step out into the hall?"

I shake my head. "No."

Her lips part. "Okay," she whispers.

Grabbing her hand, I bring it to lay over my chest. "Can you feel my heart beating?"

Kaia's gaze dips to her hand. Her steps slow. "Yes. Very faintly."

I stop dancing and tip her face up so that she looks at me. "I don't know what love is. I never have. I've been broken for longer than I can say. But Kaia…" I lick my lips, looking deeply into her eyes. "You are my heart."

Her breath leaves her all at once. Her eyes mist over. "I am?"

Nodding, I push myself to be vulnerable. To lay it all out there for this girl.

"That's what I feel. As long as my heart beats, I'll be here. Waiting for you. And I will always feel this way, even in the darkest moments when I wish it were different."

"Calum!" She presses up on her tiptoes and slides her arms around my neck. She places a kiss on my ear. "I love you."

I pull back, looking at her with a serious expression. "I'll do whatever I have to do to keep you. And if that means marriage…"

She shakes her head. "I'm eighteen. And you can't even say the words 'I love you'. Let's just take things as they come, okay?"

I lift a shoulder. "In this one aspect of my life, I'll follow your lead."

Her lips curl up. "I really, really wish we were outside. Because I want to kiss you so badly—"

I shock her by pulling her into my arms, dipping her back, and kissing her as dramatically as possible. Kaia's eyes widen and she smacks me on the arm as I pull her back up.

"What did you do that for?"

She looks around to see who noticed. Luckily it's pretty dark and there are several couples dancing who are being way more flamboyant than I was just now. I roll my eyes.

"It'll be fine."

Kaia shakes her head. "Emma is going to have something to say. When Honor was expelled, Emma sat the entire company down and told us over and over how bad it was that Honor had dated her stage manager."

I pull a face. "I fired Emma two days ago."

Her look of shock is complete. "You *what?!*"

"Well, I shouldn't say fired. I gave the opportunity to find another position on another board. To my credit, I could've done a lot worse. She threatened to blackmail me—"

A high pitched scream comes from the corner of the restaurant. I look to where there is a lot of commotion; panic stricken people rush away from that corner.

A little sourness washes through my stomach. I stalk forward, unable to see the cause.

And then he darts out from behind a wall, holding a shiny black gun. I squint at him.

It's Crispin, the little blond asshole that assaulted Kaia. And he has a fucking gun.

"Kaia!" he calls. "Ah, there you are. You and your stupid boyfriend…"

I turn my head oh so briefly.

"Run!" I command Kaia.

She isn't paying any attention to me. She seems frozen in place. Her eyes are glued to the gun, her expression horrified. "I don't understand. Why—"

Crispin charges forward, raising the gun and firing into the ceiling. I duck as the black ceiling tile explodes above me. My heart pounds. I have to do something to get this guy's attention away from Kaia… even if that means it will be on me.

"Hey!" I shout, purposely moving away from Kaia. I raise my arms out to the side and wave my hands. "You clearly have something that you want to say, but I don't know what that is. Do you want to tell me?"

Crispin looks at me with a snarl. He holds the gun out, swinging its muzzle toward me. "You. You privileged fuck. You're good looking. You have all the money in the world. Why don't you fuck off and go date some models or something? Leave the rest of us some real women to fight over. No one even likes you, Calum."

I lower my hands in a conciliatory gesture. "I get that a lot."

He bares his teeth at me. "I'll just bet you do. Tell me, what is Kaia even worth to you? Will you beg for her life?"

Without looking away from me, he points the gun at Kaia. She puts her hands up, her face gone white.

"Crispin, I think we should talk about this." Her voice trembles.

276

He laughs humorlessly. "I don't think so. The time for that has passed."

Out of the corner of my eye, I see Lucas moving stealthily around behind Crispin. He makes a gesture to me, indicating that I should keep distracting the guy with the gun so Lucas can get closer.

I step forward, desperate to bring Crispin's attention back to me. "I'll beg. You want to see it?"

Crispin focuses on me. "Yes. I want you on your knees, telling me why I should spare her life."

Never taking my eyes off his face, I get on my knees. He steps forward, leveling the gun at me. Despite myself, I start to shake. I raise my hands.

"I am begging you, Crispin. Please. No one has to get hurt today."

He lowers his gun for a split second. Lucas moves behind him, close enough to touch.

"Get fucked," Crispin says. He raises the gun again just as Lucas tackles him from behind.

The gun goes off, the sound deafening. An unseen hand smacks my left pec hard. I don't feel anything at first. Actually, I feel a lack of sensation. I look down and see neat little hole in my suit jacket. The hole tingles for a moment, then starts to burn as a tiny dribble of my blood leaks out.

My mouth opens. I gasp for air, finding that suddenly it's a struggle to inhale. My hands fly up, covering my wound.

"Calum!"

At Kaia's scream, I look up at her. She runs toward me, her face streaked with tears. I'm still stunned.

The entire world goes into slow motion, flickering as my vision starts to narrow. I feel myself falling to the side. The last thing I hear is Kaia calling my name.

"Calum? Calum!"

Everything fades to black.

36

*W*ant a little more of their love story? Get a deleted love scene right now by joining Vivian's mailing list.

Calum and Kaia's story isn't over yet, not by a long shot. Raw, gripping, steamy, and emotional… Get ready for more of their story by pre-ordering The Dancer right now.

W<small>HILE</small> <small>YOU</small> <small>ARE</small> <small>WAITING</small>, we suggest trying The Wicked Prince! Angst, drama, grit, and glamor all couched in the dazzling wealth of one royal family!

You can read a FREE prequel right now.

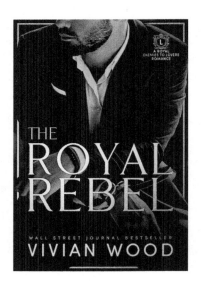

ABOUT VIVIAN WOOD

Vivian likes to write about troubled, deeply flawed alpha males and the fiery, kick-ass women who bring them to their knees.

Vivian's lasting motto in romance is a quote from a favorite song: "Soulmates never die."

Be sure to follow Vivian through her Facebook page or join her email list to keep up with all the awesome giveaways, author videos, ARC opportunities, and more!

VIVIAN'S WORKS

THE PATRON
THE DANCER
THE EMBRACE
POSSESSIVE

THE PRINCE AND HIS REBEL
THE WICKED PRINCE
HIS FORBIDDEN PRINCESS
ROYAL FAKE FIANCÉ

SAME WORLD, DIFFERENT CHARACTERS…
SINFUL FLING
SINFUL ENEMY
SINFUL BOSS
SINFUL CHANCE

HIS BEST FRIEND'S LITTLE SISTER
HIS INNOCENT FAKE FIANCÉE
HER OFF LIMITS BEST FRIEND
HER OFF LIMITS DIRTY BOSS

WILD HEARTS

ADDICTION
OBSESSION

For more information….
vivian-wood.com
info@vivian-wood.com

Printed in Great Britain
by Amazon